Thrown to the Dogs

"Jay, are you asking me to go over there every week and give your mother an injection?" I watch as his face droops into a pathetic bloodhound expression.

"And maybe take her to the doctor for her treatments once a month?" He lowers his head down as if he thinks I might throw something at him.

"Jay . . ."

"Noelle, I know this is a lot to ask. But I've got to go back to Atlanta before New Year's, and I won't be able to leave without knowing someone will be here for her."

"Jay, I'd really like to help you, but . . ."

"Noelle, sweetie. I'm kind of at my wit's end. I know it'll be awkward," he says, "but I trust you. You know how to give an injection."

"To a dog," I say. "Jay, I'm a veterinary technician, not a nurse. Can't you hire someone from the hospital?"

"She won't hear of that. That would signal the beginning of the end to her."

"But she won't mind me coming over? Jay, you do realize this is the same woman whose last words to me were 'I knew you were a mistake.' This woman, you want me to inject a needle into?" If it weren't so awful, I might just laugh.

Free to a Good Home

Eve Marie Mont

BERKLEY BOOKS, NEW YORK

THE BERKLEY PUBLISHING GROUP
Published by the Penguin Group
Penguin Group (USA) Inc.
375 Hudson Street, New York, New York 10014, USA
Penguin Group (Canada), 90 Eglinton Avenue East, Suite 700, Toronto, Ontario M4P 2Y3, Canada
(a division of Pearson Penguin Canada Inc.)
Penguin Books Ltd., 80 Strand, London WC2R 0RL, England
Penguin Group Ireland, 25 St. Stephen's Green, Dublin 2, Ireland (a division of Penguin Books Ltd.)
Penguin Group (Australia), 250 Camberwell Road, Camberwell, Victoria 3124, Australia
(a division of Pearson Australia Group Pty. Ltd.)
Penguin Books India Pvt. Ltd., 11 Community Centre, Panchsheel Park, New Delhi—110 017, India
Penguin Group (NZ), 67 Apollo Drive, Rosedale, North Shore 0632, New Zealand
(a division of Pearson New Zealand Ltd.)
Penguin Books (South Africa) (Pty.) Ltd., 24 Sturdee Avenue, Rosebank, Johannesburg 2196,
South Africa

Penguin Books Ltd., Registered Offices: 80 Strand, London WC2R 0RL, England

This book is an original publication of The Berkley Publishing Group.

This is a work of fiction. Names, characters, places, and incidents either are the product of the author's imagination or are used fictitiously, and any resemblance to actual persons, living or dead, business establishments, events, or locales is entirely coincidental. The publisher does not have any control over and does not assume any responsibility for author or third-party websites or their content.

PRINTING HISTORY
Berkley trade paperback edition / July 2010

Library of Congress Cataloging-in-Publication Data

Mont, Eve Marie.
    Free to a good home / Eve Marie Mont. — Berkley trade paperback ed.
        p. cm.
    ISBN 978-0-425-23478-5
    1. Animal health technicians—Fiction. 2. Divorced women—Fiction. 3. New England—Fiction.
I. Title.
    PS3613.O546F74 2010
    813'.6—dc22   2010008220

PRINTED IN THE UNITED STATES OF AMERICA

10   9   8   7   6   5   4   3   2   1

To Mom Mont, with love

Thank you to Jackie Cantor for her warmth and wisdom in editing this book, along with the amazing team at Berkley! Thanks also to my wonderful agent, April Eberhardt (and her reader Maria Dinzeo), for helping me improve and polish the manuscript—and for answering every question I had with patience and professionalism. For her careful reading and constant friendship, I want to thank Ashley Seiver. A special thanks to my family for providing early reads and moral support, particularly to Phil for helping create my website. To my mother-in-law, Anne Mont, thank you for reading not once but thrice and for being a true inspiration. And finally, thanks to Maggie, my loyal canine companion, and to Ken, my first reader (always) and my greatest champion.

❧

FOR SALE, Westerly: Sprawling beach house with five bed-rooms and expansive water views. The modern kitchen with granite countertops and brand-new Sub-Zero appliances is perfect for entertaining, opening onto a multilevel deck looking out on an enormous yard with inground pool and Jacuzzi. Join the nearby Westerly Beach Club for private beaches, tennis, swimming, fishing, boating, and golfing. Westerly is a picture-perfect Norman Rockwell town with a carousel, a family entertainment center, weekly large-screen movies on the beach, and more.

Everyone needs a hobby. Mine is searching through real estate web-sites. People tell me I should have been a real estate agent, but they don't really get it. I'm not looking for houses for other people to live in. I'm looking for myself.

It's not as if I'm in any position to buy one. It's more like my form of pornography—feverishly scrolling through thumbnail photos, feeling my heart rate elevate as I read the specs: nine-foot ceilings, crown moldings, a master suite, three working fireplaces, a swimming pool, a view of the bay!

Sometimes I feel I could look all day long, forsaking all other responsibilities as I imagine myself living in each house—how would my life be different? What would I do for a living? How many children would I have? Who would my husband be? Who would I be? As if a house had the power to change anything. To change me.

As a child, I loved playing house. Not that I didn't also have a rebellious tomboy in me who loved to climb trees and collect bugs in jars. But deep down I saw myself being a mother, a wife, having a house that was my sanctuary. I never got into Barbies—their blond perfection seemed too cold and remote for me. I had no aspirations to drive a pink convertible or wear a tiara, even at age seven when every little girl believes she will grow up to be a princess.

No, I preferred my Betty Crocker kitchen with its double-basin sink and stovetop oven, my dolls that ate baby food and wet their diapers, my shopping cart full of fake frozen dinners and plastic produce. Sometimes I'd make my younger brother play my husband, dressing him up in my father's old sport coats and ties, watching him pretend to make phone calls or type memos at my desk where he worked his imaginary high-powered job in the city.

If you'd reminded me of this archaic 1950s fantasy when I was in college, I would have denied it, convinced at the time that I was a raging feminist. But some say we are more ourselves at age seven than at any other time in our lives. And that we spend most of our years pretending, trying lives on for size, instead of doing what would really make us happy.

But what is that? I used to think I knew. Marriage, a big house, lots of children. But life is funny. The minute you think you know something for certain—the moment you let yourself believe everything is settled—life gets a sense of humor and shows you that nothing is ever, ever certain.

December

It's two days before Christmas, and I'm driving through Bristol to see the decorations in town. All the shops have twinkly lights around their doorways, garlands of evergreen on the handrails, trees in the windows adorned with carefully chosen ornaments (dog biscuits and plaid ribbons for Pabby's Pets, miniature wooden spoons and whisks for Krazy Kitchens). It's nice, really, this shameless display of holiday mirth, even though it's mostly for the benefit of tourists looking to find a bit of nostalgia in our quaint New England town.

I look in the rearview mirror to check on Beatrix, a half-blind cocker spaniel mix we've had at the shelter for two months now. It's difficult to place an older dog like Beatrix who doesn't have the irresistible puppy factor anymore, who's taken a few too many punches in life and maybe doesn't have the same boundless enthusiasm as the others. Sometimes I take her and others like her home with me for the weekend, just to keep them socialized in case they get adopted one day. All right, let's be honest. I take them home because I love them and would adopt them all if I could. Plus Zeke loves the company, big attention hog that he is.

On the way home I stop to pick up a bottle of wine just in case Jay wants to come in for a drink. I don't know why I'm so nervous about seeing him. It's been six months, and I know he's going to look as handsome as ever. Last Wednesday, I got my hair cut at one of those expensive salons in town, where I let myself be talked into a short haircut. Sort of flapper girl meets Grace Kelly. Since then I haven't been able to duplicate the stylist's look at all, so I leave the house most days looking more like Prince Valiant than Princess Grace.

Beatrix and I head across the bridge toward home, or what was meant to be a temporary rental house but has become my permanent residence for the past three years. It's not such a bad place, really—a tiny two-bedroom shoebox painted in gingerbread colors, with a small fenced-in backyard. I put a birdhouse out there, and every morning before I leave for work, a pair of cardinals comes to visit, the male feeding the female so it looks like they're kissing. I love that some birds travel in pairs, comforted that nature, which can be so cruel, also has this capacity for romance.

When we get home, my street is mercifully quiet. My neighbors on both sides, while lovely people, don't quite understand the meaning of privacy. It doesn't help that our houses are spaced about three feet apart. If I take the trash out, I'm bound to get into a twenty-minute conversation about weather or politics or old cars, or be accosted by one of the eighty-seven children who live in the neighborhood and seem to be selling Girl Scout cookies, wrapping paper, or bake-at-home pizzas every other day of the year.

On one side of me are the McKeevers: Dan and Danielle and their three blond, indistinguishable boys who range in age from three to six. Danielle once told me she can get pregnant just by holding Dan's hand. Of course, it might help if she didn't rely on the rhythm method as her contraception of choice.

On the other side of me are Mike and Trey, ex-military buddies in their late twenties who, after coming home from Iraq, made it their primary mission in life to perfect the art of the party. The sound of their recycling going out on a Monday morning is like some postmodern Philip Glass composition that goes on so long it's comical. Adorning their house are about seven American flags and, adorning their driveway, a motorcycle and three bumper-sticker-laden cars, only one of which will start at any given time. In their backyard sits every kind of lawn furniture imaginable—a slightly left-leaning gazebo with a half dozen plastic chairs, a gas grill, three *chimineas*, a hammock, and a ten-foot inflatable pool with a pink flamingo drink caddy.

After pulling into the driveway, I grab my wine and Beatrix and head inside to get ready. Zeke hears us come in and bounds to the front door, his tail whisking against the table where I keep my keys. Zeke is a Great Dane mix, a carousing big dope of a dog with a heart of gold. He's so sweet with all the animals I bring home, even the cats, playing with them gently at first until they adjust to their surroundings, licking their noses, crouching into play pose to let them know he means no harm.

I lead Zeke and Beatrix out into the backyard to let them get acquainted, watching them for a few minutes to make sure there are no ugly tangles. Beatrix looks so small and dainty next to Zeke, who is basically a sweet, slobbering face attached to a hulking canine body.

This dog has no idea how powerful he is, how easily he could maul Beatrix, or me for that matter, if he weren't such a gentle giant.

After confirming that Zeke and Beatrix are going to be pals, I head to my bedroom to get ready. Jay is taking me to Simpatico, a lovely little bayside Italian place with the most delicate homemade pasta I've ever tasted. That's one thing Jay and I have always had in common—we love food and drink and finding excuses to eat out even when we know we shouldn't. Jay never had to worry about his weight—he's tall and slim and likes to run. I can't imagine liking to run; when Jay used to make me go with him, I always felt like I was being chased.

From my closet, I choose the stretchy sweater with the silver threads running through it because it best camouflages the dog hair. I put on my nicest pair of jeans, the dark rinse ones that normally fit perfectly but feel a little snugger than usual. Must be the Christmas cookies. Then I apply a little raisin lipstick and a hint of blush, take a quick check in the mirror, and realize I'm looking at a fool.

I'm having dinner tonight with Jay. My ex-husband.

And yes, I still find him irresistibly attractive. And yes, I still love him. He's the sweetest, most charming man I know. He never cheated, never gambled, never did drugs, and tells me he loves me still.

So why aren't we together? Good question. And I have a good answer. An exceptional answer, actually.

My plan had been simple: go to college, find a job, get married, buy a house, have kids, live happily ever after.

The first two steps happened in quick succession. I left my family home in Connecticut for the exotic wilderness of Rhode Island, where I majored in preveterinary studies at URI. After graduation I didn't have the money for veterinary school, so I got a job as a veterinary technician at the Sakonnet Animal Sanctuary and Hospital, or SASH, one of the most progressive animal rescue facilities in New England. I loved my job, worked there for three years, got promoted to animal educator (more a meritorious promotion, as I didn't make any more money), and was ready to settle into "life as expected."

Then I met Jay. He was bringing Zeke back to SASH for neutering, and both dog and owner looked a bit apprehensive about the prospect. I remembered Zeke from when we had first found him as an abandoned puppy—all scared eyes and scruffy fur and long legs that made him look like a fawn. Now here he was six months later, already weighing ninety pounds with paws the size of small saucepans.

"Well, hello again," I said, wondering whether Jay remembered me from the adoption process. I sure remembered him. He was a bit older than most of the guys I dated, midthirties, tall with broad shoulders, cool green eyes, and the softest golden skin I'd ever seen on a man. "Didn't you get big?" I said to Zeke, who jumped up and lifted both paws onto my shoulders in the most ridiculous and endearing hug I've ever experienced. "Whoa, Zeke. Not until we know each other better."

"I'm sorry," said Jay, pulling Zeke off me.

"That's okay. Most excitement I've had all day." Did I mention I am appallingly inept at flirting?

Jay laughed anyway. "He doesn't seem to know his own strength. I'm beginning to think it may have been a mistake for me to get him. He's practically taken over my townhouse." Zeke wagged his tail vigorously, assuming we were singing his praises.

"I'm sure it was the right thing," I said. "We screen our prospective adopters very carefully. We wouldn't have let you take him if we didn't think you'd provide a good home. Besides, it's the love you give them that really matters, especially for a dog like Zeke. He's just a big baby." I knelt down again to give him a reassuring scratch behind the ears, and his tail shifted into double time.

"It's funny," Jay said. "Sometimes he'll just veg out on the sofa with me, but if he doesn't get enough exercise, he's a complete nut job."

"He'll probably calm down after the operation," I said, then watched Jay's face visibly flinch. "Sorry. Have you broken the news to him yet?"

"No, that's what makes it so terrible. He probably thinks we're just here for the atmosphere." Jay laughed weakly and looked down at Zeke. "Sorry, buddy. Has to be done."

"Do you want to come back with us while I sedate him? You're more than welcome."

"No, thanks. I have some things to do." Mmm hmm. Men are notorious babies about these things. "But when can I pick him up?"

"Dr. Robbins told you we'd need to keep him overnight, didn't she? Just to make sure there are no complications. Which there shouldn't be. Why don't I give you a call after he gets out of surgery?" I offered.

"That would be great," Jay said, pulling out a business card from his wallet.

"Oh, we have your number on file," I said, but Jay insisted on placing the card in my hand.

"I'm Jay, by the way." I looked down at the card—*Jay Salazar: Financial Consultant*. Good, I thought to myself a bit presumptuously. Maybe I'll have reason to call upon his services.

"Noelle," I said, extending my hand.

"Call me if anything goes wrong. Anything at all."

"Don't worry. Everything will be fine."

Jay smiled back at me, a smile so sweet and vulnerable that I was a little flustered for several moments after he left. I looked down at Zeke, who had the most forlorn expression on his face—hard to say whether it was due to Jay's departure or the impending loss of his manhood.

Whichever it was, things went fine for Zeke and even better for me. When Jay came back to pick up Zeke the next day, he asked me out to dinner as a thank-you for my extra attentive care of his pal. At the time I thought, gee, it must be nice to be so good-looking you can assume anyone would jump at the chance to have dinner with you, which of course, I did. We went to a trendy, dimly lit restaurant in Providence, drank a shameful number of White Cosmopolitans at the bar, then moved to a table where we shared the tuna carpaccio appetizer and for our entrées, both had the wild mushroom orecchiette ("little ears," Jay told me that meant). We talked easily about our romantic histories (mine was brief; his was extensive and funny), laughed at each other's jokes, and ended the night with a promise to do it again soon. That was in August. A year later, we were married.

You know, they say marriage is for better or for worse. They just don't tell you what worse could mean. Sure, it would have been worse had Jay been an abusive jerk or a drug addict, or something awful like that. But then at least, there'd have been someone to blame. In our case, worse was something neither of us could have predicted or controlled.

As it turned out, I couldn't have a baby. I tried. God knows I did. I visited doctors and took fertility drugs. I took my temperature religiously to find out when I was ovulating. Sex between Jay and me became as spontaneous and exciting as a pelvic exam. Nothing worked.

Turned out it was my problem, and the doctors suggested we consider adopting. But for some reason, Jay was unwilling to discuss that as an option. Some things were too important, he kept saying, but I suspected something else was at the heart of his reluctance.

I'm not saying Jay didn't love me. I know he did. But not in the "can't live without you, I'd do anything for you" sense. He had tried to convince himself he did in an attempt to have a normal life—a wife, kids, and a picket fence to boot. But since he couldn't have that life now, at least not with me, he decided to tell me the truth.

And my time of playing house came abruptly to an end.

Now you might say, well surely, Noelle, there must have been signs. You don't just marry a gay guy and not have your suspicions. But I can honestly say I must have been blind to them, seeing only what I wanted to see. And Jay has since admitted that he had become an amazingly adept actor after all his years of pretending for his family.

Of course, I didn't believe him at first. I thought he was just trying to get out of the marriage so he could find someone with a fertile uterus. I actually believed that. I went through all the denial, the crying, the pleading, the arguing, the bargaining. But in the end, I realized it was an unworkable, unwinnable situation. He loved me as a person, but marriage was never going to work for us.

I remember him saying something to the effect of "You need someone who can love you the way you deserve to be loved." At the time, it had struck me as cheesy and rehearsed, but when I considered it later, it seemed to capture fairly accurately what Jay must have been feeling at the time. Guilty. Conflicted. But certain this was for the best, both for him and for me.

We settled our affairs amicably. We filed for a no-fault divorce (because, really, whose fault was it?), sold the townhouse, then began to rebuild our lives, separately. A few months after we separated, Jay got a promotion and moved to Atlanta to work at another branch of his firm. There was never any question as to who would get Zeke. Jay insisted I keep him. My consolation prize.

About a year before all this happened, I had watched with detached empathy as the wife of a politician stood loyally by her man when he came out of the closet on national television. She had looked so anguished—devastated and humiliated but making a good show of being strong and compassionate for her husband's sake. In her case, the husband had been having an affair with one of his aides for the better part of the year, but this woman wasn't going to let it get the best of her, at least not while the cameras were rolling.

However, I am quite sure that when she got home after that particular press conference and changed out of her Jackie O. suit, she did not blithely stare at herself in the mirror and say, "What now?" Rather, I imagine she went through something resembling what I went through after finding out about Jay: uncontrollable sobbing, consecutive days spent in pajamas, brutal attacks of insecurity that left me feeling like a battered chew toy.

If this woman was being pitied by the nation, surely I was entitled to a little self-pity, too. Especially since I had been dealt a double blow—the loss of both my marriage and the possibility for motherhood.

Why had I spent so much of my childhood cradling dolls and playing house, so much of my adolescence poring through books of baby names, so much of my adulthood enduring painful menstrual cramps, if the universe was not going to allow me to have children of my own? And where would I go from here? How was I going to find some meaning in all of this failure?

The answer to these questions never appeared, but eventually, spurred by a sort of self-loathing and boredom at having spent the past six months alone with my wretched self, I brushed myself off, found this little rental house, and decided to throw myself into my work. Meanwhile, Jay moved into a bachelor's dream high-rise near Peachtree Plaza in Atlanta, got another promotion, bought himself an old Jaguar convertible, and started dating a gorgeous physical therapist named Taj.

And here I am, three years later, my divorce finally final, right back where I started, with nothing to show for myself but this oversized and ridiculously needy dog.

❧

The phone rings about three minutes before Jay is set to arrive. Caller ID says it's my mother. I really don't have time for her right now.

I answer grudgingly. She's calling to wish me a happy birthday and to tell me she'll give me my present on Christmas morning. The downside of having a December 23 birthday is that everyone tries to lump my gifts in with the Christmas presents.

I try to cut the conversation short, a near impossibility with my mother, who somehow translates "Mom, I can't talk right now," into

"I'm dying to hear about the new spaghetti pot and colander in one you bought that fell apart the first time you used it."

When Jay knocks on the door, she is still railing against the Home Shopping Network. "Mom, I really have to go," I say. "Jay's here."

"Jay? I didn't know he was home."

"Well, he is." My mother, for once, is silent. "And I'm still not ready. Look, I'll call you tomorrow, Mom. I love you," I say all in one breath so I can hang up quickly.

And I really am not ready for this. Not literally, not emotionally. Oh well, I think. I'll answer the door while putting my earrings on. It'll seem familiar. Casual. Old friends meeting up again. *Oh, come in, come in. I'll be ready in a sec,* I'll say. Oh my God, my heart feels like it's beating through my rib cage.

I open the door, and Jay is standing there—tall, well groomed, stunning as ever. A few snowflakes have landed in his hair, and I have a strong desire to brush them off and let my hand linger. He's wearing a stylish wool coat with a trendy hand-knit scarf and has on those cute wire-rimmed glasses he bought the last year we were together. His sandy hair is longer than I remember, falling a bit onto his forehead so he looks kind of dashing, kind of 1940s film star. Youthful and cocky. He smiles at me—that disarming smile—then gives me an enormous hug. I can feel myself melting into his arms. *Jay, you're back,* I think. *Hold me. I've been so lonely.* He pulls away.

"Cute haircut," he says.

"Really? I don't know."

"I like it. You look great. As always."

"So do you, of course," I say. "Too good for your own good."

"What's that supposed to mean?"

"Well, for my own good, then." I can't stop looking at him. I swear he still has a tan in December, and I'm tempted to ask whether he's started going to a salon or whether it's his new relationship that's giving him that glow.

"Zeke!" Jay shouts, moving past me and practically diving onto the floor when Zeke enters the room. Zeke is out of his head with excitement. "Zeke, buddy, I've missed you so much." Even this makes me jealous.

We decide to skip the drink at home and head to the restaurant, just chitchatting idly during the car ride about his job and mine, about Zeke, about how difficult it is to get into the holiday spirit in Atlanta when it's seventy degrees out—talking about anything we can think of that doesn't mean a thing to either one of us.

When we pull into Simpatico's parking lot, Jay shuts off the motor and turns to me. "I've really missed you, Noelle," he says, so earnestly it makes my chest hurt. He has this quality about him that keeps me tethered to him, body and soul, even though I know in every way—rationally, biologically, and legally—he's not mine anymore. I want to shout, *Can't you feel it, too? Our pheromones colliding? This attraction pulling us together?*

But of course he can't.

We sit at the bar first, like we used to. I always loved this part best—before the meal, that first drink that goes straight to your head, the soft glow of tea lights along the bar, sitting next to him, feeling the heat from his body next to mine. After my first glass of wine, it's so easy to slip into the illusion that I'm out with my husband, his face so familiar to me even now, his arm brushing mine as we reach for our drinks.

"I'd still take it, you know," I say, stupidly. I must be a bit buzzed.

"Take what?" he says.

"Marriage. With you. Even without the sex."

"Noelle . . ." he says, his voice tinged with pity.

"What, Jay?"

"That's the difference between men and women."

"What is?"

"Men need sex."

I stare down at my drink, embarrassed. "Well, women do, too," I say. "But it's not as if I've been having all this great sex since you left. All things being equal, I'd take the sex I had with you over no sex at all."

He smiles uneasily. "Noelle, you know that . . ."

"Yes, I know it all. Can't I just tell you how I feel? I know you don't feel the same. I know you found the most wonderful guy, and you don't need me anymore. But just because it was so easy for you to move on doesn't mean it's been the same for me."

"Noelle, we tried so hard."

"I know, I know. We've been through it all a million times, and I've always been so understanding. But the fact is, the minute you realized you couldn't get what you wanted out of me, you cut your losses and left." Jay's face looks wounded. I know I'm not playing fair. "I'm sorry," I say, feeling contrite. "I'm being a jerk."

"I understand." He puts his hand on top of mine. "Listen, I have something I need to tell you. It's kind of why I came home." *Oh boy.*

"Is it bad?"

"It's not bad, but in your mood, I'm not sure how you're going to react."

"All right, what is it?"

"Well, I just thought you should know that I'm moving in with Taj." There is a long silence as I take this in. The bartender is trying to pretend he's not listening. "Noelle?"

"Yes?" Blink blink. Smile.

"If it makes you feel any better, I'm selling the Jag and moving out to Marietta. I'm no longer going to be the bachelor cruising around the big city. I'm probably going to become a sedate, suburban old fart."

No, this definitely doesn't make me feel any better. "That's great," I lie. "I'm happy for you."

"Noelle . . ."

"What?"

"Please really be happy for me. Taj is so great. I want you to meet him."

"It's a little soon for that," I say.

"Noelle, we've been together for a year now. You know this."

"But our divorce was just finalized."

"So?"

"So, how do you expect me to keep up with everything? I mean, one minute, we're still trying to work things out, then you're leaving for Atlanta, and the next thing I know, I'm signing divorce papers. And now, here I am, still paying off my share of the attorney's fees while you're practically remarried."

"Noelle, we haven't talked about that yet."

I am feeling so fragile and raw, like my body's going to crack open, spilling yolk all over the floor. "Excuse me," I say to the bartender, fighting back tears. "Can I get another drink?"

"Sure thing," he says, looking at me sympathetically and making my drink much faster than usual. I hate acting like this. I hate feeling like this. "Your table's ready if you want," he says after placing down my drink. *Someone get this crazy lady away from my bar,* he must be thinking.

After we're seated, ironically at the most romantic table by the fireplace, we make the most of the distractions of looking at the menu and ordering our food.

"There's something else I need to talk to you about, too," Jay says finally.

"Great. Lay it on me," I say, feeling oddly numb.

"It sort of involves a favor."

"Okay." I begin playing with the silverware and tapping out a frantic beat with my knife.

"It's about my mom."

"Your mom?" I say. This I wasn't expecting. In fact, I'd kind of hoped I'd never have to think about her again.

"She's not doing so well," he says.

"Is it the MS?"

"Yeah," he says, stilling my hand with his own. "She fell a little over a month ago, and she didn't even tell me about it. I just happened to find some heavy-duty painkillers in the medicine cabinet and asked her about it. At first she blew it off like it was nothing, but eventually I got her to tell me. It was a pretty bad fall, apparently. The doctor said he was surprised she didn't break her hip."

"God," I say, as the waiter arrives with our salads. Neither of us seems particularly hungry.

"Apparently, she's been getting bad headaches and has been losing feeling in her hands and feet. She's afraid to drive, so she hasn't been seeing her friends or going to any of her clubs. I think she's really depressed."

"I'm really sorry, Jay. I thought she'd been doing better." I begin moving lettuce around on my plate.

"Well, she was doing better for a while. But the doctors say the condition is relapsing-remitting, which basically means the MS can come back anytime it wants with a vengeance. I never would have moved to Atlanta if I'd known it would get so bad. I'm worried about her. I'm taking her back to the doctor this week. He had her on prednisone, but she was having too many side effects." I place my fork back down on the table. It would probably be rude to start eating. "He wants to start her on a new steroid therapy. He said he's had lots of success with it recently."

"Well that's at least promising."

"Yeah. But there's sort of a catch. The thing is, she'll need to be taken to the doctor every few months for the treatment, and she's not allowed to drive home afterward. She's also going to need an injection of her interferon once a week." I nod supportively. "I know it's a huge favor, but you're the only one I know who could handle this. You're the only one I trust."

"Jay, are you asking me to go over there every week and give your mother an injection?" I watch as his face droops into a pathetic bloodhound expression.

"And maybe take her to the doctor for her treatments once a

month?" He lowers his head down as if he thinks I might throw something at him.

"Jay . . ."

"Noelle, I know this is a lot to ask. But I've got to go back to Atlanta before New Year's, and I won't be able to leave without knowing someone will be here for her."

"Jay, I'd really like to help you, but . . ."

"Noelle, sweetie. I'm kind of at my wit's end. I know it'll be awkward," he says, "but I trust you. You know how to give an injection."

"To a dog," I say. "Jay, I'm a veterinary technician, not a nurse. Can't you hire someone from the hospital?"

"She won't hear of that. That would signal the beginning of the end to her."

"But she won't mind me coming over? Jay, you do realize this is the same woman whose last words to me were 'I knew you were a mistake.' The woman who accused me of turning you gay. This woman, you want me to inject a needle into?" If it weren't so awful, I might just laugh.

"Noelle, I just need you to help out for a little while. Until I can figure out what to do. I know it's asking an awful lot."

"So you keep saying." I sit there for a long time staring down at my untouched salad and contemplating what he's asking of me. Then I sigh, feeling a horrible sense of inevitability. "If there's really nobody else . . ."

"Noelle, thank you. Thank you. You're a lifesaver," he says, sighing audibly and picking up his fork for the first time. Mission accomplished.

"Have you discussed this with her yet?"

"I'm going to talk to her about it this week. I really think she'll be relieved not to have to hire someone from outside. I mean, you are still family."

"Not really," I say. "I never really was."

"Yes, you were. And you still are," he says. He grabs my hand from across the table and squeezes it, and I can feel myself dissipating into a puddle of water. *Of course I'll do it,* I think. *I'm still in love with you.*

Then I remember why I thought Jay was taking me out tonight. For my birthday.

But he didn't even remember.

Christmas is *big* in my family. My name, of course, means Christmas, and my brother is named after St. Nicholas himself. So on Christmas morning, I brush my teeth, throw a winter coat over my pajamas, and head out to my parents' house. We have this corny tradition where we're not allowed to change out of our pajamas until we've opened our presents. This would ordinarily be fine, except that my mother has asked me to stop at the Jewish bakery on the way to pick up some fresh bread and pastry, and the customers are eyeing me up and down like I'm an escaped lunatic.

When I get onto the highway going west toward Connecticut, I notice it's begun to snow—tiny, downy flakes are flying gently into my windshield. It's so cold that my little hatchback is creaking and rattling as the glass contracts, making it sound like the car is going to shatter into a thousand pieces right there on the highway, leaving me sitting on the road clutching a steering wheel. Nat King Cole's

Christmas album is on the CD player, and every song makes me want to cry.

I have played a mean trick by bringing Beatrix along. My mother's a sucker for dogs, and she and my father haven't gotten a new one since they had to put Lottie to sleep last year. I have a feeling my mother will see Beatrix's long, luxurious bunny ears and just melt.

My parents are hilarious and adorable people—to anyone who isn't their son or daughter. Honestly, I've heard from so many people how likable and funny they are. A testament to this is the number of weekends they have booked to go on ski trips or wine tastings or white-water rafting excursions with friends. Yes, white-water rafting excursions at age sixty. They have a better social life than I do.

When I arrive at the house, my mother is fretting in the kitchen while my father and brother sit in the family room watching *It's a Wonderful Life*. Gender roles have not progressed very rapidly in the Ryan household. Both of my parents are retired, my father from thirty-two years as a policeman, my mother from twelve years of homemaking and twenty-odd years as a middle school teacher. Now my mother paints watercolors and reads *Martha Stewart Living* as her religious text, and my father watches TV and wanders around the house making sure my mother hasn't gone anywhere. He gets nervous if she goes down to the basement to do the laundry.

"Hello, I'm here," I call from the front door. "Merry Christmas." I am lugging my bags of presents and a very nervous Beatrix through the door when my mother comes out to greet me.

"Oh good, Noelle's here," she shouts as a sign for my father and brother to get their butts off the couch and come be civil. I let Beatrix off the leash, and she runs immediately up the stairs to sniff around this new, foreign turf.

"I see you brought a new boyfriend with you," she says, smirking in that annoying motherly way of hers.

"Actually, Beatrix is a girl."

"Oh, so you brought a girlfriend."

"If only it were that simple," I say.

My mother raises an eyebrow, then realizes this is hilarious. "Oh, Noelle," she says, laughing, "don't even joke about that. Your father's in the other room." (When my father found out that Jay was gay and that we were getting divorced, he hugged me stiffly, told me I'd be better off, then never mentioned Jay's name again. I swear to God.)

"You got a new haircut," my mom says, her eyes appraising me with slight disapproval.

"And?"

"Well, you know I like you better with long hair." As if short hair were a character flaw. "But this is cute, too. Very . . . hip." The way she says it, I can tell she means very unflattering.

I follow my mother into the kitchen, where the scents of bacon, fried eggs, and French roast coffee bombard my senses. I could die peacefully here in this kitchen. In all seriousness, I think my mother aspires to be Martha Stewart. Every year, she finds a Christmas theme in her magazines and decorates the house according to the theme. Mind you, when we were children, she was a big fan of cheesy plastic Nativity sets and stick-on window snowflakes and popcorn garlands, just like everyone else in this blue-collar town. But now she has her fancy display of decorations set up on the sideboard with a sign in case we don't get it. This year's is "An Irish Country Christmas": mini trees with white lace, lots of green satin, and little sheep wearing red ribbons with jingle bells. I guess there's a religious message in there somewhere—lamb to the slaughter and shepherds watching their flock by night and all that. Perhaps I'm reaching.

When I turn the corner of the kitchen and enter the family room, there they are, the two Ryan men, exemplar models of enlightened twenty-first-century masculinity, mildly sedated by spiked eggnog and Frank Capra. "Merry Christmas, Dad," I say, leaning down to give him a hug.

"Hi," he says, pulling me down next to him on the sofa. "It's just at the part where Clarence jumps into the river. Your favorite." I love this. Coming back home, pretending life has no worries beyond whether to watch Jimmy Stewart or Charlie Brown. "Happy birthday, by the way," my dad says. Still an afterthought.

"Oh yeah, happy birthday," Nick says, passing over his glass of eggnog. "Want a sip? I made it myself."

"I'm not sure," I say.

"Don't touch it," I hear my mother shout from the kitchen. "You'll be passed out halfway through church. Do you all want to open presents now that Noelle's here? We should get this show on the road."

Christmas morning is the one time of the year when we all go back to 1983. Nobody argues or fights or complains, and there's nobody from the outside world to dispel the illusion that we are the Waltons, minus a handful of children and the Depression-era clothes. Of course the minute we get to my Aunt Helen's house for dinner, the bickering begins and reality rears its ugly head once again. But for a few hours, with all of us assembled in the living room in front of a bestockinged fireplace and a fat, jolly Christmas tree, I am seven years old again.

We open presents while drinking coffee laced with eggnog and listen to carols on my parents' CD player, which my father still believes to be the latest in high-tech wizardry. Every time the CD changes, he shakes his head and says, "Random shuffle. Fantastic."

Beatrix comes back downstairs to join us, anxiously trotting from present to present, hoping there might be something for her in one of the crinkly packages. When I finish my coffee, I let her lick the mug clean.

My mother, who seems to think I'm still fifteen, has bought me a pair of tweed pants and a V-neck cable-knit sweater. I should be impressed by her restraint. If she had her way, I'd still be wearing argyle vests and knee socks.

My brother, who never has any money, has made me a picture frame using his new design technique. It's really quite amazing. He takes little pieces of punched metal and paints them various colors, then affixes them to a wooden frame using tiny screws that lock into one of two places. In the one setting, all the exposed pieces of metal form a design of two slender green trees with red apples hanging off their branches. But when you flip the frame over and turn all the screws clockwise, the trees on front change color from green to red and yellow and orange, so it looks like spring has turned to autumn. He's been trying to get a commission to sell his work in gift shops and catalogs, but mostly he just shows in small galleries and makes extra money by temping. His favorite joke when people ask him if he's still temping is to say, "Yeah, but it's not a permanent thing."

My brother has always got an iron in the fire, some new scheme that's bound to make him money, make him famous, or both. He's good with computers—he's even developed websites for dozens of his friends—but the problem is he's never collected a dime. He's generous but foolish; consequently, he's always in financial trouble, often forced to borrow money, usually from me.

I guess he gets this impracticality from my mother. Even though my parents never made a lot of money, my mother always believed that someday they would own a beautiful old house in the country, have it decorated with real antiques, and throw lavish dinner parties under a gazebo in the orchard. I guess we all have our delusions.

"Oh, Nicholas," my mother says when she opens up the necklace he's made for her. "This is exquisite. Honey, did you see this necklace Nicholas made? I always tell my friends about your work. We should have one of those parties, you know, like a Tupperware party. I'll invite all my friends and you'll show off your designs."

"That's an excellent idea, Mom," Nick says.

After the love fest for Nick has reached nauseating proportions, I ask, "So what do you think about my gift?"

"Which one?" my mother says. "The scarf is lovely. But I'm not sure about the pants. Might make me look too hippy."

"I meant Beatrix," I say.

"Oh, no you don't," my father says. "We've got enough to worry about without a new dog."

"Like what?" I say.

"Well, your mother's got her painting, and I've got—"

"What, your allotment of *Hogan's Heroes* each week?"

"Noelle," my mother scolds as if I'm five years old and not yet permitted to use sarcasm. "Your father's been quite the fixer-upper lately. He waterproofed the entire basement and turned Nick's room into an office upstairs. We've got the Internet and everything. He even bought some things on eBay." She says "eBay" as if it's a word in some remote tribal language.

"Really?" I say. It's less startling that my father did a do-it-yourself project than that he used a computer. For years, he was the only guy on his police force who still used a typewriter.

"And we're saving up for a cruise this year," my father adds. "What would we do with a dog on a cruise?"

"I could look after her," I say. "She's already met Zeke, and they get along great."

"Then you keep her," he says.

"Oh, I don't know," my mother says, but I can tell she's already softening, already imagining waking up to those adorable brown eyes, one half closed like it's winking.

"Think about it," I say, then throw in for good measure, "If we don't adopt her soon, we may have to put her down." This is entirely untrue. Ours is a no-kill shelter. If we can't find a home for the dog, we are the home for the dog. That's actually our motto. But my mother doesn't know this.

After we gather up all the wrapping paper and stack our gift boxes under the tree to reinspect later, my parents go upstairs to get dressed for church. I grab the frame Nick made me and flip the screws back and forth. Spring, fall. Spring, fall. "I really love this," I say to him.

"Thanks. I wish I could have bought you something."

"Don't be stupid," I say. He glances over at me and frowns. "What?"

"Nothing," he says. "So how are things going with you?"

"Things? Things are fine. Spectacular. Never been better. Come on, what's up?"

"Wow," he says. "Can't I ask my sister how she's doing without being suspected of ulterior motives?"

"Okay," I say. "I'm sorry. If you really want to know, my divorce is final. Jay has some gorgeous Indian boyfriend down in Atlanta, and they're moving in together. I'm taking care of Jay's evil mother, even though she hates me. And, let's see, what else . . . oh, I haven't been on a date in a year and a half. And they say it's more likely for a woman over thirty to get struck by lightning than to get married. Any other questions?"

He laughs a bit, then clears his throat. "So I guess it would be out of the question for you to lend me some money."

"Jesus, Nick. You need money? Again?"

"Oh, come on. I haven't asked you in a long time."

"I think it was September, Nick. For that art gallery show. And you still haven't paid me back."

"Look," he says, "I really thought that was going to pan out. And you know I'll pay you back. It's not like you don't know where to find me."

"Yeah, and I think I'm going to have to send someone out to break your kneecaps."

He smiles weakly, then frowns again. "I'm in some serious trouble this time. And I can't tell Mom and Dad about it."

"What is it?" I ask, waiting for the inevitable scam, scheme, or brilliant idea he's just hatched.

"Promise me you won't say anything," he says, his voice dissolving into a whisper.

"Okay, but you're scaring me. What's going on?"

"You know Dana, right? My girlfriend?"

I have met her so few times I have to scan my memory to conjure her face. Long red hair. Skinny. Quiet. "The one you brought for Labor Day weekend?"

"Yeah. Well, things have gotten pretty serious with us. I mean, we've even discussed marriage, but she's not ready for that. She still has another year in school, and she wants to start her own clothing line and all. Anyway, she just got back from her gynecologist. She'd been feeling healthy, no worries. Then at the end of her exam, the doctor says, 'You know you're about three months pregnant, right?'"

"Are you serious?"

"Unfortunately. Dana thought it was just holiday weight gain."

"Is it yours?"

"Of course it's mine," he says.

"Sorry, I was just asking." My eyes must be popping out of my skull because Nick now looks more worried than he did a minute ago. "So what are you going to do?"

"I don't know. We're discussing our options. But she might want to get an abortion."

"Jesus, Nick. This is really serious."

"I know that," he says. "Can you lower your voice? Don't you think I know that?"

Beatrix cowers by my side, tail under her legs, wondering what she's done to bring on this argument. It's no wonder. Her former owner stuck a barbecue skewer into her eye because she was begging for food beneath the grill. I put an arm around her and pull her by my side.

"Didn't you use birth control?" I finally ask.

"She's on the Pill," he says, "but I guess it's not one hundred percent."

"No, I guess not." I choke on the irony that I could not get pregnant even with a host of fertility drugs and sex at rabbitlike frequencies. And here Dana gets pregnant while on the Pill.

"Well, I'm not lending you money so Dana can have an abortion," I say. "There are too many people out there who would die for a healthy baby."

"What am I supposed to do?" he says. "I mean, I don't know whether she's going to want to marry me. And Mom and Dad will flip. You know their thoughts on sex outside of marriage."

"I wouldn't be so concerned with Mom and Dad right now," I say. "This isn't about them. Think of Dana. You need to talk to her and tell her you're going to support her, no matter what she decides to do. You know how I feel about the issue, but it's not my choice. It's hers."

"Oh man, Noelle. I really fucked up."

"Literally." And even though we know we shouldn't, we both start to laugh, that bittersweet laughter you summon when there's nothing else to do but cry.

I have decided to accept an invitation to my neighbors' New Year's Eve party even though I'm not very good at parties. I tend to shut down around lots of people. The only thing that gets me to go to this particular party is the fact that my house is roughly five steps away. If I get panicky, I can just run out the back door and go home.

Surprisingly Mike and Trey both greet me at the door, the perfect hosts. "Noelle, you made it," Trey says, kissing me on the cheek. Trey is definitely the better looking of the two—dark and wiry where Mike is more of a big teddy bear. But I've always liked Mike better. He gives me an enormous hug, then takes me directly to the kitchen and pours me an absurdly large plastic cup of pink champagne. I think twice about drinking it, then think, *What the hell,* and do a toast with him and his friends. There's a girl standing in the corner who can't be bothered to toast with us—she's tall with dark skin and a killer body, and has a single stud in her nose and a vine tattoo creeping down her left arm. Sexy. I immediately feel wrong in my turtleneck and jeans.

After spending the requisite amount of time with me to make sure I'm okay, Mike goes back to the party to mingle with the other guests, leaving me holding an empty red cup and standing next to Sexy Spice. She smells delicious. "I like your perfume," I say.

"Thanks," she says in a breathy voice. "It's imported."

"Mmm," I say, not sure what that's supposed to mean. She winks at someone behind her, then brushes past me, her long dark hair swaying against my shoulder as she leaves. "Can I pour you one while I'm at it?" a guy says to me, holding the tap nozzle in his hand. I hadn't even known he was in the room.

"Sure," I say, handing him my cup. He's cute. Messy brown hair, crinkly eyes, and that sexy clenched-jaw thing. Too cute. A turn-your-brain-to-clotted-cream cute.

"Here you go," he says, passing me the beer. "I wouldn't drink any more of the champagne if I were you. It's a hangover in a bottle." Nice voice, I think. Earnest.

"Thanks for the warning."

"Yo, Fox. Pour me a cold one, will you?" I hear someone yell from the other room.

"Are you on keg duty?" I ask.

"No, I was just standing in the wrong place at the wrong time."

"I see." I smile at him, and he smiles back, noncommittally. He seems young. Probably my brother's age. This shouldn't matter, and yet I can't help thinking that when I was in college, he was probably

32

on a skateboard somewhere, thinking of ways to intercept his report card.

"So you're . . . Fox?"

"Yeah."

"Is that your first name?"

"Last."

"Oh. That's kind of a guy thing, isn't it? To call people by their last names?" I say, babbling as I'm apt to when someone is this unsettlingly attractive.

"In my case, it's just that it's preferable to my first name."

"Which is?"

After a long pause, "Jasper."

"We have a dog at the shelter named Jasper," I say. Then, to add insult to injury, "He's a beagle."

"Really." He blinks once, his face totally impassive.

"I mean, I like the name," I say, trying to recover. "It's a nice name."

"Apparently I was conceived in the town of Jasper, Texas."

"Is that where you're from? Texas?" He nods. When I'm nervous, I tend to interrogate people like they're prisoners. Which is probably how he feels right now. "But you don't have a Southern accent."

"No, well, I've lived here for almost ten years."

"How'd you end up here?" I ask.

"For college."

"Oh, where'd you go?"

"Brown," he says. I am immediately impressed.

"Really? What'd you study?"

"Bio-med." Even more impressed.

"You have graduated, haven't you?" I ask, suddenly worried that he's even younger than I thought. For the first time, he laughs.

"Yes. Several years ago."

"Oh, good. Just making sure." Then I'm embarrassed because it sounds as if I'm hitting on him. Which I totally am.

"You haven't told me your name," he says.

"Oh, sorry. I'm Noelle. Noelle Ryan."

"I had a teacher named Ryan," he says. "Sister Ryan. A nun." Ironic, I think.

"Really?"

"Yeah. She used to rap my knuckles with a ruler."

"Are you serious? Or are you just trying to get back at me for the beagle comment?"

"No," he says, laughing. "Swear to God." He puts down the tap, which he'd been holding throughout our entire conversation, and crosses himself. "Well, I think I ought to leave the kitchen while I can," he says. "Let someone else be keg master." Oh great. He can't wait to get away from me.

"Exactly," I say, following him into the living room, where he sits down on the sofa, shoving a few pillows off, presumably so I can sit next to him. "Speaking of names," I say, trying to fill up the awkward silence that has settled between us, "do you ever wonder why nobody has any of the really famous last names? I mean, you never hear about anyone named Hitler. Or Bonaparte. Or Stalin. Did they take those names out of circulation?"

"You know, you're right," he says, smiling, and I suddenly feel a tremendous sense of well-being. I lean back into the sofa, my body facing his, thinking that my epiphany about names is one of the more brilliant ideas I've had in recent years. I sneak a glance at him again and realize what makes him so appealing is that he looks like maybe he'd been a chubby kid, the kind who had round, pinchable cheeks until he was fifteen, when everything suddenly got very lean and chiseled. But there's still a ghost of that old soft-ness there, giving me the impression that he could never be mean to anybody.

"So, you mentioned something about a beagle at a shelter. I as-sume you work with dogs?" he says.

"Yeah, I'm a vet tech."

"That sounds like a cool job."

"It is," I say. "It can be sad sometimes. There are so many un-wanted dogs and cats. But it can also be very rewarding." *Oh, please someone shut me up.* "What do you do?"

"What I want to do is write music." *Uh-oh.* "I mean, I do write music. It's just not really working as a meaningful source of income yet." *Oh dear God, he's another Nick. Run while you can. Run!* Then he breaks into a shy smile. His top teeth are a little crooked, not offensively so, just enough to render him absolutely adorable and sufficiently flawed that I can continue talking to him. "How do you know Mike and Trey?" he asks, clearly changing the subject from his unemployed status.

"Oh, I live next door. How about you?"

"I used to date Trey's sister," he says. Thud. An iron door crashes closed on my heart. But he did say "used to." These words absolutely save me. But still.

"And Trey lets you stick around?"

"Yeah, well. She dumped me."

"Oh. Still, must be awkward."

"Not really. We stayed friends." *Terrific.* "That's her over there." I turn my head slowly, hoping it won't be, but knowing it will be. The girl with the ivy tattoo. "That's Jolene."

"Jolene," I repeat, pointlessly. I am dying to ask how long it's been since they've broken up. But it's almost as if the mention of her name works as an invocation, because the beautiful siren known as Jolene begins floating (I swear, she floats) across the room and stands right in front of us, hand on one hip, pelvis arched slightly forward. Her shirt hits just above her midriff so you can see her taut, tan abdomen underneath. I am certain this is not an accident.

"Hi, Jass," she says. *She calls him Jass. How cute.* "Who's your friend?" she asks, as if to say, *I don't want you anymore, but I don't want anyone else to even talk to you.*

"Jo, this is Noelle. Noelle, Jolene." He nods up to her but doesn't stand up. Like an idiot, I do.

"Hi," I say, extending my hand eagerly like I'm interviewing at her law firm or something. "Nice to meet you."

"You're the one who liked my perfume," she says.

"Yes, that's right."

"Mmm hmm. And are you guys . . . ?" She points her finger back and forth between us.

"What, us?" I say. "No. We just met."

"Jo, Noelle lives next door. She's Trey's neighbor."

"Oh, well that explains it."

"Explains what?" I say.

"Why I haven't ever seen you before. Jass and I hang out at a lot of the same places. I know almost everyone he knows." *Just a little proprietary, aren't we?*

"Jo sometimes sings in the band with us," Jasper says. "Not so much anymore."

36

"Only because you don't ask so much anymore," she says, plopping down next to him where I had just been sitting.

"Jo, Noelle was sitting there."

"That's all right. You don't mind, do you? Jass and I haven't seen each other in a long time. We've got some catching up to do."

"But, Jo . . ."

"Look, I'm going to get another drink," I say. "Jass . . . Fox, whatever your name is . . . it was nice talking to you."

"Wait. We're playing in Providence in a few weeks. Let me give you my card."

"You have a card?" I say.

"Well, the band has a card." He hands it to me.

"The Nomads," I read. "Guess you travel a lot." God, I'll bet he's never heard that one before.

"Not as much as I'd like, I'm afraid. Anyway, we're playing the third weekend at the Loft." He says this as if it should mean something to me.

"Okay. Maybe I'll check it out."

"Do," he says. Jolene yawns.

"It was nice meeting you," I say.

"It was nice meeting you, too," he says, but I am already walking away. There is no way I'm competing with a twenty-two-year-old preternaturally pretty singer with an ivy vine tattoo scrolling down her forearm. No way.

Within ten minutes, I am in my bed staring at the TV and waiting for the ball to drop in Times Square. It's not even close to midnight. I am unbelievably pathetic.

January

There is nothing more depressing than the week after New Year's when all the Christmas trees are lying out on the curb, waiting to be turned into wood chips. Every year people bring these trees into their homes, love them and cherish them, even give them personalities— *Oh, this year's tree is so squat and fat like Santa Claus. Remember last year's looked like a scrawny old man?* We sit in front of our trees night after night, basking in their warm, soothing glow and becoming hopeful in their presence. Then, as soon as the holiday's over, we toss them out to the curb, piteous and shorn like empty carcasses left by a pack of wolves.

Perhaps I'm just in this appallingly pessimistic mood because I'm going to see Jay's mother today.

I pull up in front of her house, a beautiful restored Victorian that sits up on a hill in Tiverton, overlooking the Sakonnet River. There's even a guest cottage on the property and old horse stables, now empty. I stare up at the two flights of stairs that lead to an imposing front porch, and I'm immediately taken back to the first time I came here. The first time I met Mrs. Salazar.

Jay was bringing me home to meet the family for the first time, and Mrs. Salazar met us at the door, the perfect embodiment of the New England matriarch—tall and slim, with unusually upright carriage, a low humorless voice, champagne blond hair, and a silk pantsuit to match. Even though she was tall, she was wearing three-inch heels (in a beautiful, buttery leather) that made her tower over me. I remember her looking me up and down, mostly down in that patrician sort of way, stopping at my shoes, which like all of my clothes, were cheap and practical. I had not considered that the wife of a Brazilian shoe manufacturer might be a little picky about my choice of footwear. Shoes to me were about comfort, not class. But that night, my shoes seemed to confirm everything Jay's mother had already assumed about me. That I was blue collar. Ordinary. Tasteless. Not good enough for her son.

Jay's father was a tall and elegant man, with long slender fingers and the same honey-colored skin as Jay. He seemed to like me instantly, but then again, he seemed to be a man who had achieved such a level of success in life that he had made up his mind not to be disappointed by anything.

On the surface, everything about their life seemed perfect—the immaculate house on the hill, the tasteful furnishings, the gourmet food, the fine breeding, especially the elegance and glamour of the hosts. Jay's parents were so exquisite and aloof they gave me the impression of Julie Christie and Omar Sharif in *Doctor Zhivago*—two beautiful ill-fated lovers in a frigid landscape.

When we left the house that night, I felt exhausted from trying so hard to be likable. Despite my efforts, I told Jay I didn't think his mother liked me at all. "Nonsense," he said. "You have to understand, my mother happens to think that every member of the human race is desperately flawed and in need of her counsel."

"Or judgment," I said.

But Jay convinced me she was just wary about Jay's romantic interests, particularly as he'd had such bad luck with women in the past. Not surprising, in hindsight.

During the first six months of our relationship, Jay's mother refused to acknowledge that what Jay and I had together was anything more than a frivolous distraction. When Mr. Salazar had his first heart attack in February, Jay and I grew even closer. I had just dealt with my own father's heart attack not two years before, so I knew what Jay was going through. My father had undergone bypass surgery and had come out of the ordeal fitter and healthier than ever, so I was optimistic, persuading Jay not to fear the worst. I went to the hospital with him and offered to do what I could. Jay's mother made no attempt to hide the fact that she found my presence there distasteful and intrusive.

By April, Jay and I were engaged to be married. Of course, Mrs. Salazar was incensed. But by then Mr. Salazar's health had deteriorated, and all other concerns were irresolutely suspended. It was a terrible shock when he died that September after complications from his second heart attack. Nobody was more surprised than I, who had been so sure he'd make it through just like my own father had.

Jay was inconsolable. I thought surely we would postpone the wedding, which at that point was only a month away. But Jay was adamant about going forward with it, saying it was what his father would have wanted.

We should have slowed down, given ourselves more time to deal with the grief and take in what had happened. But we didn't. We went through with the wedding, then spent an awkward four-day honeymoon in St. Croix, where we numbed ourselves with food, drink, and sun. For a while after we got back home, Jay was so sweet and tender with me, as if the tragedy had made him appreciate me all the more.

I moved into Jay's townhouse in Bristol, not ten minutes from his mother, and we began trying to start a family. Jay kept talking about how this would make everything all right between his mother and me, how this was just what the family needed—something life affirming to bring us all together after the tragic loss we had experienced. But of course, I wasn't able to do that for her. Now she had reason to hate me all the more.

When Jay and I filed for divorce the next year, I am sure Mrs. Salazar smiled in vindication, knowing that all her premonitions about the unsuitability of our marriage had finally been confirmed.

And now I am being asked to go to her home and care for her, this woman who has shown me nothing but scorn and derision since the day I first met her.

I climb the stairs full of dread, then tentatively ring the bell. A foreboding chime. Finally after several minutes I hear the sound of footsteps and the latch clicking. When the door opens, the woman standing before me looks nothing like the imposing, frosty, calculating woman I remember. She still looks elegant in long silk pajamas and matching kimono, but she seems shorter, dissipated. She is wearing slippers instead of the usual heels, and she's also put on weight in strange places, her face splotched and jowly, like she's had a face-lift that went horribly awry. At first I'm not sure she even recognizes me, but then her eyes go wide and indignant, and suddenly the old Mrs. Salazar is back.

"What are you doing here?" she says.

"Jay told you I was coming, didn't he?"

"Must have slipped his mind," she says, turning away as if I'm not even worth the effort of speaking to. I'm not sure whether I should enter the house or run down the steps screaming, but then I remember the way she made me feel all those years ago, and a surge of outrage propels me through the door.

"He said he told you I was coming today," I say. "For your injection."

"Yes, he did mention he'd be sending you. But I told him not to. I thought he might actually listen to me for a change. I don't know why on earth he even asked you."

She's playing a game with me, I think, to see how much I'm willing to take. Testing me. "Probably because I have basic medical training, live ten minutes from your house, and everyone else said no."

She turns around to face me now, her eyebrow raised as if she's impressed at my newfound gumption. "No need to get nasty. I just don't like being treated like some kind of invalid. Jay seems to think I can't take care of myself anymore."

"Well, I'm sure that's not the case, but very few people are able to stick a needle into their own arm. Perhaps we should get started. I imagine the sooner I'm out of your hair, the better." I follow her into the living room where she has a wing chair pulled near the bay window, surrounded by a table full of books and papers. "Sit down, Mrs. Salazar," I say, trying my hand at the Nurse Ratched approach. Miraculously she obeys. "Hold out your arm," I say. "You've done

43

this before at the doctor's office. I'm just going to insert the needle here. It may take a little while, so once we begin, you'll need to hold still."

"Yes, yes, I understand," she says.

I tear the plastic off the syringe and sink the needle through the vial, drawing the medicine into the barrel, then flick the syringe until a drop falls off the tip. Then I find her vein like a pro and, before she can say another word, inject her with the needle. I take a sort of sadistic pleasure in watching her wince and turn her head away. We're all infants when we face the needle.

"Now, you're going to want to keep an eye on the injection site to make sure you don't have a reaction," I say. "And give me a call if you feel any strangeness at all. There are a few possible side effects the doctor mentioned."

"I'm not going to have any side effects," she says. "I have enough problems as it is." I almost laugh.

"All right, then," I say, gathering the spent syringe and Band-Aid wrapper for the trash.

"That's it?" she says.

"Yep."

"Oh," she says, seemingly chastened by her ten-minute ordeal. "You will be back next week then?"

"Of course."

"I mean, much as I'm sure it pains you to be here, you can't imagine how hard this is for me."

Look," I say, suddenly emboldened by some force I didn't know was in me. "I've promised Jay I would do this. No matter what your feelings for me have been in the past, I'm the one he's charged with this responsibility. I'm doing this for him."

"Don't I know it," she says, gripping the injection site with her fingers and turning her head toward the window. Not knowing what to do next, I gather my belongings and let myself out the front door.

God, that was awful, I think, heading out into the brisk winter air. But surprisingly, not as awful as I thought it would be. Perhaps I will get through this after all. If only to prove something to myself.

A few weeks pass in this way, me going weekly to the house for the injections and working long hours at the animal hospital. January is not a busy month for dog adoptions, but it is a busy month for animal neglect, so we usually find the shelter filled to capacity, with too few people willing to adopt. Every rescued dog has a story, some of them quaint and heartwarming, suitable for thumbtacking to the corkboard at the shelter to help encourage adoptions: a puppy found on the edge of a farmer's field covered in ticks, a kitten pulled out of a storm grate. But some of the stories are too horrific to utter to prospective owners: the bulldog who'd been left chained outside to a tree for four days in the glaring heat of summer without water, food, or shade or the cocoa-colored mutt beaten close to death with a wrench, brought in with a broken jaw and partially fractured skull, and so afraid of human contact that it took six months before he even allowed himself to be picked up by one of our staff.

Fortunately, my mother decided to keep Beatrix, one happy ending in a series of tragedies, and my brother's girlfriend decided to keep her baby. Love and comfort in small doses. In the context of the larger world, life still seems harsh and uncertain.

Appropriately, the weather has been cold, wet, and gray, with frequent bouts of that freezing, piercing rain that promises to turn to snow but never quite does. After the excitement of Christmas, people usually don't think of adopting a dog until springtime, so we tend to use the long wasteland of late winter to take care of fund-raising. My boss has put me in charge of organizing the annual charity function for the summer, but so far my creativity has failed me.

After a long week, I head over to Mrs. Salazar's on Saturday morning to give her her weekly injection. From the moment I arrive I can tell she's in a foul mood. "Hello, Mrs. Salazar," I say, taking off my wet boots in the foyer. "Everything okay?"

"Fine," she spits out. She looks terrible—hair unkempt, eyes rimmed with circles that look more like bruises, her gown soft and wrinkled as if it's been slept in.

"Did you sleep all right?" I ask.

"No. I slept in the chair."

"Why'd you do that?"

"Well . . . I wanted to finish that book you gave me," she says. I scan her side table where I see the copy of *The Road* I lent her. It's about two people wandering through postapocalyptic America trying to survive together. Somehow appropriate, I think.

"Did you get to finish?" I ask.

"Mmm," she says, only half an affirmation.

"So what did you think?"

"It was okay."

"Okay?" This is not a book you feel okay about when you finish. "You must have had some sort of reaction. Tell me what you thought."

"I didn't exactly finish it. I had to stop reading."

"Oh?"

"You see, I had some issues last night. It must just be anxiety or something." She shakes her head repeatedly as if she believes she can make me disappear.

"Anxiety? What do you mean?"

"It's so silly . . ." she says, looking suddenly embarrassed.

"I'm sure it's not silly. Tell me."

She sighs, exasperated. With herself or me, I'm not sure. "I was trying to read, but then all of a sudden . . . I couldn't hold the book anymore."

"Couldn't hold the book? You mean, you got too tired?"

"No, I mean I couldn't *hold* the book anymore. Like my arms gave out on me."

"Okay? I'm not sure what you mean . . ."

"See, I knew you'd make a big deal out of this." She puts a hand up to her forehead, shielding her eyes as if she cannot bear to look at me.

"I'm not making a big deal out of anything. I'm just trying to figure out what happened."

"It was as if my muscles just stopped working. Then when I tried to get up, I . . . I couldn't walk."

I am already bending down to inspect her legs as if the reason she couldn't walk might be visible. "You couldn't walk?"

"Would you please stop repeating the last thing I say! Yes, I couldn't walk. I had my legs crossed, and when I uncrossed them . . . my legs buckled. Like when your foot falls asleep, but worse."

"Why didn't you call me?" I say.

"Because it wasn't that serious. So I slept on a chair."

"Mrs. Salazar, it is serious. You should have called me."

"I didn't want to put you out."

"But that's why I'm here. That's why Jay asked me to take care of you. If you can't call me when something goes wrong, then what's the point?"

"Look, everything seems better this morning. See, I can walk now." She pushes herself up and half stands, half leans on the arm of the chair.

"But you couldn't walk yesterday. This is serious. It's something your doctor needs to know about. Look, even if you didn't want to call me, you could have called your doctor. He would have sent an ambulance for you."

She lets herself fall back into the chair, making an exaggerated sighing noise as she does so. "For God's sake, this is exactly why I didn't want anyone checking up on me. No privacy. Don't I have enough sense to decide when and if I need to call my own doctor? I wish I could give myself the damned injection instead of having you come here every week to interrogate me. Here, maybe I can," she says, grabbing the syringe from the table next to her, then staring down the tube blankly.

"Mrs. Salazar, stop this. If you don't want to go to the hospital, I'm not going to make you go. But I really think you should have yourself checked out again."

"And have the doctor tell me I'm going to need to use a walker? Or, worse, a wheelchair? I'm not going to let that happen. You may get some kind of sick pleasure out of seeing me like this, but I can tell you, I don't."

I walk over to her resolutely, pull a chair directly in front of her, sit down, and take the syringe from her hand. "Mrs. Salazar," I say. "I can assure you I get no pleasure out of this. Despite what you might think, I'm not the enemy here. Listen, let me give you your injection. I won't mention the doctor again unless you tell me you want to go see him. But please, you have to let me know if something like this happens again."

"Fine, fine," she says, making a swatting motion with her hand. *Be gone, vile fiend!* We are mythic enemies now.

I mix the interferon and give her the injection, then sit on the love seat trying to decide what to do while she seethes over by the window. "I'm going to have to call Jay and tell him about this," I say.

"Oh, for God's sake, I'll tell my own son."

"Will you?"

"Yes, I've said so."

But I don't believe her. The minute I get home, I call Jay and tell him myself.

True to form, he is completely impractical, telling me I should basically kidnap his mother and force her to go see the doctor. Of course I explain the unfeasibility of such an abduction, and he responds by telling me he trusts me implicitly to do the right thing.

"Look, Jay, this is a lot of responsibility to put on me. I don't know if this is going to work out after all."

"What do you mean?" he says, sounding genuinely surprised to hear doubt in my voice.

"She has all this animosity toward me, and I really don't know why. I'm trying to help her, and she hates me for it."

"Noelle, sweetie, she doesn't hate you. She's just the proudest woman on the eastern seaboard. Possibly the country."

"All right, but you might want to start thinking about other options. In case things get worse."

"They won't get worse," he says. Boy, this family has a love affair with denial.

"I'm just saying . . ."

"Duly noted."

"Look, don't get flippant about this. I'll be the one up here dealing with the fallout if anything goes wrong."

"I know, and I really do appreciate it," he says, his voice softening into that soothing Jay tenor. "I don't know where I'd be without you."

"You'd be up here dealing with your mother yourself is where you'd be." He laughs, but I didn't intend it to be funny.

"Listen, now that that's sorted out, do you have a minute?" he says. "I really want to talk to you about something."

My heart lurches, as it always does when Jay says he wants to talk to me about something. Given the past few "things" he's wanted to talk about, it's not surprising. "I really can't. I'm going out tonight."

"Oh, really? Do you have a hot date or something?" he says, his voice slick with smugness. He couldn't possibly believe that would be the case.

I consider making up some story, consider telling him the truth, then decide on some combination of the two. "As a matter of fact I do."

"Really? Who with?" Astoundingly, I detect a trace of discomfort in his voice—jealousy?

"This guy I met at a New Year's party. I'm going to see his band." Until this moment I had not even been entirely sure I was going to go. But talking to Jay has awakened some part of me that knows it may die if I don't get out of the house tonight.

"His band? What is he, a teenager?"

"No, he's a guitarist. Jay, don't do this, please."

"Do what?" he asks, all innocence.

"The whole protective father routine. I'm late as it is."

"Well, you need to tell me something about the guy so I don't worry. I don't want to hear they've found you chopped into little pieces in the trunk of some creepo's car."

"He's not a creepo. And I'm pretty sure he's not a serial killer. Aside from that I don't know much about him myself." And then I think to myself, it's not even a date. In fact, his ex-girlfriend's probably going to be on stage with him. But I don't tell Jay any of this. Instead I let him squirm.

"All right. But you have to call me tomorrow and tell me everything. Will you do that?"

"Yes, Jay. And you'll call your mom and talk to her?"

"I will."

We say good night, and he tells me he loves me. It's still so natural to say it back.

Subconsciously this night—"The Nomads Live at the Loft"—has been hovering over my horizon like some promised sunrise after a season of darkness. I don't know why; I have about as much chance of starting a relationship with Jasper as I have of . . . well, getting struck by lightning. Statistically speaking, even less chance.

I arrive at the club early and secure one of the little two-top tables set against the wall. Apparently this is uncool, as nobody else is sitting down. But at least I feel safe and have a decent vantage point of the stage. Despite the smoking ban, the place still smells of cigarettes but in a good way. Not stiflingly smoky, just atmospheric and heady. The bar is small but packed, a good sign.

I nurse my beer for a while, checking out the clientele, an odd mix of young hipsters and nineties Goth throwbacks with a few bikers thrown in for good measure. I have no idea what to expect. What if the Nomads are a heavy-metal thrasher band, and Jasper comes out and bites off a chicken head? Or what if they're all wearing skintight leather and playing bad power rock on fluorescent green guitars? I convince myself this couldn't be the case. Jasper had a coolness about him that leads me to believe otherwise.

When his band finally walks out on stage, I am relieved to see four unintimidating, slightly cooler than usual guys in their late twenties. Jasper looks tall and lean in a simple white T-shirt and jeans. He slides his guitar over his shoulder and walks downstage, finds me in the crowd, and smiles. I smile back, resisting the urge to wave at him like a trained sea lion.

After the lead singer gives a brief greeting to the crowd, the band begins to play—surprisingly ethereal melodies set against anthemic chords. The lead singer has a voice like molten chocolate, but I know it's Jasper's lyrics that make the song so yearning and soulful. I imagine him sitting at home with sheets of notebook paper, churning out version after version of this song right after Jolene broke his heart.

So I try to ignore the lyrics and focus on his guitar playing instead, but I'm really just staring at his arms, watching how his muscles clench as he moves his fingers up and down the frets. He is singing harmony, which is more difficult and, in my opinion, sexier than lead vocals, even though it doesn't get the same glory. I love how his voice complements the melody while going off in unexpected directions.

Then I spot Jolene. She's not on stage as I had suspected but standing right down in front of the stage with a cohort of equally tall and beautiful friends, their bodies swaying seductively to the music. She looks amazing—liquid jeans and a sparkly halter top that shows off her back and arm muscles. She must lift weights.

I am so out of my element; it's been years since I've been to a club like this. I'm wearing black, a relatively safe choice, but compared to most of the girls here, I look decidedly old. These are young women who probably work out three hours a day and drink shots of Jack Daniel's and take no shit from anybody.

As I watch Jolene I honestly want to disappear into the wall. I can't understand how two people so good-looking could break up and still remain friends. I take a long sip of my beer, which tastes stale and warm now. I'm anxious about the moment when the set ends and I have to talk to him. If I get to talk to him. Was he just being polite on New Year's Eve, or did he really mean to invite me? Or could he have been so drunk he won't even remember me?

Oh God, I think, as I consider running out of the bar before the song ends. But it's too late. The crowd is applauding loudly, and Jasper is laying his guitar down in the corner. The first set is over. He turns around and jumps off the small stage, walking directly to my table.

"Hi," he says, a little breathless.

"Hi," I say, flustered and unsure of myself. "You guys were great."

"Really? I felt like we were a little off tonight."

"Well, I thought you sounded great."

"I'm so glad you came," he says, sitting down across from me. He's even cuter than I remembered—all tousled hair and sexy cheekbones.

"I wasn't sure if you'd remember me," I say.

"What are you talking about? You're the only person I do remember from that party. Noelle Ryan, right?"

My face goes up instantly in flames. "Jasper. Fox. Which should I call you, by the way?"

"Jasper."

"I thought you liked Fox better," I say.

"Yeah, well that's before you told me about that beagle at your shelter."

I smile, look down at the floor. "I really do like the name Jasper. It sounds like 'whisper.'" This is exactly the kind of dumb thing I say whenever I'm nervous. But Jasper doesn't laugh. In fact, I think he's flirting with me. It's been so long, it's hard to tell.

For the first time, I allow myself to think of him in that way. I imagine him taking me to his apartment after the show. His clothes smell of smoke and cologne. I close the door behind us. He turns around to take my coat, and I grab him by his collar. I pull his shirt apart at the neck and rip it open—yes, rip it open, buttons popping and all—then place my hands against his chest. His body is warm against my cold hands. I grab his shoulders, pushing him back against the door. His mouth drops open a bit—he wasn't expecting this—but then he smiles and lowers his head. His lips part slightly, and . . .

I shake my head to expel this *Days of Our Lives* fantasy from my mind, then try to think of something safe and boring to talk about. "So, what do you do when you're not doing the club circuit?"

"Uh . . . you know, work, eat, live. Try to make it day by day like the rest of the world."

"Do you work?" I say, then feel foolish. "I mean, I know this is work. But do you have a day job?"

"Of course I have a day job. This gig, believe it or not, doesn't quite pay the bills."

"I'm sorry. I just thought . . ."

"That I was a bum? A rock star wannabe?"

"No, no," I say, trying to dig my way out of the hole. "It's just that I have a brother who has an artistic temperament like you. And he doesn't do much of anything."

"What makes you assume I have an artistic temperament?"

"I don't know," I say. "You play in a band, and you have that soulful sort of look to you. Look, I'm not doing too well here. I'm kind of nervous."

"Why?" he says, laughing, as if he's not taking any of this seriously.

"I don't know, really. But I think another beer might help." Whew, calm down, Noelle. He's just a guy. A really cute guy who's becoming more interesting every second.

"Then let's go to the bar. I'm thirsty, too."

We walk over to the bar and order two beers, then wander around until we find a single empty bar stool. "Here, you take it," he says. "I'll stand." Which means he is standing over me. I am staring directly at his chest. Thinking of buttons popping.

"So, what were we talking about?" he says.

"How you are gainfully employed despite foolish assumptions on my part."

"Oh, right."

"So what do you do for your day job?"

"I work for a company that uses artificial intelligence to make tools for the blind."

"Wow. I know . . . absolutely nothing about that. Like, tell me some of the things you make there."

"Retinal implants. Voice recognition software. That kind of thing." He sets his beer back down on the bar and wipes his hands on his jeans.

"How'd you get into that?"

"Well, my sister started to go blind when she was about eleven, and I've always been interested in technology. There was this professor I had at Brown who specialized in technology for the vision impaired. I was lucky enough to get to work with him. Then I took a year off after school and traveled, and when I got back to the States, Dr. Z helped me get started."

"I always wish I had taken a year off to travel. Before you know it, you're working full time and you can't get away. Where did you go?"

"Uh, let's see . . . France, Italy, the Czech Republic, India, Thailand," he says, counting them off on his fingers.

"God, you're so worldly. I've only been to Mexico."

"Well, I think I was trying to figure out what I wanted to do with my life. I've always loved to travel. But it costs a lot of money and prevents you from having a normal life, if that's what you want. Which I didn't for the longest time. When I got back and met Jolene, I got myself an apartment here. The beginning of the end, so to speak. Plants to water, bills to pay. And now suddenly I find I'm this very ordinary guy who watches *West Wing* reruns and goes to Home Depot on weekends. It's sort of depressing when you realize the person you turned into has little resemblance to the person you thought you'd be. I think that's why I started this band. I needed some outlet, you know, so I didn't forget about that guy who loved to travel, so I didn't start believing I was this boring person."

"I am that boring person," I say, nodding my head sadly. "I've always known I wanted a normal life, you know? And I love Home Depot." He smiles, assuming I'm joking. "I'm serious. You could drop me off there in the morning and pick me up at the end of the day, and I wouldn't get bored. Not once. And I'm even good with power tools. I like walking around the aisles looking at all the tools and nails and paint samples. It calms me." Jasper should start sprinting out the door right about now, but instead he's laughing at me. "I'm sorry," I say, feeling a need to apologize for my normality. "I've always been a homebody. I've always needed a place where I could find my things, you know? Somewhere along the line I started believing my heart was where my home was, instead of the other way around."

"That's not such a bad thing. If you like your home."

"But you didn't?" I ask, wondering whether I'm getting too personal.

"Let's just say Groucho Marx had it right when he said, 'Home is where you hang your head.'"

"God, that's awful," I say, trying not to laugh. "I'm sorry."

"Don't be. My mom and dad weren't exactly going to win parents of the year. My sister and I sort of had to fend for ourselves." Irrationally I want to lean over and touch his face or kiss his eyebrow. "Oh, woe is me, right?" he says. "I don't know why I'm rambling on about this, like you're my therapist or something. It's just . . . you're so easy to talk to."

"I've been told that before. It's because I ask a lot of questions. Some people find it annoying."

"Well, I don't," he says.

I begin to feel a loosening up that I've not felt in so long, that frozen part inside of me thawing just a bit. Maybe there really is something here. Maybe he feels it, too.

I turn to him and smile. But suddenly Jolene is standing next to him, her presence completely eclipsing mine. Her hand grazes his waist. She is all sex and seduction. "Hey there," she says. "Your boys are back on stage. You don't want to miss your next set."

"Oh, hey, Jo," he says. "You remember Noelle?"

"Mmm hmm," she says, totally bored. She takes out a tube of lip gloss, applies it, then smacks her lips together in the sexiest way, looking directly at Jasper. *Please don't take him just because you can.* "Hey, Jass, can I sing with you guys on my song?"

"We took it out of the playlist, Jo."

"Why?" She is pouting now, her hands poised on her perfectly narrow hips.

"You know why."

"Oh, that's so lame. It was one of your best songs." I open my eyes wide now, wondering what the hell they're talking about. Fortunately Jo explains. "Jass wrote a song about me. 'Carnival Girl.' It really was one of their best. I used to sing backup vocals on it, but now . . . hey, maybe he'll write one for you, too." Her voice is so condescending and smug I want to smack her.

"Jo . . ." Jasper says.

"What? Isn't she your new girlfriend? You've got fast turnaround time. Three months and you're already over me." Wonderful. I have started a relationship with a guy who is clearly on the rebound, whose ex-girlfriend shows no signs of going away, who in fact seems to be highly motivated to get him back, especially every time I'm around.

I take a long swig of my beer, wishing it were a shot of whiskey. Then I surprise myself. "You broke up with him, right?" I say, standing up from my stool. I must be drunk.

"Yeah, why?" she says, crinkling her face into an ugly scowl.

"Aren't you happy he's moving on? That he's not sitting at home pining away for you?"

"Well, of course," she says grudgingly. Jasper has moved closer to me and is putting a hand on my shoulder, I'm not sure whether to encourage me or warn me to stop.

"So why don't you let him get over you?" I say. I know this line of questioning is entirely out of character for me, but then again, this whole night is out of character for me.

"What are you talking about?" she says.

"You seem to like stringing him along."

"Jo, don't . . ." Jasper says.

"Look, just because I happen to go to the same club as Jasper does not mean I'm stringing him along. How about you, throwing yourself at him when all he did was ask you to come see the band? He asks dozens of people to come see the band. Did you think this was some kind of date or something?"

"It is some kind of a date," Jasper says.

I look at Jolene, whose pretty little mouth has fallen into a sulk. "I should warn you," she says, putting a hand on my arm. "Lots of girls develop crushes on Jass. He's a musician, and he's gorgeous, for God's sake."

"Shut up, Jo. You're being a bitch," Jasper says.

"It's okay," I say, grabbing my coat from off the stool. "She obviously can't hold her liquor."

"Who's the bitch now?" she says.

"Don't go," Jasper says, grabbing my arm. "We have two sets left."

"Well, obviously you and Jolene need to work some issues out, and frankly I'd rather spend my evening with my dog than spend another minute listening to the two of you." I pull away and walk toward the door.

Jo bursts into laughter, vindicated. "You're way too old for him, honey!" I hear her shout.

Jasper is following me, trying to catch up with my nearly bionic legs. I'm exhausted, and it's not even ten thirty. "Wait," he says, grabbing hold of my arm again. I don't want to turn around and look at him because I know it will melt my resolve. But I do anyway. Oh boy.

"Listen, Jasper," I say, trying to be cold and aloof. "I am going to leave now."

"Why? Don't let Jolene get to you. She's incredibly immature."

"Yes, but maybe she's right. Maybe I am too old for you."

"Come on, how old could you possibly be that it would make a difference?"

"Try thirty-three."

"So what? I'm twenty-eight. Five years. It's nothing. Besides, Jolene's just drunk. And jealous. It really is over between us."

"It doesn't seem that way. I think you both have some complex feelings to sort out."

"Noelle," he says, looking straight into my eyes. "There is absolutely nothing complex about my feelings for Jolene. It was honestly just a physical relationship."

"That does not make me feel any better," I say.

"Look, I'm sorry about tonight. This was a disaster. Let's try it again. The right way. A proper date, just you and me."

I stand there holding my coat, trying to decide what to do. "You've got to get back on stage. Your band mates are waiting for you."

"Here," he says, grabbing a coaster from a bar table and writing his number on the back. "Please call me. I really want to see you again." His eyes are so vulnerable, his voice so sincere, that I have to resist the urge to kiss him passionately on the mouth. Instead I play it Katharine Hepburn cool.

"Good-bye, Jasper," I say with film noir poise, and let him watch me walk away. But I make sure I grab that coaster from his hand before I leave.

When I get out onto the street, the world seems dreary, wet, and dirty, a depressing excuse for a planet. I feel like the walking embodiment of it. I am going home alone. Again. I am miserable.

And despite everything, I really like this guy.

February

✣

FOR SALE, Newport: Spacious four-bedroom colonial with all new gourmet kitchen, three fireplaces, and magnificent views of the Sound from both your rooftop deck and your entertainment deck off the kitchen! The finished basement has a comfortable family room, home gym, and access to huge backyard. Located in an excellent school district and close to shops, restaurants, and beaches.

It is a bitterly cold day—dull gray and snowing—and when I step inside the Salazar's house, it feels about fifty degrees. Mrs. Salazar is sitting in her chair under an afghan, half asleep. "Hi, Mrs. Salazar. Are you awake?" Which I know is a stupid question, and I deserve the answer she gives me.

"Unfortunately."

"It's kind of cold in here. Do you want me to turn the heat up?"

"No, no. This is the way I like it. With the price of oil, I'm willing to freeze."

"Suit yourself," I say, wondering why she's worried about the price of oil. I go over and set up her infusion, then give her the needle. Quick and easy now: swab, prick, plunge, and remove.

After I finish, I ask her if she'd like the television on. "I do have a remote," she says. "Stop treating me like a helpless animal."

"Sorry," I say. "Occupational hazard."

"Oh, that's right," she says, as if it's just occurred to her that I work with dogs. They're actually a hell of a lot easier to deal with than she is. Even the ones who were trained to be vicious.

"It's supposed to snow today. Do you need anything from the store? I'd be happy to run out for you," I say, trying to remain upbeat.

"I think the refrigerator's almost empty," she says. "God, I actually miss food shopping. Does that seem crazy?" I think this is the most honest thing she's ever said to me.

"No, not crazy. I like it, too."

"I used to go without a list, just picking whatever looked good that day. Dominic loved my cooking. He was always excited when I came home from the store. He'd stand in the kitchen like a little boy, rubbing his hands together, wondering what I'd brought home for him." She stares out the window with a faraway look in her eyes.

"Do you want to come with me?" I ask, hoping with all my heart she says no. "I mean, the weather's not ideal, but . . ."

"No, I don't want to go. I was just being nostalgic. Foolish, isn't it?"

"Here, why don't you make a quick list of what you need?" I say, handing her a notepad. "In the meantime, I'm going to light a fire for you."

"Just don't set the house on fire," she says, getting in one last dig.

I ignore her and spend the next ten minutes getting a roaring fire going. This is something I'm particularly good at. Then I grab my coat and head out the door.

Predictably, the grocery store is mobbed. "Gonna be a pretty wicked storm today," I hear one customer telling another. "A nor'easter. Expecting ten to fourteen inches." The weather forecasters have been notoriously inaccurate this year, always hyping a big storm that never materializes. I'm not about to fall for it. However, I do start moving the cart around the store at a slightly faster clip and pick up a bag of rock salt.

When I get outside the store, the snow is falling heavily and quickly in big, fat flakes that stick to the ground. Perhaps two inches have fallen already. I pull my car out of the parking lot, skidding a bit as I turn, cursing myself for buying this tiny hatchback instead of the all-wheel-drive station wagon my dad had recommended. The wagon had cost six thousand dollars more, and it was August at the time. I wasn't thinking of snowstorms.

Carefully I pull onto the Salazars' street, a steep uphill road that curves around for about a half mile. I'm afraid for a minute that my car's not going to make it up the hill, that I'm going to slide back down and end up in the bay. But I'm able to make it about halfway up before my wheels start spinning.

"Oh shit," I say out loud. I put the car in reverse and cut the wheel to try to make a rut so my tires can find some footing, but my car starts backsliding. I put it into first gear, cut the wheel in the opposite direction, and the car lurches onto the curb. Good, I think. At least it can't go anywhere.

Forgetting to put my gloves on, I grab the grocery bags and haul them up the sidewalk past eight other mailboxes before I reach her house. By the time I get to the top of the stairs, my fingers have deep red indentations from the heavy bag. I bang off my shoes, then head inside, quickly dropping the bags onto the floor.

"Watch it, watch it," I hear her yell from the other room. "Don't break those eggs. I was really looking forward to an omelet today."

"I won't break your precious eggs," I mutter under my breath.

After taking the bags into the kitchen and unloading them, I go back into the living room. The fire is blazing, and the room feels warm and smells of wood smoke. "I'm a little worried about getting out of here in my car," I say.

"What do you mean?"

"Well, if you haven't noticed, there's a pretty bad storm outside. There's about three inches out there already."

"There *are* about three inches," she corrects me. "And, anyway, if you're a self-respecting New England girl, three inches should mean nothing to you."

"No, not if I had all-wheel drive. But my car is a fishtail nightmare. I nearly skidded out a few times on the way here, and I couldn't even make it all the way up the hill."

"Going down will be easier," she says.

"Are you suggesting that I back down the hill in reverse? Because there's no way I'm going to be able to get up the hill or turn the car around. And even if I could, my tires would just slide the whole way."

"Oh, for God's sake. There was one blizzard years ago when Dominic and I drove all the way to Newport and back, with twelve inches of snow."

"Yes, but I imagine you were driving the Land Rover."

"Yes, that was a great car. I was so sorry when Jay sold it. I wish he hadn't. Well, I suppose if you don't know how to drive in this weather, you'll have to stay. I don't know what we're going to do with one another." *Or to one another,* I think. "Do you know when it's supposed to stop snowing?"

"No," I say. "I heard some people talking—they said ten to fourteen inches were expected."

"Oh, wonderful. A slumber party."

"Look, I'm sorry to have to impose, but I really don't see what choice I have."

"We always have a choice," she says philosophically, but I don't think she's talking about the snow anymore.

"Let me go call my neighbor and see if he can watch Zeke for me."

"Zeke?"

"My dog? Jay's dog? Surely you remember him."

"Oh, right. The Great Dane. He was a big dog."

"He still is."

"It's a shame Jay couldn't bring him with him to Atlanta, but then again, I guess they probably wouldn't want a big dog now that they're considering adopting."

"Adopting?" I say. "What are you talking about?"

"Didn't Jay tell you?"

I walk over to her chair so I can face her. "Tell me what?"

"Jay and Taj are thinking of adopting a little Indian girl. Last I spoke with him, they were talking about flying to Delhi to begin adoption proceedings."

"I don't believe it." I am trying very hard to remain calm.

"Why not?"

Can she really be ignorant of the fact that I begged Jay to consider adopting? "I'm just . . . surprised, is all. I didn't think they'd be ready for that yet. How do you feel about it?"

She considers this for a moment. "Jay has made a decision about how he wants to live his life, and although I can't approve of it, I understand it's what makes him happy."

My mind is racing. If she is trying to get a rise out of me, the last thing I want to do is oblige her. "Well, I'm happy for them."

"Are you?"

"Sure."

"I would have thought it might upset you," she says.

"Is that why you told me?" I glare at her, daring her to say yes.

She pauses for a long while, then looks away from me. "You know, I'm not sure why I told you. It wasn't really my place."

I'm almost taken aback by this answer, this sliver of regret from a woman who has knives in her heart. "I'm going to call my neighbor," I say flatly, and leave the room.

When I get into the kitchen, I am so upset I have to steady myself on the counter. Tears immediately spring to my eyes, and I squash them back in with my fists. *Don't let her do this to you,* I think. *This is what she wants.*

It must get tiring, all that anger and vitriol. *I'm not the enemy!* I want to shout to her. But it wouldn't matter. She needs someone to play the part, and it might as well be me.

After I call and talk to Trey, I feel a little bit better. He's going to bring Zeke to their house and let him play in the snow. Good. At least somebody will enjoy the day. I put on a fresh pot of coffee and take out the eggs. And damned if I don't start making that woman an omelet.

I whisk the eggs, a bit too vigorously perhaps, then pour them in a sizzling skillet, slowly adding diced tomatoes, sautéed mushrooms, Swiss cheese, a sprinkle of Parmesan on top. It's a thing of beauty. I carefully slide the omelet onto a plate, then set it on a tray with a cup of coffee and a glass of cranberry-orange juice. *Here, choke on this, lady.*

But when I take the tray out to her, she appears to be sleeping. Quietly I approach the side table, leave the tray there, and head back to the kitchen, sitting down on one of the stools around the island and staring out the picture window at the snow falling in the enormous backyard. The stables look so picturesque, the perfect image of Victorian gentility. My mother would love it here, I think. The evergreens that surround the property are weighted heavily with snow, their boughs leaning down like obliging footservants.

There is something wonderful about this house, about this kitchen, despite the pervasive gloom that has seeped in since Mr. Salazar's death. I can imagine how it must have looked when Jay was a little boy—full of sparkling light and a promise of days spent playing in the yard or swimming down at the beach. I have always wanted a kitchen like this, with gleaming copper bowls hanging from the ceiling and a cozy breakfast nook where my family would meet for coffee and morning chatter. I allow myself to imagine us here, my family, the imaginary one of my dreams—little Emmy and Jenna (identical twins, age four) sitting at the breakfast nook eating cereal and conspiring like little girls do, and earnest Charlie (a precocious seven) sitting at the island with his Daddy, helping him work on a crossword puzzle. The daddy always used to be Jay, but he's gotten vague in recent months, a sort of generic male figure to be determined at a later date. Whether this fantasy will ever come true is doubtful, but I like to summon it every now and then, believing that someday I still might get what I want.

I decide to call Jay and confront him about this adoption issue. There are just too many questions I have, and if I don't call him now, I'm going to drive myself insane. Thankfully he answers after one ring.

"Jay, it's me," I say, my tone icy.

"Hey, sweetie, how are you? Is my mom okay?"

"'Okay' is not the word I'd use to describe her today, but she's fine. No problems."

"Oh, good. I get nervous every time the phone rings anymore. So what's up? Anything new with the guitarist?"

"Jay, this isn't a personal call."

"Oh," he says, chuckling a little. "Should I go get my lawyer?"

"Jay, this is not a joke. Your mother told me you and Taj are thinking of adopting. Is it true?" There is a long silence on the other end. Jay knows that without the benefit of his handsome face in front of me, he can't get away with nearly as much.

"God, Noelle. I wanted to tell you myself. I'm going to kill her."

"I'd be happy to take care of that for you."

"Listen, honey, I was going to tell you. But it's complicated." I used to like these little endearments—sweetie, honey—but now they seem false and patronizing.

"Well, life is pretty complicated, so why don't you tell me about it now?"

"All right. But let me remind you, we're only talking about it at this point. We haven't done anything formal." My knee is bouncing frantically up and down off the footrest. "See, about a month ago, Taj got a letter from his aunt in India saying that the Indian government is begging Western couples to adopt Indian girls."

"But I thought you didn't want to adopt," I blurt out. "I thought you said you'd never consider it."

"Noelle . . . this is difficult. I didn't think I wanted to adopt, but I think I was just stalling because . . . I mean, I knew what I really wanted, and I guess deep down, I knew that if we had adopted a child together, I would have been . . ."

"Stuck?" There is another sickening pause.

"No, you're misunderstanding me."

"Look, Jay, don't sugarcoat it. That's what you thought. And there's nothing wrong with it, I just want you to be honest with me. I'm a little hurt, but I can handle it."

"Noelle, if you knew the situation, I think you'd understand. There are eleven million abandoned children in India, mostly girls. Sometimes they just get dumped outside an orphanage. Most of them end up as beggars or prostitutes. It's horrible. The Indian government just increased the number of children available for adoption, and they've decreased the waiting period to forty-five days."

"And?"

"And we called an agency because we were so excited to get started on this, but they told us we can't adopt because we're gay."

"What? That's ridiculous."

"You know it, and I know it, but that's their policy."

"So why do they have to know you're gay? Why can't one of you adopt on your own?"

"Because we're male. If I were a single woman, I could adopt, but single males aren't permitted."

"What difference does it make whether you're gay? God, this kind of thing makes me so angry," I say, surprised and relieved to find that my indignation at the injustice of it all is overriding my sense of bitterness and jealousy.

"I know. I think this is probably the first of many battles we're going to have to fight."

"Jay, I'm really sorry you're going through this." I am trying so hard to be sympathetic.

"Look, I really didn't want to get into this yet. I've barely had time to discuss it with Taj, but . . ."

"But what?" There goes my heart, lurching up into my chest, a fireball of anxiety.

"You wouldn't consider it, would you?" he says, tossing the words out casually like he's asking me to try sushi for the first time.

"What?" I say.

"Adopting for us?"

"Oh God, Jay. Are you serious?"

"It's just one of many ideas we've been thinking about. I know it's a lot to consider, but I just wanted to see if that might even be a possibility." I can hear him breathing on the other end, waiting to hear what I'll say. My head is spinning with disbelief and outrage and sadness and sympathy; I don't know which emotion to grasp onto.

"Jay, this is extraordinary. I just don't think . . ."

"Listen, don't answer me now. It's too important a decision, for both of us. For all of us. I'm sorry to spring this on you so unexpectedly. It's just . . . we don't know what else to do."

"Jay, I need to think about it. About lots of things. Okay?"

"Sure, sure. Noelle, just know that I love you. You have been the best thing to happen to me."

"Jay, I need to get off the phone with you now," I say, feeling the lump rising in my throat. I cannot allow myself to cry over the phone.

"All right, all right. I love you. Love to my mother . . ." I hear him say right before I hang up. It's the first time I haven't said *I love you* back.

I sit frozen on the stool for minutes, my head full of cotton and my eyes full of tears.

Jay and Taj want to adopt. But they can't. And why shouldn't they be able to? It's absurd. And yet what do I have to do with Jay's life anymore? Why me? Why does he always turn to me? I'm not his wife. We don't have a life together. I can't be his life raft all the time.

I throw the phone down on the counter and head back out to the living room to check on Mrs. Salazar. I can't tell if she's still sleeping or not, but I do notice that the omelet is gone. Every last bite.

"Noelle," she says suddenly.

"Yes?"

"Was that Jay?"

"Yes."

"How is he?"

"He's fine," I say, trying to betray nothing in my voice. I don't want to give her the satisfaction.

She seems about to say something, then lifts the empty plate and lets it drop back on the table with a reverberating clang. "The omelet was delicious. Thank you."

"You're welcome."

"I didn't know you could cook. Jay never mentioned it."

"It's just an omelet," I say, wanting to throw the plate at her face.

"I know, but it's a damn near perfect omelet," she says.

"Wow, a compliment from Mrs. Salazar? High priestess of hospitality?"

She raises her eyes and glares at me. "For God's sake, are you going to call me Mrs. Salazar until I keel over and die? My name is Margaret."

"Margaret," I repeat. "Sorry."

"And I'm tired. You don't have to entertain me."

"Right."

"Dominic had a whole library full of books if you want to take a look," she says. "It's across the hall and through the double doors." And she makes a shooing motion with her hands.

Anxious to be out of her presence, I take her up on this offer and am surprised at what I find. Rich walnut bookshelves filled with leather spines in masculine colors of burgundy, gold, and forest green; maps on stands; even one of those sliding ladders for accessing hard-to-reach volumes. Sitting at the far end of the room by a fireplace is a beautiful antique desk with brass office accessories and a globe of the world as it looked shortly after 1492.

Something about the entire setup reminds me of Gatsby's library with its thousands of volumes of books, all with their pages uncut. As much as the Salazars have always appeared to me as landed gentry, I've never really thought of any of them as being truly intellectual. Jay rarely read in his free time, preferring to exercise or play video games when an idle moment hit him. And Jay's father was, at heart, a businessman, one who traveled so frequently I doubt he ever spent much time in here. So was this Margaret's sanctuary? And if so, would she so freely give me access to it now?

I wander along the shelves of books, searching through titles both familiar and obscure. There is a section of large, illustrated books like Richard Burton's *The Arabian Nights*, Malory's *Le Morte D'Arthur*, Cervantes's *Don Quixote*. Then smaller, leather-bound classics like *The Sound and the Fury*, *The Sun Also Rises*, *The Red Badge of Courage*. Some art books splayed open on stands to showcase a carefully chosen image. More maps and antique charts.

I make my way around to the desk and sit down, running my hands along the polished surface. A few photos sit in gilded frames: one of Jay as a boy and one of Jay as a man, one of Margaret standing on the beach in her younger days, one of the Salazars' wedding day. None of Jay and me. Hardly surprising.

I tilt the wedding photo toward me and study it. It is black and white, with the magical sheen of all wedding photos taken before 1970. There stands Dominic, tall and handsome and beaming, his arm around Margaret, an artlessly beautiful woman at the time, so young, and not wearing the elaborate Cinderella dress I might have expected, but a simple, empire-waist dress with a garland of flowers in her hair. She almost looks like a hippie. This seems unfathomable, reconciling the free-spirited-looking girl in the photo with the dry, embittered woman sitting out on that chair in the other room.

Cautiously I pull out the side drawer of the desk, half expecting to find a revolver or evidence of tax evasion but instead discover several stacked photo albums. I pull out the first one, a baby book filled with photos of Jay and hand-pasted artifacts like his birth certificate, his handprints and footprints, notes meticulously taken about his first year. *Likes to hear himself talk,* says one note. *Outgoing and joyful most of the time. Cries when he wants attention, mostly crocodile tears.* Boy hasn't changed much, has he? Then there are the endless photos of him for every milestone occasion: Jay at his birthday party wearing a cowboy hat, Jay on the beach when he had white-blond hair, Jay in a T-ball uniform standing in the outfield staring at the sky.

Underneath I find another album, this one older with yellowed pages and black-and-white photos. I flip through until I find a picture of a girl standing alone and immediately recognize the face with its gorgeous bone structure and hair, the intelligent, downturned eyes, the slightly dissatisfied mouth. She is wearing a tutu and standing at a ballet bar, looking impatient for her mother or father to please just snap the picture already. As I go through the album, there are other photos of her as an older girl still wearing the dress and ballet slippers, one of her dancing in the backyard with her sister, one of her onstage as one of the characters from *The Nutcracker*—not the leading girl in the pink gossamer gown, but perhaps one of the spices in a brown crêpe tunic. Maybe Coffee or Tea.

When I hear a creaking noise coming from the other room, I quickly place the albums back into their drawer and close it slowly, hoping not to make a squeak. I grab a book from nearby, *Jane Eyre*, and pretend to be reading it. But no one enters the library. After a few minutes, I actually get into the story, perfect for a dreary day stuck inside someone else's cavernous house, watching the snow pile up outside the windows.

After a few hours, Mrs. Salazar (now Margaret), comes into the study.

"How are you feeling?" I ask her.

"I'm feeling a bit better actually," she says. "The tingling sensation comes and goes, but I haven't felt it all day. I might even be up to making something for dinner. Were you able to get the pork chops and potatoes on my list?"

"Yes," I say, realizing I'm ravenous.

"And of course I'll throw a salad together, too."

"Let me do that," I say.

"No, that's all right. I'd really like to. I was thinking I might like to watch a movie tonight, and I wondered if you might like to join me."

"Sure," I say, standing up out of some strange feeling of obligation.

"Do you like oldies? Hepburn–Tracy? Gary Cooper? Astaire?"

"Anything you like is fine with me," I say.

"Well, come on. You must have an opinion. For example, Jimmy Stewart or Cary Grant?" she says.

"Jimmy Stewart."

"I thought so. I prefer Cary Grant. So much more polish. What about Katharine Hepburn or Audrey Hepburn?"

"Katharine. No question," I say.

"Then *The Philadelphia Story* it is. And maybe *Top Hat* after that if we can make it through."

"Sounds perfect," I say, smiling.

"It's just dinner and a movie. I haven't asked you to the prom," she says, turning around and closing the door behind her. But inside I'm smiling. This is progress.

That night, Margaret makes us dinner and pours us wine, and we share a dinner in front of *The Philadelphia Story*. Trying to talk to each other over a meal would be asking a bit too much from both of us at this point. After dinner, she sets out some sheets and towels for me and shows me the guest room. Later, I make us some popcorn and we begin watching *Top Hat*, marveling at what an amazing team Fred Astaire and Ginger Rogers made.

"He's so incredibly smooth, he looks like he's floating," I say.

"She does everything he does, but backward . . . and in high heels," Margaret says. I laugh. "I can't take credit for that line," she adds.

"It's still a good one. Did you ever dance yourself?"

Margaret smiles at first, but then her face gets reflective. "A long time ago. Tap and ballet. I remember I had this pair of toe shoes— they were so worn out, my mother had restitched them probably twenty times, but I loved them. I thought they were magic slippers, and if I didn't wear them I wouldn't be able to perform at all. Then one day I came home from school and was getting ready to go to rehearsal, and I couldn't find them. I looked everywhere, tore my room apart, and when I came back downstairs my mother was standing there with a new pair of shoes in her hands. She had thrown my old ones in the trash. I was furious—threw a temper tantrum and yelled at her until I thought she was going to beat me. I didn't go to rehearsal that day, and I never went again. I gave up dancing just to spite my mother for throwing away my magic slippers." She laughs lightly. "I know it wasn't really her fault, but I never forgave her for that." I am absolutely silent, not wanting to break the spell of this unexpected intimacy. "I haven't thought of those slippers in a long time." She shakes her head as if dispelling a painful buzzing in her ear. "Well, couldn't get my foot into one of those slippers now even if I wanted to." I smile weakly at her, then look away.

We watch a bit more of the movie, but after about ten minutes, Margaret is asleep in her chair. I let her stay there, covering her up with some blankets. For a few moments, I linger in the darkened living room, the light from the snow outside tinting the room an angelic blue color.

Finally, I take our dishes to the kitchen, rinse them and put them in the dishwasher, then head to the guest room to turn in for the night. It's strange, but even in this house that contains such painful memories for me, I feel oddly at home. I fall asleep almost when my head hits the pillow.

March

I'm on my way to one of my most dreaded places—not the DMV, not the gynecologist, but the mall. Every year around late winter my mother insists on dragging me out for a shopping excursion even though I have told her repeatedly that I detest shopping. All that groping of clothes and checking of tags and looking at yourself in the mirror—it's masochistic really. And nothing ever fits properly, so I end up feeling deformed.

When I get to the mall, my mother is waiting in the lobby of Bloomingdale's wearing a pink scarf the color of Pepto-Bismol and pearl earrings. I wonder when it was that she turned into a little old lady from Charing Cross Road. The first thing she says to me is that I look pale.

"Yes, Mom. I'm Scotch-Irish. I'm supposed to look pale in the middle of winter. Why are we here again?"

"I know you," she says. "You always get SAD in the winter." She doesn't mean sad as in gloomy and depressed, although those emotions do come into play. She means SAD, as in seasonal affective disorder. She's convinced I suffer from this affliction because I never want to go out in winter and often stay in my pajamas until noon. But everyone in their right mind does the same when it's twenty-two degrees out and the sun hasn't shone in six months. "Shopping always gives me a lift," she continues. "And all the cruise wear is out now, so we can imagine we're in the Caribbean."

"Does that work for you?" I ask, never failing to be amazed by my mother's capacity for self-delusion.

"It does," she says. "I feel better when I'm wearing something floral in bright tropical colors like turquoise and peach." Colors, I think to myself, I would never wear.

When we enter the store, my mother immediately goes into Vanna White mode, stopping to show off various accessories that she thinks would boost my pale complexion or asking me if I'd like to try a makeup sample with her. Shopping with my mother is often an exercise in cultivating serenity in the face of absurdity. Just listen and nod and say "ooooh" and "ahhh" every now and then, and try not to have any real opinions.

Eventually, I surrender and go into the dressing room to try on a few items my mother has selected for me: a floral wrap skirt with a matching bustier that puts me in mind of Ginger on *Gilligan's Island*, and a coral-colored silk dress with lots of knots and gathers meant to make you look like a Grecian goddess, I suppose. Unfortunately in my midwinter's state of pallor and flab, it merely makes me look like an oversized shrimp in desperate need of cocktail sauce. Or a cocktail.

"Hey, Mom," I say, carrying all my miserable failures out of the dressing room to reshelve, "let's go have lunch. All this shopping has made me hungry."

"But you haven't found anything. I'm still on a quest."

"Look what happened to Ahab. You need to know when to quit," I say, and she reluctantly agrees to go with me to that shameless cornerstone of fried factory food and false cheer: T.G.I. Friday's.

When the waiter comes to greet us, a little too cheerfully I might add, my mother pauses to consider what she'd like to drink. She looks up at the waiter, a cute, slightly effeminate guy with the longest eyelashes I've ever seen. "I've always wanted to get a martini for lunch, like that 1940s actress. What was her name?" She looks to me.

"I have no idea."

The waiter says, "Oh, I think I know who you're talking about. She was in that movie . . ."

"Right," my mom says. This is one of the most ridiculous conversations I've ever heard.

"Yes, it always looks so stylish when the frosted glass gets put on the table, the three olives leaning against the side."

"I know exactly what you mean," the waiter says. I can already tell he's getting a huge tip.

"But I'm afraid I'm too old for a lunchtime martini."

"Not at all," he says. "In fact, you sort of remind me of that other actress. What's her name? You know, the one from that movie with the bank robbers and the old cars."

"Which one is it?" my mom says, her ears peeled for a compliment.

"The guy wears suspenders, and the girl wears a beret. They're famous bank robbers, I think. Clarence Darrow or something?"

"Clyde Darrow?" I say. "You mean *Bonnie and Clyde*."

"Yes, that's the one."

"Oh, you dear," my mom says. "You think I look like Faye Dunaway. But she's just stunning."

Her last comment hangs in the air like a piece of bait. "And so are you," he says. "And definitely not too old for a martini. We actually have a delicious Cosmo if you're in the mood."

"No, really, I'm afraid I'd keel over on the steering wheel on the way home."

"Not such a great idea, then," I say. "I'll have a Diet Sprite."

"Oh, that'll be fine for me, too," my mother concedes, finally.

"Right away," Waiter of the Year says, and then he's off to start earning his 30 percent tip.

"Well, he's just adorable."

"Yes," I say. No real opinions, no real opinions.

"So, how are you?" she says. "How's work?"

"Work's fine," I say. "I'm working on our summer fund-raiser."

"That sounds like fun."

"It isn't. But it's keeping me busy."

"Keeping you from brooding, which is good. I don't even know if you have a boyfriend." Tick-tock, tick-tock.

"Mom."

"What?"

"My love life is . . . nonexistent at the moment. So let's talk about something else."

"I really wish you'd let me buy you a pretty outfit. All you ever wear are jeans and oversized sweatshirts. Let's try again after lunch and see if we can't find you a nice skirt and blouse. Something feminine."

"Mom, I don't really do well in skirts."

"Why? Is it your legs? You've got your father's legs, it's true. But some heels would be very slimming."

"Mom."

"What? I'm only trying to help." The waiter comes back and sets down our drinks. He's brought my mother's Sprite in a frosted martini glass with three cherries. "Well, would you look at that? Look, Noelle. A Sprite martini. Thank you so much!"

"It was my pleasure," he says. "Are you ready to order?"

"Oh, I'm afraid we've just been gabbing. We haven't even looked at the menu yet."

"Not a problem," he says. "I'll be right back." And then he spins around as if on point shoes and jogs back to the kitchen.

"So cute," she says again. "Don't you think he's cute?"

"A little young."

"Well, of course. But there's nothing wrong with that. Look at Demi Moore."

"Mom, seriously. Don't be disgusting."

"I'm not talking about me, silly. I'm talking about for you."

"Mom, he's probably nineteen. And probably gay."

"Oh, you're just being overly sensitive about that."

"No, Mom. Did you see the way he spun around?"

"He's got charisma."

"Okay, Mom."

"Look, I'm just saying it wouldn't kill you to smile and flirt a little. I can't help but wonder sometimes if you're not . . ."

I stare at her in disbelief. "What?"

"If you're not . . . well, you know?" And this part she whispers. "A lesbian."

If my jaw had an actual hinge, it would be clattering on the floor right now. "Mom, are you serious?" I say, trying to decide between laughing at her and throwing my drink in her face.

"There wouldn't be anything wrong if you were," she says.

"Well, I know that. But why on earth would you think I was? Because I like wearing jeans?"

"No, but my friend Debbie, you remember Debbie McMenamin, right? She just told me that her daughter came out to her and Chuck over Christmas break, and it got me thinking. Maybe there was a reason Jay chose you."

"Mom, we are not having this conversation."

"I just started wondering. I don't know how these things work. I mean, you don't seem to date anyone."

"Mom, I just finalized my divorce!"

"I know. But Sheila Nolan's son was already on three dating sites by the time he got served with divorce papers. And then, there's your job."

"What about my job?"

"Well, it just seems like an awful lot of lesbians like dogs."

"Mom, really, you're embarrassing yourself. More than half the population likes dogs. They're the most popular pets on the planet."

"But what about your thing with hardware stores?"

"Mom, I like wandering around in them."

"Well, there's no harm in me asking. Because there'd be absolutely nothing wrong if you were a lesbian."

"I am not a lesbian, Mom!" I shout. And this is the moment our waiter decides to come back for our orders.

"Ready yet?" he says, smiling sheepishly at my mother.

"Well, I am," she says. "But I think my daughter needs a little more time."

"No, I'm fine," I say. "I'll have the club sandwich."

"That comes with a cup of soup or a small salad."

"I'll have the clam chowder," I say, and my mother raises her eyebrow at me as if this somehow confirms her suspicions even more. Because, of course, all heterosexual women would have chosen the salad.

My mother does indeed order a salad, Asian chicken to be exact, then winks at our waiter who's beginning to annoy me at this point. We sit there in uncompanionable silence for about five minutes before my mother finally cracks.

"Your father and I are taking salsa lessons. Did I already tell you that?" This is the new thing she says all the time—*Did I already tell you?*—another sign that my parents are getting older.

"No, you didn't," I say. "Dad agreed to take dance lessons?"

"Yes, with a little arm twisting on my part. I told him it was for his health. Salsa dancing is good for the heart and circulation."

"Well, that's great. How many lessons have you had?"

"Only two. The trouble is, your father is so rigid. I'm always trying to get him to be a little more spontaneous. I'm really much better at leading than he is."

"You never were good at following someone else's direction."

"What does that mean?"

"Nothing," I say, immediately pushed into defensive mode. "Just that you're independent. Take charge." I follow this up with a women's power fist.

"I just like to move where my feet take me, and your father's not so good at keeping up with me. I guess we need a lot more lessons before we'll be ready for the recital."

"You have a recital? When?"

"Oh, not until the end of the year."

"Wow. I didn't know it was so serious."

"You could come sometime if you want. We're allowed to bring guests. And there are quite a few men without partners," she says.

"Mom."

"All right."

In her own way, my mother means well. But you know what they say about the road to hell being paved with good intentions. And after we finish lunch, I feel as though I've been through the seventh circle of hell: retired moms with single daughters.

Work at SASH is busier than ever with our spring spaying and neutering campaign under way, loads of new adoptions, and the charity benefit to plan. I've started dog training sessions on weekends, with Zeke as my demonstration dog. He loves his role, the big showoff. It's good for him, too, because at home, I tend to be quite lax about the rules, treating him more like a person than a dog. He needs to be reminded that occasionally I need him to obey a command and at least make me look like I know what I'm doing.

The beginning of the workweek is uneventful. On Monday, we get a phone call from a woman overreacting to her dog's sneezing. "I think our puppy has kennel cough," she says. "I need to bring him in."

"Okay, ma'am. Has he stayed in a kennel lately?"

"Well, no, but . . ." You get the picture.

But Friday is a particularly grueling day. It starts off ordinary—a few distemper shots, a spaying, some routine checkups. But after lunch, it all goes downhill. One of the new volunteers gets bitten by a miniature pinscher and decides to quit. Then a couple and their daughter bring in their three-year-old retriever, Becks, who is suffering from bone cancer. The family have decided it's time to put him down, and Dr. Robbins agrees.

Kate Robbins is our best vet—strong, capable, and able to balance the practical demands of the job with emotional sensitivity for the owners' feelings. I have to assist her in euthanizing Becks in front of his owners, including the ten-year-old daughter, who grabs hold of her dog and weeps and weeps and calls his name over and over again through muffled sobs. It's probably good that she's able to grieve so openly. Most people feel they have to be stoic because it's only a dog or a cat. But I've seen a grown man cry over the death of his beloved parrot who lived to be fifty-five and had been the man's companion for almost his entire life. No one can define what grief for a lost pet should look like. And even working at a place like this and having assisted in dozens of euthanizations, I still ache each time for the pet, but even more so for the owners and the loss they feel at losing a cherished family member.

To make matters worse, the executive director of SASH comes to my desk at a quarter to five (on a Friday, no less) demanding my plans for the charity benefit by Monday. Joe is neither a veterinarian nor an animal specialist; he's a businessman in charge of making sure the facility stays solvent. I rarely have dealings with him—he likes to hole up in his office where he doesn't have to smell pet odors or hear cats mewing or wade his way through distressed owners—

but since I've been put in charge of our new fund-raising venture, he's been wanting to meet with me at least once a month to check on my status. Sadly, my status has not changed since our last meeting in February, and even more sadly, Joe is not sympathetic.

"Well, I'm still thinking some kind of charity ball," I say. "Maybe two hundred dollars a couple and we can auction off prizes or something."

"Noelle," he says, "your plan sounds a little vague. Auction what prizes? Are you going to get donations from local businesses, and if so, when are you going to start soliciting them? Do you have a venue chosen? A theme?"

"A theme? I hadn't really thought about it," I say.

"Look, people with money want to feel useful, want to feel special. You have to promise to ply them with food and alcohol, make them feel really good about themselves, and show them a good time. Dancing. Entertainment. Something. A theme can help. What about a *101 Dalmatians* theme?"

Oh my God. Is he serious? "Well, that's one idea."

"Come on, can't you just see all those society women getting their hair done like Cruella de Vil and wearing spotted fur coats."

"Wearing a fur coat to a charity function to rescue abused dogs and cats seems like a conflict of interests," I say. I've only very recently allowed myself to get sarcastic with Joe. I know I'm too useful to him to fire.

"All right, so they'd wear faux fur, but you see my point."

"Actually, I don't think that's such a great idea. After the remake of *101 Dalmatians* was released, hundreds of people flooded the pet stores looking to get Dalmatian puppies, then realized how difficult they were to train. So many Dalmatians ended up at shelters that year."

As I am giving myself a self-righteous pat on the back, Joe says, "Then how about *Lady and the Tramp?*"

"What, and serve each couple a plate of pasta and meatballs with no silverware?"

"Well, I don't know! This shouldn't be my responsibility, Noelle. I'm not a creative type. Here, look through these," he says, slamming a pile of papers onto my desk. "Press releases from former charity events. You should have already pored through these yourself."

"I'm sorry, Joe. Really. I've just been so busy with the new training classes and looking at grants to apply for, not to mention the regular duties of my job . . ."

"Hey, this is a regular duty of your job. Remember, that's why we gave you a promotion." I want to laugh in his face. "You knew special projects would be included. You said it was what you wanted. So you're going to have to figure this one out on your own."

Great. I have three months to plan and organize a charity benefit to improve our facility so we can protect and shelter more abandoned cats and dogs. That's why I'm here, I have to keep reminding myself. Because for all this extra work, I will receive not a cent more in salary nor a day off in time.

At the end of my shift I am still sitting at my desk sulking when our receptionist, Tara, comes back through the hallway. "There's someone looking for you out front," she says. "A guy. Cute."

Oh, God, I think. *Jasper.* Who else could it be? I run into the ladies' room and check myself in the mirror. Disaster—my hair in an unkempt ponytail, face devoid of any makeup or color for that matter, scrub jacket covered in dog hair and a little blood. Quickly

I splash some water on my face and pull the rubber band out of my hair. Then I take off my jacket, under which I am wearing a boring gray T-shirt. Not sexy, but not repulsive either. It'll have to do. After spraying myself with some perfume, I head out to the waiting room.

It's him. Hands in his pockets, back toward me, checking out our adoptions bulletin board. "Hi there," I say, and Jasper turns around. Yep, still adorable.

"Hey," he says, breaking into a smile. "I hope it's okay that I stopped by."

"Sure," I say. "But what are you doing here?"

He looks down at the floor and shuffles one leg in his jeans. "I came to see you."

"How did you find me?" Tara looks over at me as if to say, *Why don't you go over and attack the guy instead of giving him the third degree?* She has a point.

"You did tell me where you worked," he says, sounding a bit hurt. "Did you not want to be found?"

"No, not at all," I say.

"Well, I hadn't heard from you, and I wanted to see how you were doing." We both stand there awkwardly for a few minutes, and I'm at a complete loss for something to say. The last two times I was with him, we were surrounded by people and music, and I'd had the benefit of several alcoholic beverages in my system. Now it's just the two of us here in this quiet, sterile waiting room, and I cannot speak.

"I guess I'm doing fine," I say finally.

"Hey, did you ever adopt out Jasper?" he asks, mercifully. I can handle this one.

"Oh, the beagle? Yeah. We had a little trouble with him, actually. The first family that adopted him had to bring him back because their daughter was allergic. The next guy said he barked too much. Then someone's other dog didn't get along with him. I was beginning to get really worried for him. Not that we'd put him down. We don't euthanize dogs here. But I didn't know where he was going to end up. I thought about keeping him myself, but finally this retired guy took him in. He said he'd be able to spend a lot of time with him and train him, get him comfortable in his new surroundings. So many people think it's going to be easy to introduce a dog into their home. But it's hard work. I can't stand when people just come in here looking for some cute puppy, not realizing what they're getting themselves into." When I look at Jasper, he is grinning. "I'm sorry," I say, "I'm getting on my soapbox again. You don't need to hear this. I'm sure I'm preaching to the choir."

He takes a step closer to me. "How do you know?"

"What?"

"How do you know you're preaching to the choir?"

"Well, I assume you like dogs."

"You assume, huh?"

"Well, yeah," I say, worrying that I've made him angry.

"For all you know," he says, looking at me with mock seriousness, "I could be very, very anti-dog."

"But you're not," I say, laughing. He's laughing now, too.

"But how do you know? You thought I was a bum, remember?"

"I know I did. But knowing people's animal preferences is sort of my specialty. I've worked this job long enough to know a cat person from a dog person from a bird person from a non-animal person, and I can tell you're a dog person. Definitely."

He is smiling broadly now. "You happen to be right."

"Aha! I knew it."

"In fact, I can't understand how anyone isn't a dog person. Dogs rule."

"Yes, they do." I shrink my voice into a whisper. "The executive director of this organization doesn't even like animals. I swear I have no idea why he got involved with this place. You'd think he worked for a Fortune 500 company the way he struts around here barking orders at everyone. And he's always talking about bottom lines like he thinks we're working on commission or something. I mean, hello, it's called a nonprofit."

"Well, even a nonprofit has to raise money," he says. "And it's hard to be in charge of an organization's finances, particularly a non-profit's. Your options are limited. I don't imagine he makes a ton of money."

"Oh, don't feel sorry for him. He makes plenty of money. I heard a third of our budget goes toward his salary. And for what? So he can sit on the phone in his office using phrases like 'status assessment' and 'budgetary restrictions' and go out on his Starbucks run every afternoon for his Iced Caffè Lattes? Then he gets on my case because I can't juggle eighteen thousand responsibilities on thirty thousand a year. Sorry, I didn't mean to drop my salary, but there we are. And now I have to plan this charity function for him by Monday, and I have no idea what I'm going to do."

"Wow," he says, walking closer to me. "You seem a little stressed out."

"Do I?" I say, involuntarily stepping back. I don't want him seeing me too close up right now.

"I can help you," he says. "That is, if you want help. I have a little experience with marketing and fund-raising."

"You do?"

"What is it you're trying to raise money for?"

"Well, we want to put a new wing on the facility, one that will have animal housing with soundproofing and natural light and homey features like furniture and carpeting. It'll have an exercise room for the animals to play in during bad weather and classrooms for dog training and humane education classes. I'm definitely excited about it, I just don't know how to organize an event for a bunch of rich, suburban women who think having a Chihuahua fit into their purse is the highlight of pet ownership."

"So you're having trouble identifying with your target donors. I really am good at this kind of thing. Are you hungry?"

"What?" I say.

"Why don't I take you out to dinner and help you brainstorm?"

"Really? You'd do that?"

"Sure. It sounds like fun."

"Well, I am starving," I say. I'm still running on that Pop-Tart I had at 7 A.M. "Can you give me, like, ten minutes to go clean up a little?"

"Sure, I'll just talk some more with Tara," he says. I look over at Tara, with her healthy blond looks and athletic body that looks so cute in scrubs.

"You know what," I say. "I'm actually all right. Let's go eat."

In the parking lot, Jasper asks me for a restaurant recommendation, as he lives in Providence and doesn't really know this area. My first thought is Simpatico, but then I think, too romantic, too expensive. I end up taking him to an Irish pub in Bristol where we sit at a high-top table in the upstairs bar, staring out at the harbor. Both of us order a Guinness and a burger, mine topped with mushrooms and Swiss, his with cheddar and onions. I am already reading into this choice. Onions? Could he possibly have romantic feelings for me and order onions?

"So, tell me about this charity function. What were you thinking?" he asks, taking a sip of his stout, then leaning toward me with an elbow on the table. For some reason, this feels too intimate. I tell him about Joe's lame *Lady and the Tramp* theme, but somehow Jasper is able to make it sound workable. "I could see couples finding it fun to play uptown girl and downtown boy. Besides, you could get some strolling violinists and accordion players for entertainment and have a bottle of Chianti on each table."

"That's not bad," I say. "A bit cheesy, but . . ."

"A lot of people like cheesy," he says. "But you know, you're only catering to the kind of crowd that can afford two hundred dollars a plate. I know a lot of people who'd be really into the idea of supporting a local animal shelter but would never in a million years attend a charity ball. Have you ever thought of running a different kind of event?"

"I can barely contemplate organizing one. How on earth could I plan for two?"

"With my help," he says. "I could plan the other one."

"Jasper," I say, thinking he's ridiculous for suggesting this. "You don't have to be so nice. You're going to ruin all other men for me."

He leans his head slightly to the side. "Well, that's sort of the point," he says, and I have to look down at the table.

"So, you really are a dog person?"

"Really, Noelle. From the moment you told me where you worked,

I've wanted to get involved in some way. I had a dog growing up, the cutest little sheepdog-collie mix named Munchkin. Cassie and I loved that dog."

"Cassie?"

"My sister. And then one day we came home from school, and the dog was just gone."

"What do you mean, gone?"

"I don't know. My mom had been at work all day, but my dad was unemployed at the time and spent most days lying on the couch watching game shows. When we asked him what happened, he said Munchkin had run away. But I didn't believe him. He never liked that dog. My dad was kind of an alcoholic asshole."

"So what do you think he did with her?"

"Oh, I don't know. Drove her out to some field and let her loose? Gave her away?"

"Do you think he might have taken her to the pound?"

"Cassie and I called every shelter and SPCA in the area. Whatever he did, he made sure he got rid of her for good. And I never forgave him for it. We never got another dog after that."

"No, you wouldn't, would you?" I say, still gazing at him, wishing I could heal whatever wounds he's suffered. When he notices me staring, he abruptly changes the subject.

"So, about this fund-raiser. I know the owners of the Loft, where you saw my band play. I'll bet they would love to get involved with something like this. My band could provide the entertainment, so that would be free. And people could pay a cover charge—not two hundred dollars but something reasonable. Young people have a lot of money these days."

"Really? Not the ones I know. We're all in debt up to our eyeballs."

"Well, I know a lot of young people with money to spend. Jolene's crowd? Man, they burn through money. And we'd have to come up with something fun for them, too. A theme. They're kind of a hardcore crowd—leather and punk and anarchy. That kind of thing."

"So how about an S&M theme?"

"Yes!"

"I was joking," I say.

"But it could actually work. We could make it an S&M party. Strays and Mutts."

I begin nodding my head. "I love that idea. And we can tell everyone to wear collars and leashes."

"Exactly." I smile at the thought of Jolene tied to a fence post.

"This actually sounds kind of fun. But are you sure you'll have the time to help me plan?" I say. "I mean, you do have a day job."

"Ha-ha, yes, I do have a day job. But don't worry about me. I love to multitask," he says, jotting down some ideas on a cocktail napkin.

"Hmm, notes on a napkin, phone numbers on a coaster. Are bar accessories your primary means of communication?"

"Pretty much. Speaking of phone numbers on coasters," he says, putting his pen down and staring at me. "Why didn't you ever call me?"

I take a sip of my beer and look up at him guiltily. "Jasper, I don't know why I didn't call. I wanted to, so many times."

"And?"

"And I guess I thought you might need some more time to get over Jolene."

"Jolene?" he says. "Not her again."

"I don't know. I was nervous about starting something."

"Noelle, I'm only talking about a phone call," he says.

"I know. But I've been really busy lately."

"Okay, you can stop right there," he says. "If you don't like me and you don't want to have anything to do with me, just tell me. I can handle it. But please don't tell me it's because you're busy. No one is too busy for a five-minute phone call to say, hi, how you do-ing, I really enjoyed your band. Trash the bitchy ex-girlfriend, and we'll talk."

I laugh, but I also feel tremendously guilty. I have no good ex-cuse. He's all I've thought about for a month, and I didn't call him because I'm a coward. "How is the bitchy ex-girlfriend, by the way?" I say. "Oh, sorry."

"It's okay. I said it first," he says. "Do you really want to know how she is, or are you just being polite?"

"Polite. I don't care in the least how she is. I mean, providing she isn't dying of some rare disease where you need to tend to her nightly. I guess I was more asking how the two of you are."

He drops his head back, exasperated, as if he can't believe I'm still harping on this. I can't believe I am either. "We are not together. Just like we were 'not together' on New Year's."

"But are you more 'not together' now than you were then?" I say. I can't make myself stop.

"I guess so. We're not hanging around in the same places any-more. I've tried to keep my distance from her. Ever since that night at the club when I thought I'd blown it with you."

"Well, you didn't blow it," I assure him.

"It seemed like I did when you never called."

"Fair enough," I say. "But I did intend to. I was just . . ."

"What?"

"Scared, I guess."

"Scared of what?"

"Of dating again. I didn't tell you that night, but I just got through a divorce."

"Oh. I'm sorry." His face takes on just the right shade of sympathy and warmth.

"It's okay. It's just that it's really hard for me to start thinking about getting out there again. I know that's such a stupid phrase, 'getting out there,' but that's how I feel. I mean, I thought my life was settled, and then all of a sudden I'm thrust back out into this dating wilderness. I didn't think I was ready for it."

"That's fair," he says. "I just wish you'd have told me so I didn't have to sit home all last month wondering why you hated me."

"You did not do that."

"No? Give my sister a call. She'll tell you what a loser I've been, sending her e-mails and calling her to ask what I did wrong."

"I thought only women did those kinds of things," I say.

"Another assumption," he says, giving me a look that's so adorable I want to melt off my chair. "Guys can be obsessive, too."

"Well, there's a bit more to the story," I say. "But I hesitate to tell you because I don't want you to dart out the door."

"What?" he says.

So I take a deep breath and tell him why Jay and I got divorced. Not about my infertility but about the one important factor Jay neglected to mention that made it impossible for us to have a viable relationship with each other. After another Guinness, I tell him about taking care of Jay's mother, too, and about how stressful the past few months have been for me. I cannot, for the life of me, shut myself up.

"There, it's out there," I finally say. "Are you sorry you asked?"

"Not at all," he says. "In fact, it explains a lot. Sort of massages my wounded ego."

"Yes, I'm sorry about that. You must have thought I was such a bitch."

"No, I knew there must have been an explanation."

"I can't believe I just told you all that, and you're still sitting here," I say, laughing with relief.

"Unlike you, I don't scare easily."

"Well, I promise next time I won't say a single word about myself. I'll go back to interrogating you. How's that?"

"Does that mean there will be a next time?" he says, smiling.

"I guess it does."

"Excellent. And, not that I don't believe you, but why don't you give me your number? Just in case you *intend* to call me again but get too busy."

"Smart-ass," I say. But I write down my number on his napkin.

When we get out into the parking lot, he walks me to my car, and there is an awkward, electric moment when I'm not sure if someone's going to get kissed, and if so, who's going to do the kissing. "Thank you so much for your help tonight," I say.

"Any time. I'm happy to help. Now you can go in on Monday and tell Joe you've got everything taken care of."

"That'll feel great."

"Just remember, I've got your number now. I'm going to be calling you to work on this, so be ready to hear from me."

"I will," I say, getting the feeling that the kissing moment has passed. I turn around to unlock my car door when he touches my shoulder and gently pulls me back around.

"And Noelle," he says. "I understand you're not ready for a relationship yet. And I'm in no hurry. I'm an extremely patient person. Just know, whenever you are ready, let me have the first shot. I know we didn't start off on the right foot, but I feel like we're improving every time we meet."

"Okay," I say, shivering in the night air, hoping he never takes his hand off my shoulder.

"That means after another dozen meetings or so, we'll be perfect," he says, and I laugh. "Good night." He stands over me, hesitating a moment.

"Good night," I say, abruptly turning away to get into my car. Then he is walking away, and I'm sitting alone, staring at my dashboard and clutching my shoulder, wishing I could get that moment back again.

April

FOR SALE, Portsmouth: Renovated country house nestled on a hillside, with three bedrooms, beautiful country kitchen, and sunny living room opening onto deep wraparound farmer's porch for quiet evenings watching the sunset. Backyard features rose garden and views of protected land filled with beautiful wildlife.

On Saturday morning, I am sitting on the couch by the front window with Zeke sprawled out on my lap like an afghan. The sun is streaming in, so Zeke's fur feels sleek and hot, like warm velvet, a security blanket for the soul. I kiss the soft indented spot just above his eyes, and once I start, I can't stop kissing him there. If he were a seven-year-old child, he'd be squirming wildly now, embarrassed. But since it's Zeke, he takes it all with a sweet tolerance.

Sometimes I worry about how attached I am to this dog. About the fact that the primary relationship of my life is with a canine. That at the end of a terrible day I look forward to nothing more than coming home and lying on the bed, under the covers, with a giant Great Dane.

At around eleven thirty, I have to pry myself off the couch to go pick up Margaret from her steroid treatment at the hospital. Almost as soon as she gets into my car, I can tell she's in a foul mood. "How are we feeling today?" I ask.

"*We* are not feeling anything because *we* are not a joint entity. *I* am actually feeling quite well."

"Sorry about using the first person plural. Won't happen again," I say. Despite the minor progress we've made in the past few months, I have to keep reminding myself that our relationship is like that of two former rival nations that have entered a truce for the purposes of their mutual benefit: we don't really trust each other; we try to meet somewhere in the middle but usually end up miles apart anyway.

I really have been trying to be more understanding, spending time researching MS on the Internet, that vast virtual filing cabinet of faulty information. But I've actually found a lot of reputable websites about the disease, and I'm beginning to understand that some of what I interpret as bitchiness in Margaret is really just irritability from the medication she's on and fear about the progression of the disease. Not that Margaret isn't sometimes a bitch in her own right, but a lot of MS patients have fear and denial and anger about their diagnosis that can manifest itself as cruelty. Or resentment. I think that's where Margaret is now, saying to herself, *How dare this happen to me? I always exercised and ate right and followed the rules. Why me?*

Why now, when I have only so much time left to live? This isn't what I signed up for. In a way, I know just how she feels.

During this brief period of understanding and good will among enemy nations, I turn to Margaret and say, "Look, it's a beautiful sunny day. Do you want to go get some coffee at Tradewinds?" Shockingly, she turns to me and says yes. It's these little breakthroughs I live for. I drive us back to Tiverton, where we park across from the marina and walk over to the café.

I love Tradewinds, an all-organic coffee shop with a huge outdoor seating area with a dozen Adirondack chairs all facing the bay. In warm weather, the baristas set up a coffee bar outside and serve iced coffee and homemade lemonade. It's still a bit chilly for that, but I can smell spring in the air, feel the potential for future balminess.

We take our coffees out onto the lawn and warm our hands with the steaming cups. "I'm not sure I'm going to be able to sit in one of those," Margaret says, eyeing an Adirondack chair. A cute guy wearing a biking helmet, jersey, and bike shorts overhears us and pulls a bench from the porch over to us.

"Thank you," Margaret says, placing her purse on the bench and slowly sitting down.

"Yes, thanks a lot," I say, looking up to see that it's Dan, my next-door neighbor, the walking sperm bank. "Hey, Dan," I say. "How are you?"

"Good. Just getting some coffee," he says.

"Did you want to join us?" Margaret asks, looking slyly at me. I wince slightly. I notice a pretty girl on a bike by the curb, waiting for him. The girl is not Danielle.

"No thanks. Actually, I was just leaving," he says, walking away quickly before I could even introduce him.

"Isn't it nice that there are still decent people in the world?" Margaret says as I pull up a chair beside her.

"Yes. Yes it is," I say, taking a sip of my coffee.

"He was cute."

"What?"

"That man. He was really cute. And he was checking you out. You should have been more friendly."

I begin laughing. "He was definitely not checking me out."

"Yes, he was. And what would be the harm in flirting with him? Are you going to pine away for Jay for the rest of your life?"

"No," I say, laughing a little, shocked by her question. "But that guy was my neighbor, and he's married."

"Oh," she says.

"And that wasn't his wife."

"Well, in that case, I guess you shouldn't flirt with him. But I do think you should start flirting with someone before you forget how."

"Margaret . . ." I say.

"What?"

"Do you have any idea how awkward it is getting dating advice from your ex-mother-in-law?"

"No more awkward than getting an injection from your ex-daughter-in-law," she says.

"Fair enough." I cup my hands around my coffee, chuckling a little over this strange encounter. Margaret, however, does not let the moment pass.

"Really, though. How come you're not dating anyone?" she says.

"How do you know I'm not?"

"Because you have that frustrated, dried-up look about you."

"Thanks a lot."

"I'm not trying to be mean. I'm trying to help you."

"Look, Margaret. I'll have you know that I am seeing someone. Well, I think so anyway, and . . . I'm really not comfortable discussing this with you."

"You don't have to get so defensive. I'm just telling you that you don't look like someone who's sexually fulfilled. And knowing what we both know about Jay, you probably haven't been for years."

"Margaret!" I say, practically doing a spit-take with my coffee. I have always thought of Margaret as this snobby, repressed WASP of a woman who probably slept in a separate bed from her husband and wore a full-length flannel nightgown to bed. Now here we sit having a frank, albeit extremely disturbing, conversation about my lack of a sex life.

"Oh, don't act so shocked. The fact is I knew about Jay long before he ever told us. My husband didn't, God bless him, though I don't know how he could have been so blind."

"I was."

"Well, you were in love. Who expects you to see something when you're so hopelessly over the moon?"

I cradle my coffee close to my chest and look at her. "So . . . you knew about Jay?"

She turns her head and stares out at the bay, bringing a hand up to her throat. "I know what you're thinking. Why did I let him marry you?" she says, looking at me. "How could I stop him? He hadn't even been honest with himself yet. He was still trying to convince himself he could have a normal life. I thought, if he wants to try it this way, I shouldn't be the one to stop him."

"But Margaret . . . you accused me of turning him gay."

She places her coffee cup onto the bench next to her and begins wringing her hands together. "That was inexcusable. It was a difficult time with Dominic being sick. I know it's no excuse, but it's the only one I have."

My mind is reeling from this revelation. She knew all along that Jay was gay, and not only did she let him marry me, but she blamed me when the marriage failed. "Noelle, I really am sorry," she says. "I hope you can forgive me someday."

"I just . . . I don't know what to say."

"What is there to say? Your husband is gay, my husband is dead. Neither of us got what we bargained for."

"But you were so mean to me."

Margaret pushes herself up straight on the bench, takes a deep breath, and exhales. "I was never really much of a peach to any of Jay's girlfriends. I guess that's how a mother gets with her only child. I didn't want anyone taking him away from me, and I didn't think anyone was good enough. But with you, I know I must have seemed particularly cruel. I'm not sure why."

"You really damaged me," I hear myself say. "I honestly never felt more awful than I did at your husband's funeral. You screamed at me to get out of your son's life."

She shakes her head, embarrassed. "I think subconsciously I knew you were a sweet girl, and I didn't want you to get hurt. I didn't want you to get involved with us. I know that sounds like an excuse coming as it does now, but I wanted to send you running. We were too complex and inclusive a unit, all of us, with too many secrets among us. Hermetically sealed, you could say. You just didn't have a place there." Although I am agitated and angry, I sort of understand what she's saying. It doesn't necessarily make

108

anything any better, but it's the explanation I've been searching for all these years. "Did you know my parents didn't approve of Dominic?" she says after a pause. "In fact, they threatened to cut me off if I married him."

"Why?"

"He was Portuguese and Catholic, and his family didn't have any money. They didn't think he'd make anything of himself," she says, chuckling to herself.

"I guess he fooled them."

"We both did, in more ways than one. He got rich, and I got pregnant." She stops and looks at me, going for maximum shock value. "Are you stunned?"

"A little," I whisper, my breath caught somewhere in the back of my throat.

"I was quite a rebel back then. I'm sure you can't imagine it now, but I was actually something of a free spirit, always searching for a cause. This was back in the late sixties when you had to have a cause. Dom was more straitlaced, more traditional. When he found out about the baby, he said he wanted to marry me before anyone found out. So we eloped. We were happy for a time. Really happy. He called me Mags back then. Can you imagine?" No, I couldn't. I couldn't imagine this beautiful, blond, blue-blooded woman being called Mags or being a hippie or being pregnant out of wedlock. None of it made any sense. "But marriage sometimes changes things," she says. "Especially if you're not ready for it."

"My brother's girlfriend is pregnant," I blurt out. Margaret raises an eyebrow and leans imperceptibly closer to me. "His girlfriend wants to keep the baby, but he's not so sure."

"It's a tough decision," she says. "They need to know what they're getting into. And they'll need all the support they can get. Are your parents involved?"

"They don't know yet. I mean, my parents are great, but they're pretty old-fashioned. Particularly my father. I'm the only one who knows."

"It must be hard for you," she says.

"Well, my brother's always been the type to get himself into these situations. And he usually comes to his big sister to rescue him. I'm used to it."

"I didn't mean it that way," she says. "I meant . . . it must be hard dealing with your brother having a baby when you . . ."

I turn to face her. "Can't?"

"Yes," she says. "I'm really very sorry. You'd probably make an excellent mother."

Trying not to tear up, I look out to the bay, brisk and wild, churning with foam like it's looking for a fight. I think back to that story Margaret told me about giving up her ballet lessons over a pair of missing shoes. Back then, it probably meant so little to her to give up ballet, believing as she did that her whole life was ahead of her, taking for granted that one day, when she felt like it, she'd be able to dance again.

And now here she sits looking down at two legs that won't work the way they're supposed to, knowing she'll never dance. It's quite a different thing when you realize you can never do something again.

⁓

When I get home from Margaret's, there's a message on my voice mail from my neighbor Danielle, asking if I can stop by for a bit. I let Zeke outside first, then head next door, a little uncomfortable with the fact that I just saw her husband at a coffee shop with another woman.

Their dog, a crazy Jack Russell named Bebop, does circles around my legs, barking like a maniac. I have this tendency to correct other people's dogs even though I know it's probably rude. I bend down to his level and talk to him in soothing tones. "Okay, Bebop, sit for me. Sit." He does, and I praise him. "Good boy, Bebop."

Dan bought Bebop from a breeder, spending more than five hundred dollars on him because Danielle wanted a dog that looked like Eddie from *Frasier*. Meanwhile, we had about five Jack Russell mixes at the shelter that year, all of them equally adorable and probably far healthier and of a better disposition than Bebop. Breeds that become trendy or popular have a tendency to be overbred, thus often having more health problems. But a lot of people, for whatever reason, insist on having a purebred dog.

"Thank God you're here," Danielle says, walking into the room, her toddler hanging from her thigh. "I need major help."

I cannot help but notice the compact bulge barely concealed underneath Danielle's shirt. She notices me noticing. "Yes, I'm pregnant again," she says, laughing in a trill that for some reason infuriates me.

"Really?" I say, forcing my face into a fake smile. "Congratulations."

"We're hoping for a girl this time. Obviously," she says, nodding down to the three-year-old barnacle on her thigh. I feel like screaming at her, *Who cares if it's a girl or a boy so long as you have a healthy baby?* But of course, I just smile at her like an idiot. "Anyway, we're beginning to set up the nursery, but I'm starting to get nervous about Bebop. He's gotten so possessive of me lately. He's already barking at my stomach like he knows the baby's in there."

"He probably does," I say.

"And he's been showing some other strange behavior, too."

"Like what?"

"Like peeing in the house when I go out for just a few minutes. Barking when someone else comes near me. He almost bit Dan the other night, for trying to touch my stomach. I don't know what to do."

She sits down on the sofa and places her hands on her firm, round belly. She looks perfectly contented in her turquoise maternity blouse and leggings, her skin pink and glowing.

"How far along are you?" I say.

"About four months."

"Well," I say, taking a seat across from her, "it seems Bebop wants to be your protector while you're pregnant. He wants to guard you. Russells can be quite territorial. If he perceives somebody as a threat, he's going to defend you."

"Do you think he has some sixth sense that I may be in danger?"

"No, I don't think so," I say. "I've heard about this happening before. But you want to minimize the protective behavior. The best way to do that is to try and get him to be more independent. Does he still sleep with you and Dan on the bed?"

"Yes," she says. "Well, actually Dan's been sleeping on the sofa because sometimes Bebop growls at him when he tries to get into bed."

"That isn't good."

"I know," she says, looking genuinely distressed. "Do you think we should put him down?"

"Put him down?" I say, hearing my voice lurch above a civilized volume.

"Yeah. Do you think we should put Bebop to sleep, before the baby's born?"

"No, I don't think you should put Bebop to sleep. You just need to train him and make him feel at ease so he's not so on edge. Has there been a lot of tension in the house?" I say, feeling the acids churning in my stomach. *Is your husband having an affair that you're aware of?*

Danielle looks at me, then drops her eyes to the floor. "No, not really."

"Well, the worst-case scenario is if he doesn't improve, I'll take him to the shelter and find someone to adopt him."

"Oh, Noelle, I just don't have time to worry about Bebop along with everything else. Dan thinks we should get rid of him, but I don't know. What do you think?"

I am so angry I can barely speak. I hate this careless attitude toward animals, as if they exist merely to satisfy our human whims and desires, as if they don't have emotional lives and feelings of their own. "If it were up to me, which I know it's not, I would work with Bebop so he's ready to accept a different role in the house once the baby's born. I can help you with it, but you and Dan are going to have to be consistent about training him. No more letting him sleep in the bed. And you should try to get him used to the idea of being alone sometimes. Did you ever think of crate training him?"

"No, it seemed mean to put him in a crate, like a tiny jail cell."

"Oh, but putting him to sleep isn't mean?" I say. Immediately, I regret my outburst, even though it's true. "Sorry, it's none of my business."

"No, I know. You're right. It's just that Dan's been so irritable lately. We seem to be fighting about everything. I'm not sure he even wants this baby."

Oh boy. Why do I seem to invite these kinds of shocking Jerry Springer revelations? "I'm sure it's just the stress of it all. And Bebop's bearing the brunt of it," I say, trying to bring this conversation to safer footing. "That's probably why he's been acting so strange. But if you give him a place he can go when he's feeling anxious, a crate with his blankets and chew toys and treats, I think it would really help."

"I'll try anything," she says. "Do you think you could come over a few evenings a week just to help us get started?" There is an uncomfortable moment of silence as I consider how to say no.

"Well," I say. "I've been really busy lately."

"It'll just be for a little while," she pleads, "until Dan and I figure it out on our own."

"Well, I guess I could do it for a little while," I mumble. "I've got a few days off coming up for Easter . . ."

"Oh, thanks, Noelle. You're the best."

Yes, Noelle. You are the best sad, spineless sap out there, and we'd love to take advantage of you again sometime soon.

On Tuesday, we have to confiscate seven dogs from a rural compound in Middletown, where the owner had been training them for dog fighting. All of the dogs have been checked for serious injuries, and they're being temporarily housed in a separate part of the facility to keep them isolated until we can have them evaluated. Tara and I are going back to feed them and fill their water bowls, so I have to steel myself for what I'm about to see.

Seven dogs, all pit bulls, all terrified, but dealing with the fear in their own ways.

As we walk down the rows, a few of them come right up to the front of their cages, barking and snarling at us. And who could blame them? When you've seen enough abuse at the hands of humans, I guess you start distrusting them all. One of the dogs is at the back of his cage, and I can tell he so desperately wants to greet us, his tail half wagging, then going between his legs. It's heartbreaking to see this dog, so barrel-chested and tough, with the face of a fireplug, acting so deferential and terrified of us. The awful thing is, some dogs are so loyal and so blindly hopeful of human goodness that they'll wag their tail at night for the same person who kicked them that morning.

Two of the dogs are lying back in the corner of their cages, looking up timidly, but afraid to even stand up. One begins to quiver when we approach her cage with the food.

"This is just so sad," Tara says. "How could anybody do this to an animal?"

"I don't know. It disgusts me," I say.

"What do you think is going to happen to them?"

"Joe wants to bring in an animal behaviorist to analyze their aggressiveness, see if maybe some could be placed in foster homes for socialization."

"Don't you think fighting dogs would be too violent to be placed in a home?"

"Well, nobody really knows for sure. So few fighting dogs ever live long enough for us to find out."

"Nobody's going to want these pit bulls, though. Especially with their track record."

"That's not necessarily true. Did you know that before pit bulls got the reputation as gang dogs, they were known as worker and companion dogs. Pit bulls worked as armed service dogs during the Civil War and World War I; some even worked in Hollywood."

The dog who had been lingering at the back of his cage tentatively makes his way to the front, but then his neighbor snarls and lashes out, and he runs back into the corner, terrified. Tara goes to stand by the opposite end of the cage, kneels down, and begins talking in soothing tones. "Come here, sweetheart. I won't hurt you." He whimpers, wags his tail once, and sits down. "Oh, I'd take this one home in a heartbeat," she says. "Maybe if that specialist says he's okay, I'll adopt him."

"That would be great. But what about these guys?" I say, pointing to the ones who've been so beaten by life they've decided to keep everyone away with their growls and bared teeth. "They're every bit as terrified. What's going to happen to them?"

"We'll probably have to send them away," Tara says. "You know, there's that place out in Utah. For hopeless cases."

"I'd hate to think there are any hopeless cases," I say. But I fear, in this instance, she might be right. Who's going to look into the face of one of these dogs and see love and potential friendship behind the snarling lips?

Reluctantly, I make the trip home for Easter because my mother is having her annual ham dinner. I have always hated Easter, even as a child. I thought the Easter bunny was a fraud, painted eggs smelled like sulfur, and white chocolate was a vile abomination of one of my favorite foods. I know Easter is supposed to be the most holy day on a Catholic's calendar, the Resurrection, the miracle of miracles, but I cannot bring myself to get into the spirit. Maybe it's the secular part of Easter that bothers me—the eggs and the bunny rabbits and all those symbols of spring and fertility.

Or perhaps the real reason for my bitterness is that my next-door neighbor is pregnant, my ex-husband is pressuring me to adopt a baby for him, and my brother's girlfriend is going to give birth in two months. I'm surrounded by maternity clothes, baby magazines, endless conversation about infants, even though I will never, ever be able to have one of my own.

Oh, and then there's my mother's Easter theme this year: Beatrix Potter characters. "Get it?" she said on the phone to me, near bursting with excitement. "Beatrix is our dog, so we're going to dress her up like Peter Rabbit, and I'm going to make a display of vegetables for Mr. McGregor's garden, and make cookies in the shapes of . . ." I stopped listening somewhere around the Flopsy and Mopsy pot holders.

After enduring the ham dinner served on Beatrix Potter dishware, I pull Nick aside in the den. Beatrix follows us in. I am happy to see that she now has that calm, proprietary sense dogs get when they feel at home somewhere. *This is my dog bed. My water bowl. My toy. But I'm so happy you're here.*

"Nick," I say, petting Beatrix's ears, "I want to give you some money. It's just a loan, for the baby."

"Aw, thanks, Noelle. We could really use it."

"But Nick, it's just for baby items. Not for some scam or investment or for gambling. It's for Dana and the baby."

"I know," he says. "I'm laying off the schemes for a while."

"Have you told Mom and Dad yet?"

"No," he says. He gives me a dejected look, the same look he gave me when he was seven and he "accidentally" ripped the head off of one of my dolls.

"Are you going to wait until you have a baby attached to your hip and tell them it's a growth? I mean, Jesus, Nick."

"You probably shouldn't say that word today," he whispers, "or you're going to end up in h-e-double hockey sticks."

"Nick, in two months, you are going to have a *b-a-b-y*. You have to tell Mom and Dad."

"I know, I know," he says.

"Today."

"Will you stay and do it with me?" he asks, scrunching his face into a pathetic frown.

"Yes, I'll stay. But do it soon. I've got work tomorrow."

"So do I," he says.

"Really? You got a job? Where?"

"Still temping, but I have a pretty good gig at one of those eBay stores. I'm helping them maintain their accounts."

"That sounds promising. Maybe they'll hire you full time."

"No, the job's only for another three months. Their normal person is out on maternity leave."

"Are you kidding me?" I say. It's like some sick cosmic joke.

"Yeah, what's the big deal?"

"Nothing. Never mind. Look, let's go in and get this over with. Mom's had her brandy already so maybe she won't freak out."

"What about Dad?" Nick says, his eyes growing enormous.

"I don't know what to say about Dad. Let's just hope he's feeling the divine spirit of Jesus' forgiving power."

"Amen, sister," he says.

We are so going to hell.

❧

Here is an abridged transcript of the conversation that took place at my parents' house on the evening of Easter Sunday:

Nick: *Mom, Dad? I want to tell you something.*

Mom: *What is it, sweetie? Did you get a job?*

Nick: *(under his breath) No. Well, uh . . . Dana's pregnant.*

Mom: *Noelle's pregnant? Oh my goodness! When? Who? (Mom hugs me; Dad folds his arms tightly across his chest.)*

Me: *No, Mom. Not me.*

Nick: *Not Noelle, Mom. Dana.*

Dad: *Who?*

Mom: *Dana. You know, Nick's girlfriend that we never see.*

Dad: *I thought they'd broken up.*

Mom: *No, dear.*

Nick: *Hello? Did you hear me? Dana is pregnant.*

Mom: *Is it yours?*

Nick: *Yes, Mom. It's my baby. (More shrieking from my mother. My dad's arms go even tighter across his chest.)*

Mom: *Oh dear, and you're telling us on Easter Sunday.*

Nick: *What difference does it make when I tell you?*

Mom: *Oh dear.*

Me: *Aren't you going to say something other than 'Oh dear'?*

Dad: *What do you want us to say to him, Congratulations?*

Nick: *No, Dad. I don't want you to say anything. I just thought you should know.*

Mom: *Oh my poor Nicky.*

Dad: *Poor Nicky?*

Mom: *What are you going to do?*

Nick: *We're going to have the baby.*

Mom: *Well, of course you are, but are you going to get married?*

Dad: *They have to get married.*

Nick: *Actually, we don't.*

Dad: *That's what you do when you get a girl in trouble. You marry her.*

Me: *Not necessarily. It's not 1955 anymore.*

Dad: *Stay out of this, missy.*

Me: *Dad, you're being ridiculous.*

Mom: *Now, hon, let's not get too upset.*

Dad: *Upset? You expect me not to get upset? Our twenty-seven-year-old unemployed son knocks someone up, and you expect me not to get upset?*

Nick: *Dad, we're going to take care of everything. You won't even have to be involved.*

Mom: *Oh, dear, this is something. Oh, Nicky. My poor Nicky.*

Dad: *Poor Nicky, my foot! This one knocks up his girlfriend, and this one marries a gay guy. Can't we all just have a normal life?*

I'll spare you the rest of the conversation because it contained a lot of expletives, and it really wasn't very productive. But at least Nick told them, for better or for worse.

And my father's question has sort of been hovering over me for the past few weeks: can't we all just have a normal life?

Then again, what does a normal life look like anyway?

May

Today Jasper is driving down to Tiverton to meet us at the beach, and Zeke is so excited that he gets to come with. We're going to this outdoor seafood restaurant that serves crabs to you on big picnic tables covered in brown paper. I wasn't sure whether Jasper would go for such a rustic place, but he'd gone online to look up restaurants in the area, and asked me if I'd ever been there.

"Marilyn's Crab House? That's the best!" I said. "You want to go there?"

"Sure, it looks great," he said. "Why?"

"I don't know. I just didn't see you as a picnic-table-and-no-utensils kind of guy."

"There you go again," he said.

"I know, I know. I won't assume anything."

Now as I sit on the beach waiting for him to show, I'm feeling nervous again because I'm not really sure where all this is going. I keep glancing back to the road, looking for his car, and Zeke keeps pulling me, as if to say, *What gives? I'm usually the sole focus of your attention!*

Finally I see Jasper standing on top of the seawall, peering out to spot us. He's wearing jeans and a loose-fitting white shirt, and when he takes off his shoes and begins walking toward us on the sand, I swear he looks like a commercial for men's cologne. Calvin Klein's Hotness for Men. I throw a piece of driftwood for Zeke so I can stop myself from staring.

"Hey," he says, when he finally reaches us.

"Hi there."

Zeke comes bounding back to greet him, and Jasper bends down to pet his ears. "Hey, Zeke," he says. "My God, you're a horse!"

"I know. I think he's still growing."

"Why the name Zeke?" he asks. "I mean, not that it doesn't suit him."

"Jay named him. He was actually Jay's dog before he was mine. But when Jay moved to Atlanta, he let me keep him."

"That was nice of him," he says.

"I guess." We begin walking down the beach, heading closer to the shoreline. Zeke plunges in when he realizes where we're headed, then comes out of the water, enormously pleased with himself. When I lean down to scrub his wet muzzle, he shakes from head to tail in delighted convulsions, scattering water all over the two of us.

"Zeke!" I say as Jasper laughs.

The beach is surprisingly empty, perhaps because it's a bit chilly out. Seagulls are darting between the masts of boats in the distance, cawing out in joy that summer is finally around the corner.

"It's so nice to be on a beach again," he says. "Even though Providence is only thirty minutes away, I hardly ever get down here. I don't know why."

"I live five minutes from here, and I don't come as often as I'd like. But it's nice to know I can. I don't know how people live in landlocked states."

"I didn't see a beach until I was sixteen," he says.

"Really? There are beaches in Texas, right?"

"Yeah, but I lived closer to Dallas than the coast. Anyway, my parents weren't real big on family vacations. I didn't even know what the ocean looked like, apart from pictures. As soon as I got my driver's license, I set out to see as many as I could. But maybe if I'd lived here, I wouldn't have been so anxious to get away." He turns and gives me a warm and open smile.

"What was your favorite place you visited?"

He digs one foot into the sand and kicks it a little. "Wow, that's a tough one. I'd have to say India. I went with a buddy of mine right after college. God, we were so young. And poor. We stayed in this tiny little shack on the beach for less than five dollars a day, and there were these yellow flowers that grew right along the dunes by our cabin. These big, beautiful flowers, the kind you drew as a kid, you know?"

I couldn't help but smile at the image. "Seems like a good place to do some soul searching. If you want your soul searched, that is. Me, I think I'm happier not knowing what's going on in there." He laughs, and I can feel him looking at my profile. I immediately change the subject.

"So, are you hungry?" I say.

"Starved," he says and smiles.

❧

Our waitress is sunny and chipper, if a little clumsy, bringing us two Coronas but immediately knocking one onto Jasper's lap.

"Oh my God, I am so sorry," she says, grabbing a pile of napkins to wipe up the spill, then blushing when she realizes she's wiping Jasper's crotch.

"That's all right," Jasper says, standing up and laughing. "Really, it'll dry quickly. Don't worry about it. I'm just sad we wasted a whole Corona."

The girl laughs self-consciously, then excuses herself to get him another beer. The entire front of his pants is completely soaked, but he sits back down and resumes his conversation as if nothing happened. Jay would have made us go home to change. He was always incredibly fastidious that way. One time he got a tiny sauce stain on his shirt while we were out to dinner. He said it was okay, but when we were at the movies later, he looked down at himself during the previews and said, "I've got to go wash this out."

"Okay," I'd said. "I wonder if they have any club soda at the concession stand."

They didn't. We ended up leaving the movie.

"So I checked with George and Rita at the Loft," Jasper says, "and they're on for the S&M night."

"Really? That's great," I say. "I found a venue for the *Lady and the Tramp* ball. The Newport Country Club."

"Sounds sufficiently swanky."

"Yeah, we have it reserved for June twenty-second. A Sunday night."

"Oh, that's the night George and Rita suggested, too. They're not usually open Sundays, so they said it'd be a good night to host a special party."

"Oh," I say, a bit disappointed. "That's too bad."

"Why?"

"I was kind of hoping you could come to the ball with me. I hate going to these functions alone."

"Oh, that's right," he says, pursing his lips together in concentration. "Can't you ask someone else to go with you?"

"I can't really think of anyone else I'd like to take," I say, then feel myself blushing. "So what about you? Who are you going to take to the Loft?"

"Probably no one."

"Do you think Jolene will be there?"

"Maybe." Involuntarily, I frown.

The waitress comes back with another Corona and our crabs, and we spread them out over the table. "Wow, there's nothing better than this, is there?" Jasper says. He picks up a crab in his left hand and grabs a small knife in his right, carefully cracking open a claw so the meat stays intact, sucking the meat out, then taking a swig of beer. "Do you let Zeke have the claws when you're done?" he asks.

I nod, watching as he bends down to hand Zeke the shell. *Who is this guy?* I think. *And why are things so easy with him?* Things with Jay were never this easy. I mean, I loved him and all, but everything was always an ordeal, a production. If Jay were a piece of music, he'd be a lavish orchestral soundtrack with complicated rhythms and dissonant tones. Jasper would be—oh, I don't know—a song by the Eagles like "Take It Easy" or "Tequila Sunrise."

Even his job seems so laid-back and stress-free. Over lunch he tells me he's been experimenting with a new video game system for the blind that uses music and sound cues to let players know what

125

to do next. There's even a remote that responds to the player's arm movements instead of a touch pad and joystick.

"Gives me a great excuse to play video games at work," he says.

"You sound just like my brother. He's always looking for a way to make money by playing."

"What's he like?"

"Nick?" I give out a one-note laugh. "He's very different from me. Sort of shiftless and irresponsible but in a lovable way. He's the baby of the family, you know, so it's not necessarily his fault. But he's got a really good heart. You two would probably get along well." And then I feel the need to backpedal. Is it too soon to be alluding to Jasper meeting members of my family? "What about your sister?" I ask quickly, hoping he didn't catch my blunder.

"Cassie?" he says, smiling. "She's crazy. But in a good way."

"Not in the Bellevue way?"

"No," he says, laughing again. "She was kind of wild growing up. I was always the more serious one. After she started going blind, my parents had no idea what to do with her, so they sent her off to this special school that was a half-day drive away, so I hardly got to see her anymore. And then a few years later, I left Texas for good."

"But you guys still seem close."

"Not as close as we used to be. I try to go down to visit her when I can, but it's not as often as I'd like. I guess my job is sort of a way for me to make up for not being there for her." His face grows distant and pensive.

"I was actually thinking about your sister recently," I say.

"Really?"

"Well, not Cassie specifically. But I was wondering whether my boss might consider letting me start a guide dog training program at

SASH. I know he'd like the idea, but I don't know whether he'd be willing to take on another initiative right now."

Jasper cracks another crab claw and pulls the meat out clean. "Cassie had a guide dog assigned to her at school, and it really helped a lot. I can give her a call to see if she might be able to help." Jasper is back, fully present and too good to be true.

"Oh . . . okay," I say. "I was just going to start by researching some grants."

"Well, if you need any help writing them, I've written a lot of grants for OpticGate." I smile at him, but a concerned crease must be forming over my eyes because his face suddenly looks hurt. "Sorry, sorry," he says after a pause. "I'm doing it again."

"Doing what?"

"I have this tendency to want to solve problems for everyone. I like to fix things."

"Want to come over to my house sometime?" I say, smiling to lighten the mood. "I've got a list of DIYs on my refrigerator door that will knock that impulse right out of you."

He takes a long swig of his beer. For some reason, this is inordinately sexy. Either that, or I'm really hard up. "So, are you inviting me over to your house?" he says.

"Not until I know you a little better."

"Well, then we should plan our next date so we can get to know each other better. Do you bike?"

"I used to," I say. "Not so much lately."

"You know the bike path in Bristol that goes to Providence?"

"Yeah," I say. "I used to ride it occasionally, but I've never gone all the way before."

"No?" he says, a crooked smile appearing on his face.

I feel immensely stupid for saying this. "Well, I mean, I never went all the way to Providence before. I never had anyone to visit in Providence."

"Well, now you do," he says. "And from now on, you have an open invitation. Any time you want. I mean it. I can't say I'd look forward to anything as much as you showing up on my doorstep."

"And where exactly is your doorstep?" I say.

"Is there a napkin around somewhere? I'll write it down," he says, smiling.

"Somebody really needs to buy you a BlackBerry."

"Where's the fun in that? This way, you get to remember all the places you've been with me. Think of them as souvenirs of our relationship."

Relationship, I think to myself. "You sure you want to get involved with a nut like me?"

"Definitely."

I raise an eyebrow at him, daring him to tell me why.

"You're one of the nicest people I've met in a long time," he says. You genuinely care about people."

"How do you know?" I say, giving him my best deadpan stare. "I could be very, very anti-people." He starts laughing, hard enough that I can tell he's not just humoring me.

"Trust me, I know."

"Well, sometimes I don't. I don't have a lot of faith in people. The dogs I've known have been a hell of a lot more loyal."

He is leaving the tip for the waitress when I suddenly feel his hand on my arm. "Not all people will disappoint you, Noelle," he says, and despite all the fresh air, I am finding it hard to breathe.

❧

The following Wednesday, I get home from work feeling utterly weary and repellant. All I want to do is take a shower, lie down on the couch with Zeke, and read a good book. I am just about to strip off my filthy T-shirt when the phone rings. I almost don't answer, but finally relent. It's Margaret, and she sounds panicked.

"What's wrong?" I say.

"I can't walk," she practically yells into the phone. "Remember this happened before? Well, it's happening again. I can't walk, and I'm terrified."

"All right, Margaret," I say. "Don't worry, I'm coming over. Don't move."

"I can't move, for God's sake," she screams, but I hang up on her.

I quickly drive over to Tiverton, breaking a land speed record for used hatchbacks made in Korea. When I let myself into the house, I call Margaret's name and hear her yelling something from the kitchen. As I get closer, I can make out a string of profanities. "Margaret, what happened?" I say.

"I don't know. These goddamn legs are useless. Might as well cut them off and put me in a wheelchair for all the good they do me."

"Come on, now. You know this happened before, and you were fine later. Let's get you up off the floor."

She reaches her arms up to me, surprisingly allowing me to help her to her feet. "Thank God I hadn't turned the oven on yet. I can't even reach the switch from here. I could have burned the whole house down."

"No, you couldn't have. Because you keep the phone on the

counter like I told you to, so you were able to call me. Do you think you can manage to get down to my car, or should we call an ambulance?"

"No, no ambulances," she says. But when I try to get her down the porch stairs, I can tell it's going to be impossible for me to carry her weight by myself, and I'm worried about her falling again and injuring herself more. In my most diplomatic voice, I convince her that we should call an ambulance, just to be on the safe side, and miraculously, she consents.

I have always been pretty good at handling a crisis, staying calm, not letting others know that my insides are churning about like the Tilt-A-Whirl. But this feels terrifyingly real to me, like when my mother called and told me my father had suffered a heart attack, only now there's nobody else around to share my burden.

Margaret's doctor meets us at the emergency room entrance with a wheelchair and immediately takes her back to a temporary holding room. "Call Jay," she yells to me as she disappears around a corner.

Okay, call Jay. I can do this.

After finally calming my voice, I call his cell phone, but only get his voice mail. "Hi Jay, it's Noelle. Don't worry, everything is fine. But your mother was just admitted to the hospital." That sounds very reassuring—*everything's fine, but your mom's in the hospital.* "We're not sure what's wrong yet, but the doctor is with her now. Give me a call when you get a chance."

I hang up the phone and immediately realize I want to call Jasper. I'm not sure why—he's never even met Margaret—but I just have a feeling he'd make me feel better. So I call him, too.

"Hi, Jasper. Are you busy?"

"Still at work but trying to get out of here," he says. "Are you okay? You sound a little frazzled."

"Actually, I'm at the hospital. Margaret had a fall. She couldn't get up, her legs weren't working, so we came here in an ambulance. I'm not really sure why I called you . . ."

"Noelle, slow down," he says. "I'm glad you called. Are you okay?"

"I'm fine, I guess. A little shaken."

"Of course. Where are you, in the emergency room?"

"Yeah."

"Do you want me to come down?"

"Oh, no, no," I say. *Yes, yes.* "Thanks, but it's not necessary. I just . . . wanted to hear your voice."

"Good. I'm glad. Is it helping?" he says.

"Yes, it is. I feel better. Oh, there's her neurologist. Listen, I better go. Can I call you later?"

"Of course. Please do. No matter what time it is. Okay?"

"Okay."

I hang up and go over to talk to the doctor who tells me he doesn't know much yet, that I should have a seat or maybe even leave for a while and come back later. But I'm too nervous to leave. So I sit and wait. And wait. And wait.

Finally after two hours, a nurse wheels Margaret out in a wheelchair. "Is she okay?" I ask the nurse.

"She's fine for now. We knew this kind of episode was always a possibility. The interferon must not be working as well anymore," she says. "The doctor would like to start her on a different course of drug therapy."

"Yes," Margaret says. "One I'll need every day."

"Pills?" I ask.

"Injection," she says, smirking at me.

"Oh."

The nurse comes around so she can face Margaret, then crouches down so she's at her eye level, like she's about to speak to a child. "You know, Mrs. Salazar, we have nurses we can send out to your home to give you the injections. It's an expense, but Medicare will pay for some of it."

"Yes, it may be time for me to start thinking about something like that," Margaret says. My heart plummets.

"We have to be careful since you live alone," she says in a singsong voice that must be infuriating to Margaret. I myself would love to wad her mouth full of cotton balls. "If you have another episode and you're not near the phone . . ."

"Can we not refer to what happened to me as an episode?" Margaret says. "It makes it sound like I'm a character on a medical drama."

"I'm sorry," the nurse says. "What would you like me to call it?"

"Listen," I interrupt before things turn ugly, "can I have a moment alone with Mrs. . . . with Margaret?"

"Sure," the nurse says, blinking at me twice and putting on a falsely cheery smile. She walks away behind the check-in desk.

"Margaret, I can still come to give you the injections," I say to her once we're alone. "There's no need to hire a private nurse."

"Nonsense," she says. "I'm not going to make you come all the way to the house every day, along with everything else you have to do. That's ridiculous."

"It's not like it's so far away," I say. "Your house is ten minutes from where I work. It's really not a problem."

"Noelle, thank you. That's very kind of you, but I have to face the facts. This is it. The monster's got me."

"Don't have a negative attitude," I say. "You've had months when you felt perfectly fine. And you will again. You're just starting a new treatment to see if that works better for you."

"You know, I had a dream the other day. All of my teeth began falling out, one by one. I've had that dream before, but this time it was different because you were there, and you kept picking my teeth up off the floor and telling me I could glue them back in. And I'd say, 'No, Noelle, it's not going to work.' But you kept pushing them in, forcing them there with glue. You wouldn't give up."

"So what does that mean?" I say.

"Just that maybe I need to know when to say when. When to give up."

"No, I don't think it meant that at all," I say. "I think it was trying to tell you that you don't have to lose your teeth because I'll be there to help you put them back in."

"Ever the optimist," she says, shaking her head. "Oh, did you get Jay on the phone?"

"I left a message on his voice mail." She sighs and brings a fist to her mouth. "Do they know yet if you'll have to stay overnight?"

"Yes. They want to give me my first dose and see how I respond to it."

"Good. When are they going to move you to a room?"

"As soon as one opens up."

"And they're going to make you wait out here until then?"

"I don't know."

I walk over to the desk to find the nurse who wheeled her out. "Excuse me," I say.

"Just a minute," the receptionist says, putting one call on hold and answering another. I can see our nurse, Miss Condescension, back by the filing cabinet. I know she hears me, yet she shows no sign of acknowledging me. "Yes, how can I help you?" the receptionist says after getting off the phone.

"I need to speak with Mrs. Salazar's nurse," I say, clearing my throat and nodding toward the woman behind her.

"Kelly Ann?" she says.

"Yes, I'll be right with you," Kelly Ann says without turning around. Frustrated, I walk back over to Margaret.

"Boy, she's just bursting with friendliness, isn't she?" I say.

"Well, I wasn't so nice to her."

Finally Kelly Ann comes out from behind the reception area. "You needed to see me?" she says as if she's never seen us before in her life.

"I just wondered how long it would be until Mrs. Salazar gets a room."

"Well, technically I'm not her nurse. Debra's her nurse. But I can go check for you."

"Would you? We'd really appreciate it," I say, giving her a sincere smile for her phony one.

"You should leave," Margaret says. "I'm sure they'll find a room for me eventually. I'll be fine."

"Not until I know you're in a room," I say. "Are you hungry? Do you want anything from the cafeteria?"

"Do you think they have Bombay Sapphire?" she asks.

"Probably not."

"Well then, no."

"I'm going to run down and get a cup of coffee. Just hang tight. I'll be right back," I assure her.

On my way down in the elevator, I give Jay another try. I'm exhausted and confused, not sure exactly what I should do. Thankfully, he answers this time. Quickly and calmly, I tell him where we are. He is panicking already. I explain to him everything I know, which isn't much.

"Listen," he says, "I'm coming home. We're going to sit down and talk everything over. Can I talk to her?"

"I'm in the elevator. Do you want me to have her call you?"

"No, that's okay. I'll call her later, I'm late for a meeting. But I'm booking a flight for the end of the week. I should be up there by Saturday, Sunday at the latest. Tell her that, will you?"

"All right," I say, sighing in relief. "Bye, Jay."

"Love you, Noelle."

"Love you, too."

Good. Jay's coming home. He'll know what to do. Because right now, I haven't got a clue.

June

FOR SALE, Jamestown: Shingle-style house with lots of warmth and character, featuring hardwood floors and stained-glass windows, two bedrooms, plus living room with wood-burning stove and exposed beams. Light-filled kitchen has beautiful views of salt pond. Enjoy your own little piece of heaven.

The following Saturday, once Margaret is back home and showing a positive reaction to her new medication, I meet Jasper halfway between Providence and Bristol along the bike trail. It's a gorgeous day, the sun shining overhead in a sky streaked with cirrus clouds. A cool breeze is coming off the water, bringing with it the briny smell of sea life.

By the time I'm halfway along the trail, I feel disgusting with my matted ponytail and flushed and sweaty face. Why do I always look like a ravaged refugee whenever I see him? I spot him up ahead coasting down a small hill, wearing a weathered gray T-shirt, sweat streaks along the sides. It's one of the great injustices in life that sweat looks sexy on a man but revolting on a woman.

"Hey, Noelle," he shouts, riding up to meet me, then braking right along my side.

"Hi," I say, breathlessly.

"Phew, I'm out of shape. I'll have to start doing this ride more often."

"Me, too," I say, but I really am out of shape. Jasper has about 2 percent body fat and looks as if his heart rate hasn't crept above eighty.

"So, where to?" he says. "Are you thirsty? Hungry?"

"A little. There's a great sandwich place down in Bristol if you don't mind coming down that far."

"Not at all," he says. I turn my bike around, and we set off down toward Bristol's waterfront, stopping at the deli I recommended to pick up a few sandwiches to share. We sit on the rocks watching the rough chop rock the boats in the harbor and talking about the fund-raisers—plans, progress, what's left to be done.

Jasper gives me some literature Cassie sent him about guide dog training, along with the name of a trainer who'd be willing to come up and work with SASH. "This is great, Jasper," I say. "Tell Cassie thanks. I'm definitely going to call this guy. I'd love to get certified myself."

"You'd be a great trainer," he says. "You're so patient. And compassionate. You're, like, the nicest person I know." I can already feel the heat rising to my face.

"Oh yes," I say to diffuse any sparks that might be flying. "I am the Florence Nightingale of veterinary technicians."

"You're also really funny," he says.

"Mmm hmm."

"And beautiful."

"Yeah, right," I wisecrack. "Particularly the stylish way I wear a ponytail through my baseball cap. That takes a lot of planning."

"Are you always this gracious with a compliment?" he asks.

I brush a few crumbs from my lap. I am suddenly feeling very self-conscious. "I'm actually atrociously bad at accepting compliments," I say, unnecessarily.

"All right, then," he says. "You give one to me. I'll show you how it's done."

I laugh. "Now that's not even fishing for a compliment. You're just going out there and demanding one. Okay, a compliment. Let's see, you are . . . incredibly generous with your time."

"Yes, I know. This is no fun for me at all. I'd much rather be at work," he says, prompting a dubious smirk from me. "Go on."

"All right. You are infinitely calm, and I feel calm when I'm with you."

"Good. Keep going." His teasing look has turned more serious, and I can feel my chest begin to tighten.

"Except when I don't feel calm around you, like when you look at me that way."

"What way?"

"You know what way. That sexy see-right-through-me way. It makes me nervous."

"That's good, too," he says. His T-shirt is still clinging to his chest in places, and I have to force myself not to stare.

"It looks like it could storm out there, doesn't it?" I say, pointing across the bay toward some gray scudding clouds. "Should you be getting back?" *What the hell is wrong with me?*

"No," Jasper says, a bit abruptly. "I mean, I'd like to spend more time with you, if that's okay."

"Sure," I say, standing up and straddling the jagged rocks with my hands on my hips. I feel a bit unsteady.

"Have you ever been to Blithewold Mansion?" he asks.

"Oh, yeah. It's only ten minutes from my house."

"Would you take me there?"

I smile and nod. "I'd love to."

The ride down to Blithewold doesn't take more than a few minutes, but I have to admit I'm exhausted both from riding and from holding my breath. When we arrive at the mansion, Jasper still looks as if he could swim across the channel and run a marathon.

We walk into the visitors' booth and are greeted by a man who could be Truman Capote's heterosexual, horticultural brother. He hands us a brochure and map and begins to ply us with a history lesson on the family who owned the house and the various types of plants and trees to be found on the estate. I can feel my eyes glazing over but manage to maintain eye contact and nod my head a lot.

When we are finally given permission to explore the grounds, we step outside, stopping to look at the map to get our bearings. "Should we tour the mansion or see the gardens first?" Jasper asks.

"Let's do the gardens first, in case it rains," I say. "There are several really nice ones from what I remember. There's a rose garden and a rock garden and . . ."

"And apparently three thousand species of trees and the largest sequoia on the east coast," he says. "Did you know the word 'sequoia' has all five vowels in it?"

"No, I did not." I laugh at his earnestness, enjoying this slightly dorky side of Jasper's personality.

The mansion is situated on an enormous lawn that slopes down toward the water, an open vista of rolling green running itself right down to the bay. The view as we wander to the seaward side makes me think of a garden party from a Virginia Woolf novel. I can practically hear the string quartet and clinking champagne glasses. "Can you imagine living here?" I say.

"Not really." He looks at me expectantly, his arm hovering for a moment away from his body, almost as if he's had the brief urge to grab my hand.

"I mean, imagine having all this as your backyard. Or raising kids here," I say, then want to impale myself. What the hell am I doing bringing up kids on our second date?

"But you'd never be able to find them," Jasper says, smiling, and I immediately sigh with relief. "Besides, would you really want to live in a house that had forty-five rooms, with servants' quarters and long, narrow corridors that echoed when you walked through them at night to find the bathroom?"

I laugh. "I think I could get used to it. I mean, I love houses. Especially ones on the water. I look for them all the time."

Jasper looks at me with a questioning face. "What do you mean you look for them?"

I wonder whether I should share my strange hobby of compiling house descriptions on the computer and decide, in the interest of full disclosure, I should. "Promise you won't think I'm nuts?"

"Well, no, but maybe I like nuts." He stops walking and gives me his full attention.

"I like to go to real estate websites and collect descriptions of the houses I like," I say, spitting the whole sentence out like the words are on fire.

"Houses you'd like to buy?"

"Maybe in my dreams. No, it's more like window-shopping. For the future."

"I see," he says, turning around so he's facing me, then proceeding to walk backward while he talks. "So, you look at houses you'd like to live in someday."

"It's not even that, really," I say. "I guess I imagine myself living in them. Imagine how my life would be different."

He squints his eyes, trying to figure me out. "But your life wouldn't be any different," he says. "You'd still be you but with a better address. A bigger bedroom."

"I think a house, if it's the right one, can sort of transform a person, don't you? I think we're influenced by a sense of place. I mean, look at these gardens, look at that view. Don't you think you'd see the world a little differently if you woke up to that every morning? Knew all of this was yours?" His face still has that slightly disapproving look, and for a moment, I'm worried that I'm coming off like some kind of materialistic snob. "Look," I say, trying to explain myself. "I don't want you to think I'm one of those gold diggers interested only in wealth and big cars and fancy houses, because that's totally not me. I just think a house can be a touchstone, the one place you go every day to restore yourself. The one place you go to feel safe." I am rambling, to be sure, but I think it's working because his slightly disapproving look has transformed into a grin. He steps forward so he's standing two inches from me.

"Noelle, I could never think of you as a gold digger," he says. "Remember, you thought I was a bum, and you still went out with me."

"Very true."

A crackle of thunder echoes across the bay, sending tiny shivers down my sides, and the breeze kicks up, cooling beads of sweat along my neck, inside my elbows. Jasper looks up at the sky and lifts his palms to catch the first raindrops. "Let's duck in there for some tree cover."

"Isn't it dangerous to be under trees if it starts lightning?" I ask.

"Don't you ever do anything dangerous?"

"You know I don't," I say, and he breaks into that crooked smile of his.

"Well, now's your big chance to live dangerously." And this time he does extend his arm and gently takes my hand and leads me back along the path into a little grove of trees.

We follow the path as it snakes its way through tiny grottos and flower gardens until it comes to a beautiful hollow with a koi pond, Japanese fountain, and stone bench. Jasper guides me over to the bench and sits down facing me, one knee propped up on the bench, one dangling down near the stones at the pond's edge.

Briefly I let my mind contemplate the warm, salty smell of him, think about running my tongue along that sexy spot right beneath his Adam's apple. Another roll of thunder bellows, closer this time. I shiver involuntarily. "Relax," he says. "You're fine."

"I'm relaxed," I say.

"Oh yeah, you look real Zen."

"What do you mean?"

"Look at you. Your arms are crossed, and you have your body entirely closed off to me."

"I do not," I say, but then I realize he's right. My body language is giving me away. Oh my God, am I my father's daughter? I uncross my legs and turn slightly toward him. "Is that better?"

"Oh, much better," he says, laughing. "Very intimate." He pulls up his other leg so he is sitting Indian-style, facing me. The rain that had been pitter-pattering in soft thuds just a few minutes ago is now slapping against the rocks and pinging off the pond like machine-gun fire. "Wow, this is turning into quite a storm," I say.

"Are you getting too wet?" Jasper asks, his voice softer now in the rain.

"I'm okay."

"Are you cold?"

Despite the chill of the rain, my face feels flushed and my thighs feel like they're on fire. "No," I say. We are both soaked now, the rain hitting us from all angles, pouring in sheets so heavy we can hear it on the bay. It sounds like applause.

Slowly I turn to look at him. His face is all warmth and intention. Smooth golden skin dampened by rain, strong hard jaw, soft full lips. "I really want to kiss you right now," he says, giving me a look that turns my insides to melted butter. How does a girl respond to that? Well, any normal girl would tackle him on the spot. But me? I stay glued to the bench, unable to move, unable to speak.

His face is close to mine, so close I can feel the heat from his face, smell the salt on his skin. I turn my body into him now, steady myself with one hand, then feel his hand on my arm. I am liquid mercury, overheated, leaking out of the glass bulb.

His other hand grips my cheek, cold and wet, an electric jolt to my system. I want to bury my head in his neck, taste his skin, his lips, his tongue . . .

And then, my goddamn cell phone goes off. Honest to God.

I refuse to answer it at first, on the grounds that I am very, very busy. But the inconsiderate person rings back again. Jasper and I laugh it off, but it's hard to recapture that emotionally charged moment when my phone will not cease its infernal ringing.

"Maybe you should answer it," Jasper concedes.

"It might be Margaret." Reluctantly, and I do mean reluctantly, I grab my cell phone from out of my purse, see from the caller ID that it's Nick. "This better be important," I grumble to Jasper.

"This better be important," I say into the phone.

It is. Nick is at the hospital with Dana. She's just had her baby.

Of course, I am thrilled for them and eager to go meet my niece, and yet there is a fairly large part of me that wants to cry, because I will have to leave this beautiful man sitting in front of me, and leave this possibly once-in-a-lifetime moment.

Jasper is a good sport, riding back with me to Bristol, putting my bike on the rack for me, giving me a disappointingly chaste kiss on the cheek. He's going to wait out the rain in a café and attempt to ride back to Providence later this afternoon. We say good-bye and agree to call each other soon. I watch him ride away in the rain for a few seconds, then jolt myself back into gear and get in the car heading out to Connecticut, feeling a strange mixture of frustration and anticipation. My brother has a baby. My baby brother! I have that familiar lurching in my gut, a tiny stab of jealousy in the pit of my stomach.

But as soon as I reach the hospital, all resentment fades away.

There's a little sign posted outside Dana's room: WELCOME, MIRANDA! 7 POUNDS 8 OUNCES. I go inside to find my father, Mr. Hands-Across-His-Chest, holding the baby on his lap and cooing—yes, cooing—at the baby, letting her hands grip his pinky fingers as he shakes her arms up and down in a grandfatherly dance. I have such an ache just then for this to be my baby, for it to be me lying on the bed exhausted and proud and bursting with love.

"Noelle," Nick says, coming over to the door to hug me. His grin is wide and dopey, full of pure, unadulterated happiness.

"Congratulations, Dana," I say, walking over to the bed. "She's so beautiful."

"Thanks." Dana sighs, glancing down at the baby and smiling.

"Hello, little Miranda," I say, bending over my father, who glances up at me.

My mother comes up behind me and puts an arm around my shoulder. I flinch from the pressure, imagining a voice inside her saying, *When will it be your turn?*

"Do you want to hold her?" my father asks. "Everyone else has gotten a turn."

"All right," I say, as my father gets up from the chair and hands the baby off to me like a football. She has more heft that I expect, fitting perfectly into the cradle of my arms, a warm lump of wriggling limbs. "Wow, she's really active."

"She takes after her daddy," my mom says. "Nicky never slept. Just fussed and moved and cried."

"Let's hope she doesn't take too much after her daddy," Dana says, grabbing at the baby's big toe. "You're going to sleep like an angel and eat anything that's put in front of you and be so brilliant people will be fighting to have you come work for them and be so beautiful all the men will want to marry you." It is such an intimate moment between mother and child that I almost feel like a voyeur.

After a long visit, my parents and I finally decide to leave the three of them alone to have some quiet family time. My parents walk behind me, arm in arm, reluctant to leave the room. I have that familiar twinge in my chest, that unsettling feeling that's a combination of helplessness and despair and desperate, reckless desire.

"Is anyone else starving?" my father says. "Want to go grab a pizza?"

"Sure," I say.

"You look awful, sweetheart," my mother says to me in the elevator. "Are you getting enough sleep?"

"I came here right after a long bike ride, so I'm covered in sweat."

"Oh, is that all?" she says.

Of course that's not all. I just left a near-perfect romantic moment I may never be able to recapture. I'm heartsick because my brother has a baby and I never will. Margaret's condition is worsening, and my ex-husband is coming to town tomorrow. "I'm fine," I say.

Out in the parking lot, I get in my car and follow my parents to a little pizza parlor, complete with red and white checkered tablecloths, glass dispensers full of garlic, oregano, and Parmesan cheese, and menus with colorful maps of Italy on them. My father orders us a pitcher of beer, my mother orders a glass of Chianti, and the three of us toast Miranda. The pizza has thin crust with basil baked right into the dough, fresh tomato sauce, and gooey mozzarella cheese, the kind that stretches out so long you have to break it off with your hand.

It is here in this corny yet cozy Italian restaurant that I decide to tell my parents something I should have told them years ago. It is an anguished ten minutes, but after I've told them, after I see their looks of shock turn into looks of tender sympathy and understanding, I fall into a state of relief so immense that I feel like I've been drugged.

"You're not angry?" I say.

"Honey, why on earth would we be angry? I just wish you'd told us sooner. We could have helped you through it. This all must have been very hard for you," she says.

My father is silent, but I can see from his face that he'd do anything to heal me if he could. He wishes he could wrap his arms around me and comfort me, if only that was the kind of man he was. As it is, he pours me another beer.

It is a week later, and I am standing onstage in front of a microphone, my palms sweating, my mouth parched as a stone, red splotches no doubt beginning to appear on my neck, which has begun to itch as if it's covered in poison ivy. This is me when I have to speak in public, and it's not a pretty sight. After introducing myself, I can almost feel myself leave my body, like I'm watching myself give this speech to a group of three hundred wealthy benefactors, each one looking grim and humorless. But then I find Jay in the crowd. Since he was home visiting anyway and since Jasper is at the Loft tonight, Jay agreed to be my date. He is smiling warmly from his chair in the middle of the room, nodding his head in that encouraging "you can do it" way. Oddly enough, it does the trick.

I hear myself saying, in an inelegant Muppet voice, "Your presence this evening will fund improved lodging for the animals, an expansion of our rescue operations center, and classrooms for animal training classes, all of which will allow us to save more animals. In addition, through your donations and independent grants, we hope to be able to launch a new animal rehabilitation program to train abused and neglected animals to work as therapy and guide dogs for people with disabilities. In this way, your generosity will allow SASH to continue to strengthen the magical bond that has always existed between human and animal, between man and man's best friend."

Applause follows, and I relish the few seconds in which I do not have to speak. How I wish I were at the Loft right now, listening to Jasper's band play, downing beers at the bar, watching people dance in their leashes and dog collars.

"So without further ado, I bid you a wonderful evening of Italian food, music, dancing, raffles, romance, and *Lady and the Tramp.*" More clapping as an enormous screen drops from the ceiling and the famous scene from *Lady and the Tramp* begins playing. The two dogs stare at each other timidly over the plate of pasta while violinists and accordionists play "Bella Notte" behind them. As the Tramp nudges the meatball over to Lady, actual violinists and accordionists come out from behind a curtain and begin playing live music to the tables.

It is all incredibly silly, yet people seem to love it. Those grim looks in the audience have transformed into delighted, childlike expressions of joy and wonder. Lady and the Tramp have just touched noses on the screen and are looking away shyly as the piece of spaghetti breaks in half. Couples who probably haven't sat down for a meal together in months are now holding hands, laughing, clinking glasses of Chianti, even tearing up at the sight on the screen.

149

I return to my table, where Jay sits waiting for me in a beautiful Calvin Klein tuxedo, with a platinum vest, tie, and pocket hand-kerchief. He looks like a matinee idol, like he should be swirling me around in a waltz across a moonlit dance floor, speckled with diamonds. Me dancing like Ginger Rogers.

"You did great, sweetheart," he says, putting an arm around me as I sit down next to him.

"Did I? I have no idea what I actually said."

"Well, you said everything you rehearsed to me last night. Cheers," he says, giving me a kiss on the cheek and clinking my glass.

Joe and his wife are seated across from us. Even Joe looks happy. And why shouldn't he be? We've made a lot of money tonight. He raises his glass to me and smiles. I don't think I've ever actually seen Joe smile before. It's certainly not the warmest one I've ever seen in my life—more one of those toothless smiles where the skin looks stretched to capacity—but at least he's trying. His wife is sweeping some lint off his tuxedo jacket. It doesn't take too long to figure out who wears the pants in their relationship. Joe's wife, Sally, is one of those women who doesn't ever let her husband finish a story. She's always interrupting him, editing him, trying to make his story more interesting, trying to make him more interesting. Maybe that's why he acts like such a tyrant at work.

"I'm so warm," I say. "I become a human sprinkler when I'm nervous."

"You want to go outside for some fresh air?" Jay asks.

"Yes."

I allow Jay to grab my hand and lead me out onto the veranda of the country club. It's a startlingly clear night, full of stars and the first June fireflies. We stand there gossiping about all the rich couples—what they're wearing, how much they're drinking, what the captions under the society page photos will say tomorrow.

"I'm so glad I'll never be like that," I say.

"Although the money wouldn't be bad."

"No, I'd take a little more of that," I say. "It does make things so much easier, doesn't it?"

"Definitely," he says, taking my hand in his and gently rubbing my knuckles. This is yet another of Jay Salazar's patented seduction moves. I cannot help but imagine him doing the same to Taj. "I have a proposition for you," he says, smiling seductively. I look up at him with skeptical eyes. "I wasn't going to tell you yet, but you did such a great job out there, and I'm feeling a little buzzed."

I laugh a little, then clear my throat, growing impatient. "What, Jay? What is it?"

He pulls my hands close to his chest. "See, Taj and I have been living together for a while now. And his house is gorgeous. And enormous, way too big for the two of us. Extra bedrooms and everything. And it's right near this nature park, and it has a pool, tennis courts . . ."

"That's great, Jay. And I live in a hovel. What's your point?"

"No, you're misunderstanding me," he says. "Let me finish. Taj and I have discussed the idea of you adopting a baby with us."

My eyes shoot wide open. "What?" I nearly choke on my champagne.

"Look," he says, "you and I always wanted a baby, right? But we couldn't have one together. Now we can! We could adopt together. Maybe you could even come and live with us."

"Jay, that's crazy . . ." I begin to say, pulling my hands away from his.

"Who's to say what's crazy or not crazy? Look, I know I'm getting ahead of myself. Taj hasn't even met you yet, but I know he'll love you as much as I do. Noelle, I want you to be happy. And you want me to be happy. Doing this for us would make us all happy."

My mind, which had already been reeling, now catapults. "But, Jay, . . ."

"Besides, you'd love Atlanta. You always complain about the cold and the snow and the ice."

"No, I don't." *Yes, I do.*

"Atlanta's beautiful and sunny. Spring begins in February. No more scraping ice off the windshield. No more shoveling out from twelve inches of snow."

"But what about my job?" I say, trying a different tactical approach.

"You could easily get another one."

"But I like my job," I say. "I'm committed."

"I know you are, but you'd be committed anywhere you worked. That's the kind of person you are. And you've kind of reached a ceiling here. Now that you've made them all this money, what the hell are you going to do? Where's the challenge? You keep doing all this work for them, and when was the last time you got a raise?"

"I . . ."

"Not a promotion," he says, making quotation marks with his fingers, "but a raise. An actual raise." I open my mouth to speak, but no words come out. "See? They don't appreciate you. Atlanta has tons of animal shelters and veterinary hospitals. It'd be so easy for you to get a job or even go back to veterinary school if you wanted. But if you didn't, Taj and I make enough money that you wouldn't have to work. You could just stay home and raise the baby."

"What, and be your nanny?" I say, my voice getting edgy.

"No, be the baby's mother! Don't you see?" he says, taking my hands again.

"No, I don't see," I say, feeling a bit queasy all of a sudden. "How would I be the baby's mother if you and Taj were the adoptive parents?"

"We'd all be the parents. We'd be an unconventional family, for sure, but what family isn't when it comes down to it?"

"I don't know, Jay," I say, blowing air out of my mouth as if breathing into a paper bag.

"I know you'll have to think about it. We all do. But really, No-elle. *Think* about it. We could be so happy, all of us." He kisses me on the cheek, and leans on the railing next to me. I stare out into the harbor, the lights of the tall ships gleaming in the water.

It seems an absurd idea, and yet, I do so terribly want a family. But Jay and Taj and me? With a baby? I allow myself to envision all sorts of crazy high jinks, the three of us crowding around to change the baby's diaper for the first time, laughing when we realize we've put it on backward. All of us dancing in the kitchen to Sister Sledge's "We Are Family" while we cook chicken cutlets and baked potatoes. Taj uncorking the wine, making a triple toast to the baby. It'll be like that movie, *Three Men and a Baby*. But it'll be *Two Men, a Woman, and a Baby*. *Two Gay Men, a Single Woman, and a Baby*.

"But what about Margaret? What about your mom, Jay?"

"That's something else I wanted to talk to you about," he says soberly.

"What?"

"Don't you think it might be time to look into some other op-tions for her?"

"Like what?" I say. Months ago I would have been relieved to hear this coming from him, but now my stomach clenches at the thought of change.

"Her doctor says the situation with you coming over every day isn't practical."

"What's not practical about it?" I say. "If I'm willing to do it, and your mother doesn't object, why isn't it practical?"

"I just think she's going to need a higher level of care from now on," he says. "There are places, beautiful places . . ."

"Nursing homes?" I say, scrunching my face into the most unpleasant of scowls.

"No, not nursing homes. Assisted-living residences, where somebody would be on call night and day in case she needed anything."

"Assisted-living residence, nursing home—what's the difference? She's still not able to live in her own home and be independent. She would hate that."

"I'm not so sure anymore. A few things she's said lately have led me to believe she might be more open to it than you think," Jay says, running his fingers through his hair. This gesture used to turn me on so much, but right now, it just irritates me. I feel like yelling at him, *Get a haircut, you floppy-haired pretty boy!*

"Look, you put me in charge of taking care of her," I say. "You left, and I've been here to give her the shots and take her to the hospital and talk to her when she's feeling down. For almost six months! Now you come home for a few days and think you know what's best for her?"

"She is my mother," he says. "And you're not going to be able to take care of her forever."

"Why not?" I say.

"An injection every day? More hospital visits? And God knows what else. It's crazy. And it wasn't really fair of me to ask you in the first place." Was this the admission of guilt I'd been waiting to hear all these months?

"What about hiring a visiting nurse?" I say.

"A nurse isn't going to do the shopping and cleaning. My mother shouldn't be living all alone in that huge place anymore. Besides, if she sold the house, she'd have enough money to go into one of the really nice places."

"You expect her to sell her house now, too?"

"It's worth a lot of money," he says. "It would help all of us in the long run. You'd get your life back again."

"I don't know, Jay," I say. I feel a massive headache coming on. "Can we discuss this later? We really should include Margaret in this decision."

"You're right, you're right. I'm sorry to throw this all on you." He kisses my forehead and grabs my hand. "Let's go back inside and enjoy the rest of the evening."

There's a fire bursting in my stomach, and my legs suddenly feel like melted metal, all fluid and flimsy. We walk back into the ball-room together, and I whip a glass of champagne off a server's tray, down it like I've seen people do in the movies. Sickeningly sweet, but it goes straight to my head just like I want it to.

At the end of the ball, Joe actually comes over and kisses me on the cheek. "You'll never guess," he says to me in my ear.

"What?"

"We just got a telegram from an anonymous donor saying they're going to match whatever we make here tonight."

"Are you kidding?" I say. "Who do you think . . ."

"I have no idea. Probably some wealthy old biddy who loves dogs.

I don't know, and I don't care. All I know is you may just get that rehabilitation center after all."

"Really?"

"Especially if that grant comes through." He grabs my arms and shakes them, and I can't make out whether he's happy we'll be saving more animals or just happy about getting a hold of more money. For some people it's all about the thrill of acquisition.

Shockingly, he invites Jay and me over to his house for a nightcap, but I beg off with a headache and ask Jay to drive me home. Jay lingers outside my door as if he wants to come in, but I'm not sure what could possibly be served by this, so we say good night.

Finally after he's gone, I go inside, let Zeke out and back in, splash myself with water, get in my car, and drive all the way to Providence.

※

Every time I walk into a bar alone, I feel terrified all over again, like I'm thirteen and walking into the cafeteria by myself because my best friend's home with the flu. Tonight I feel especially out of my element as everyone at the Loft is wearing black leather and chains (not really my best look) and resembles a gang member's pit bull. This was sort of the idea, I know, but it is intimidating all the same, especially since I'm still wearing a silver strapless gown and heels. Might as well put a target on my head.

While I'm standing in the doorway trying to decide whether or not to bolt, a guy in a black leather vest and motorcycle hat, sporting a spiked collar and leash, comes over to me as if he knows me. As he gets closer I can see he's far older than anyone else in the bar, probably in his late forties or early fifties. He has a doughy face covered partially by a thick black mustache, but mostly he looks sweet and kindly, a Hell's Angel with a heart of gold.

"Sweetheart," he says to me, "did you walk into the wrong place? You'll get eaten alive here. We're having a special benefit for dogs. We don't usually look this scary."

"I know," I say, shouting over the music. "I'm a friend of Jasper. He organized this for my shelter."

"Oh," he says, laughing. "You must be Noelle."

"Yeah," I say, surprised Jasper's mentioned me.

"I'm George. I own the place," he says, pulling me farther inside. I guess I'm staying.

"Nice to meet you," I shout. "And thank you so much for offering to host this. It looks packed in here!"

"It is. We've had about four hundred people through here tonight, at twenty dollars a pop. And a few people have thrown hundred-dollar bills into the bowl in front of the stage. Jasper thinks we might have made over ten thousand."

"That's incredible!"

"Yeah, well, you invite people to an all-you-can-eat-and-drink buffet, and tell 'em they can dress up in S&M gear—well, suddenly you've got yourself a full house."

I smile at him gratefully. "Jasper told me you donated all the food and drink tonight. We really appreciate it."

"Rita and I love dogs. Besides, Jasper's the one who's been doing all the work. You should have seen him hanging posters, enlisting all of us to call everyone we knew, getting beer and liquor companies to come in with free samples and raffle prizes. Jasper's good people. Well, come on in and have a drink on me," he says, taking my arm and leading me over to the bar. "We don't bite, even though we look like we do."

Nobody even bothers to stare at my inappropriate attire. They all seem to be having too much fun. "Hey, Rita," he calls to an attractive blonde behind the bar. "Come here. I want you to meet someone."

Rita introduces herself to me as George's partner; she is every bit as nice as he is, if not a little more sly and sarcastic. The two of them actually start stripping off accoutrements of their outfits to give to me so I don't stick out so much. Rita even pulls off her black Doc Marten boots and offers them to me.

"You really don't have to—" I start to say.

"Nonsense, here take 'em. I've got five other pairs. They look cute on you."

Once I am properly attired and situated with a beer, Rita grabs my arm and says, "Come on. Let's find that boyfriend of yours."

"Oh, he's not my—"

"Yeah, yeah," she says, winking.

An all-female band is onstage, playing a weird hybrid of French cabaret and punk music. After scanning the band members and finding no trace of Jolene, I give myself permission to like them. The lead singer, who stands all of five feet two inches, with a huge mass of curly dark hair almost as big as her body, has a voice that can go from a kitten whisper to a growl in mere seconds.

"Wow, she's fantastic," I say.

"That's my niece," she says. "Isn't she beautiful?"

"She is," I agree.

"So, where is he?" Rita says, turning around to scope the crowd for Jasper, but I'm actually the one who sees him first.

"I guess I should have called first," I say, trying not to show that I am tremendously disappointed—no, crushed is more like it—that Jasper is talking to Jolene.

"Nonsense," Rita says. "There's nothing going on there. Take it from me. Jo's nothing but trouble. She's dated every musician that's come through this place. That's how she is—she goes through men like toilet paper. And treats 'em just as shitty. Don't you even worry about her. Nice girl like you is what he needs. You go over there and talk to him."

"I had kind of decided I'd rather die, actually, but thanks."

"No, no, you're coming with me," she says, grabbing my arm rather forcibly and dragging me over against my will.

Jolene sees me first and rolls her eyes like she cannot believe I have just materialized in her bar. "Here she is now," she says to Jasper. "Speak of the friggin' she-devil."

I look at Rita, and we both start laughing, although I am certain this is not the most appropriate response if I want to ingratiate myself with Jolene. A bit late for that anyway.

"Noelle, hi," Jasper says, looking genuinely happy to see me, if a bit rueful about his present company. "Good, you met Rita."

"Yep," Rita says, "and I think Jolene needs to come with me and get a martini, on the house."

"Rita, don't do this to me," Jolene says, already beginning to pout.

"I'll make it dirty for you, the way you like it," Rita says, winking at me again and pulling Jolene away from Jasper so the two of us are standing alone, or as alone as you can be in a bar packed with two hundred people. Jasper is wearing jeans and a black leather jacket, and his hair is spiked up into little points spray-painted blue.

"Nice look," I say, smirking at him.

"You, too," he says, glancing down at my biker/beauty contestant outfit. "I didn't think you'd make it."

"I didn't either. It was sort of spontaneous," I say. "If you can believe that. Dumb move, huh?"

"What do you mean?"

"You know. The ever-present ex-girlfriend," I say, turning in the direction of the bar.

"Noelle, I don't know how many times I have to tell you," he says. "It's over between Jo and me."

"Maybe someone should tell her that."

"I just did," he says. "But she says she regrets breaking up with me. The minute someone else shows an interest in me, she gets this insane desire to hook up with me again. It's a game to her. So I told her about us."

"What about us?" I say, suddenly feeling defensive.

"Well . . ." *Exactly*, I think. What is there to say about us at this point? "I just told her we'd been spending a lot of time together. And that she needs to lay off. Stop calling me."

"She's been calling you?" Oh God, I'm starting to sound like a jealous girlfriend. This is exactly why I didn't want to get involved with anybody in the first place.

"Only when she's feeling lonely. When she comes home from a bar at two in the morning, empty-handed. Believe me, it doesn't happen very often."

"It just gets very frustrating that almost every time I see you, there she is. It's hard to believe there's nothing going on between you two."

"Trust me," he says.

"It's difficult for me to trust you when I was married to a man who lied to me for two years."

We are standing inches away from each other, not by choice but by necessity. He takes the leather jacket off and slings it over a nearby chair. I am trying to maintain some semblance of strength and grace, but the band has just slowed their tempo, launching into a sultry Billie Holiday–style ballad that makes my spine want to collapse and curl into a ball.

"I'm not Jay," he says, and we stare at each other for a few weighted seconds until the tension seems unbearable, a bridge of heat between us siphoning away any resistance I have left.

He seems to sense my softening stance, approaches me in such a way that before I'm even aware of it, I am dancing with him, laying my head in the crook of his shoulder, swaying softly to this haunting melody, our bodies so close I can feel his ribs against my chest. He smells different tonight, like sweet smoke and pine needles, and I tilt my head to smell his neck, brush my lips against it, feel his body push into me, hear a faint outtake of breath.

"I wish we were alone," he says, and I nod, pressing my nose into his chest, dropping my hands slowly from his shoulders to his back, feeling for the bottom of his T-shirt, sliding my hands gently onto his warm stomach. Abruptly he pushes me away.

"Sorry," I say.

"No, it's okay. It's just . . . been a while."

"A while?"

"You know, so I'm kind of . . . easily aroused," he says, smiling.

I am speechless. Could it really be that this beautiful, sensitive man has not had sex in . . . a while? And what does "a while" mean for him? Does it mean the same as it does for me—something verging on two years?

"I wish we could leave," he says, "but I guess that would be irresponsible."

"Seeing as we're the ones who organized this entire evening?"

"Exactly." I feel a little lightheaded myself. "This sounds really lame, but do you mind if we just talk for a little while?" he says, smiling. I smile back, look down at the ground.

"Mind? Yes. But will I? Of course."

"Okay, good," he says, grabbing my hand and walking me to the bar. Jolene has disappeared for the moment.

We sit down, order a few beers, then turn to face each other. "Did you ever see a couple at a bar, and they're so into each other they're practically having sex on the dance floor?" he asks.

"Yeah," I say, blushing slightly.

"And you think to yourself, man, they must really be drunk. Now I'm a bit more sympathetic." I laugh nervously. Take a sip of my beer. "So tell me, what's the least sexy thing we can talk about?"

"The gasoline crisis. Existential philosophy. The net proceeds of a fund-raiser, perhaps."

"Oh yeah, I didn't even get to ask you about your night. How did it go?"

"It went really well," I say. "I was nervous, but I got up there and gave my speech, and people opened their wallets and bought lots of raffle tickets, and we made quite a bit of money. In fact, someone sent an anonymous telegram promising to match the amount we make tonight."

"Really?" he says. "Good, good. I'm glad it was a success."

"Yeah, my boss actually kissed me."

"Should I be jealous?"

"Well, it was just on the cheek," I say.

"That could be pretty sexy," he says, leaning over to me and brushing his lips against my cheek. I am holding my breath. "There I go again," he says. "Sorry. Who'd you end up taking? Margaret?"

"No, she wasn't feeling well, so . . . I took Jay."

"Oh." Jasper looks at me, beer bottle raised to his mouth. "Jay, huh?"

"Yeah, he's home for a short visit. We've been talking about Margaret and what the future holds for her." There is a long moment of silence during which I pray he will say something. Anything. "Of course, I wish I could have taken you, but you had to be here." I laugh to make light of an awkward situation, and Jasper shakes his head. "What?" I say. "What were you just thinking?"

"Nothing."

"No. Tell me."

He takes a big breath. "I just find it ironic that you were giving me the third degree about Jo earlier when you spent all night with your ex-husband."

I purse my lips together, uncomfortable with this conversation. "Well, it's a little different," I say.

"Really? How is it different?"

"Well . . . Jay's gay."

"Okay, so that means he's not into you, but it doesn't mean you're not into him. The first time I ever went out with you, you admitted you still had feelings for him."

"And you admitted Jolene still had feelings for you."

"Yeah, but isn't it better that she have feelings for me rather than I have feelings for her?" he says. He stares at me hard, probing me, and for a moment, I can't speak.

"But I don't have feelings for Jay," I say with as much conviction as I can muster.

"He's still an awfully big part of your life."

"Yeah, well, we used to be married," I say.

"Okay, so it's normal for me to feel a little jealous about his place in your life, right? Especially if we're going to move forward in this relationship."

"Exactly what is this relationship?" I say, getting a little too defensive.

"I don't know." He looks sullen and upset and just a little bit angry. "A few months ago you told me you weren't ready for anything. I've been waiting for that to change, but I don't know if it has because you never tell me anything. Everything's always a joke with you. But I have no idea what you're really ready for."

And there is the question. What am I ready for? I think I'm ready to plunge in and try a full-fledged, mature, romantic relationship for the first time since my divorce. But there is that thorny issue of Jay and the possibility of adopting a baby together.

And before I can hear the little voice that is trying desperately to tell me to shut the hell up, I find myself divulging everything. "I think I'm ready to try to be with you," I say, "but there are some . . . issues that have been preventing me from committing to the idea."

"Issues? What issues?" he says.

So I tell him about Taj and Jay wanting to adopt a baby and possibly needing me to help them do it. Jasper looks like he's trying very hard not to react to what I've just said.

"Why can't they adopt in the States?"

"Well, I imagine they could. In certain states, anyway. But I guess they really want an Indian baby. There's a humanitarian crisis there."

"I understand that," he says. "But there are lots of unwanted babies here in this country, too. I mean, I can't believe he'd ask that of you." His jaw looks like he's chewing on rocks.

"Well, Jay and I have a very close relationship. I mean, we were married for five years."

"But three of those years were spent waiting for your divorce to go through. And two of those years, the man lied to you. You just said it yourself. I mean, come on, Noelle, how could you even consider that? Don't you want to have a baby of your own someday?" he says, and my stomach flips. "I'm sorry. It's none of my business," he says, placing his empty beer bottle on the table. I stare at the puddle of condensation pooling around the bottom.

"No, I do want your opinion. That's why I told you," I say, desperately wanting to rein in this conversation, wishing I could shove the stupid words back in my mouth.

"Look," he says. "I guess I don't know you as well as I thought I did. And I definitely don't understand enough about your relationship with Jay to know whether you guys could make that work or not. I just think adopting a baby together is a big deal. It's your life, you know?"

"I know."

"And he can't ever love you the way you deserve to be loved." *Did he really just say that?* Ironically, that line prompts an indignant impulse in me to defend Jay.

"But he does love me," I say. "Tonight, he asked me to move to Atlanta. Move in with them."

Jasper's face visibly tightens. A new band has taken the stage, and their screeching guitar chords send my head spinning. "Move in with them?" Jasper says. He is actually grinding his teeth now, livid. "Are you all crazy? What kind of life would that be for you?"

"A meaningful life!" I say. "A life spent helping someone else live his dream."

"Yes, Noelle. Helping someone else live his dream! And what about yours?"

The music is building into a frenetic crescendo, the lead singer's vocals a bansheelike wail. "What is this?" I say, turning toward the stage to see Jolene and her hyperkinetic, hypertoned body thrashing around onstage like a brunette Gwen Stefani. "Great," I say, tossing my head back. As she thrusts her pelvis into her guitar, I can hear her sing, "You know you see my face when you sleep with her, dream my lips when you kiss her. Ooooh—come back to me where you belong to be."

" 'Come back to me where you belong to be?' That isn't even good grammar," I say. "Did she write this about you?"

"I don't know." His voice is icy.

"Yes, you do," I say, keeping my tone equally cold.

"Noelle, this isn't about Jolene!" he yells, and I pull my head back, stunned. The two of us stare at each other for a few excruciating seconds, until I finally manage to say something.

"I'm sorry," I say, feeling a sickening but inevitable feeling of defeat, the tears beginning to well at the corners of my eyes. "I'm so sorry. This isn't going to work. I'm just . . . really sorry." Somehow I manage to put some money down on the bar and clomp out of there in my borrowed boots, trying to flee before I fall apart completely in front of him.

Half of me is hoping he will follow me out of there, chase me down the street, tell me this is all his fault. But it's not. In fact, none of it is his fault. I'm the one with the baggage, with the crisis of my own that I've dragged him into. He doesn't deserve any of this.

It's a miracle I am able to drive home without crashing into a telephone pole or driving off an embankment. When I finally get back to the house, I collapse onto the sofa, where Zeke follows me, his canine intuition kicking in, and then I'm uncontrollably sobbing into his fur, the kind of heaving, hiccupping crying that seems like it won't ever stop and doesn't end up making you feel any better.

When I wake up in the morning to the phone ringing, still on the sofa and still wearing my silver dress and boots, I feel a spark of hope as I imagine Jasper's voice coming over my machine to apologize, to say let's forget last night ever happened and start over again.

But it's only Joe. He tells me not only did the two events last night make over forty thousand dollars, but the anonymous donor did indeed wire a money order to the shelter this morning for a matching amount. We made over eighty thousand dollars in one night.

Joe is ecstatic. And despite the fact that this should make me happy as well, that this should make me realize my life is worthwhile and that I'm a good human being after all, all I can think about is Jasper.

I feel sick to my stomach, embarrassed, guilty, confused. I want to call Jasper and talk to him about everything, but I can't. I'm the last person he'd want to talk to right now.

And he's absolutely right.

The week that follows, I try to distract myself with work, all the work I've created for myself over the past months—writing grants for the guide dog training program, calling and speaking with the trainer Cassie recommended, helping Danielle train Bebop, going daily to give Margaret her shots, and mostly, dealing with cases at SASH.

Sometimes my job is almost too heartbreaking to endure. On Monday, we have to euthanize a sheltie who ate lethal amounts of chocolate. On Wednesday, one of our dog-fighting rescues, Sheba, of whom I had grown particularly fond, is deemed too aggressive to rehabilitate and is sent to the animal sanctuary in Utah for "lost canine souls." But the worst comes on Thursday, when a woman brings in a miniature Doberman she witnessed being dragged around behind the back of a truck.

He survived, but he's so severely injured that it will take months for him to heal properly and be ready for adoption. All I want to do is cradle him in my arms and explain to him that he is safe now. That nothing will ever hurt him again. That for as long as he's with us, he will have a home.

Today I stand in the waiting room in front of our corkboard staring at a photograph of one of our former strays, a dachshund named Phoebe. In the picture, she's now tending five puppies of her own and, surprisingly, a piglet whose mother had ostracized him from the litter. The piglet lies snuggled against the other pups, its skin as tender and fuzzy as a peach. I look at the picture for a long time, awestruck by the ingenuity of nature.

Maybe there isn't one right way to go about motherhood. Maybe that's why we're so adaptable, so prone to find new ways of surviving, of thriving. Maybe the photograph is a sign telling me that Jay's suggestion to adopt a baby for them isn't so absurd; it's just another example of human resourcefulness and love.

Or maybe I'm just so desperate to have a baby that I'm doing my best to convince myself this is the right thing to do.

July

❧

Margaret has been responding well to her new treatments. She's even letting me take her to the annual Fourth of July parade in Bristol. The people of Bristol plan for the parade all year long. Then, sometime in early June, the quaint little town of quiet bookstores and cafés begins to transform itself into a patriotic extravaganza of red, white, and blue—flags, floats, costumes, boat sails, street paintings. People come in from all over the northeast, and even farther away, to celebrate Independence Day in style, or at least in a stupor. I warned Margaret that it could get a little raucous. A lot raucous, actually.

Bikers decked out in patriotic gear begin riding into town about a week before, camping out on storefront steps and down by the waterfront. We've even had a few Hell's Angels visit over the years. People begin drinking at least two days in advance and seem to drink continuously until the Fourth in order to avoid ever getting a hangover. And the fireworks display over the river is spectacular. It's been a while since I've attended, because you really have to be up for it, almost in warrior mode to survive all the crowds and craziness. But Margaret insisted this was something she really wanted to do.

I pick her up a little after nine and we head into Bristol, driving about two miles per hour down Main Street and getting an up-close and personal view of all the carousing. Women in red, white, and blue tube tops and short shorts are sitting on men's shoulders to get a better view, kids of all ages are running around like bandits, trailing streamers and sparklers behind them. A few elderly couples sit on their front porches, squinty-eyed in the morning sun, holding tall sweating glasses of lemonade. I envy their easy contentment.

We turn down a side street to look for parking, driving around for blocks until Margaret finally convinces me to pay the ten dollars to park in a lot. Since the parade won't begin for another half hour or so, I usher Margaret inside a bar. This is not the kind of bar I would normally frequent, nor the kind of bar I'd normally take Margaret to, but Tara's brother owns it, and she invited us to come watch the parade from the roof.

When we get inside, there are a half dozen guys sitting at the bar, beers already in hand. There are no rules about when to start drinking on the Fourth. The bartender sees us and laughs, the sight of us in this place incongruous to him. "You must be Noelle," he says, wiping his hands on a rag, then reaching out to shake my hand.

"Mitch?"

"Yep, that's me." He reaches over to shake Margaret's hand as well.

"Mitch, this is my friend Margaret," I say. My friend Margaret.

"Tara's already on the roof," he says. "I'll walk you up there. Hey, can I get you something first?"

I decline, but Margaret takes him up on the offer, asking for a Bloody Mary.

"Really?" I say. "Should you be drinking with your medication?"

"Oh, stop worrying about me," she says. "I want to live a little."

"All right," I say, throwing my hands up to God. "Then I guess I'll have one, too."

"Fourth of July comes but once a year," Mitch says. "You gotta celebrate like the locals do."

Armed with our morning fortification, we follow Mitch up the stairs, past the upper-level apartment door and straight up to the roof. Tara is lying out on a chaise lounge in her sunglasses, holding some kind of fruity beverage complete with a frozen drink umbrella. "Hey, Noelle. You made it."

I introduce Tara and Margaret, then look out over the roof top. In the distance, you can see the harbor, flecked with white caps sparkling in the sunlight. Closer to the edge, Main Street unfolds in all its pomp and circumstance.

"Grab a seat," Tara says. "Mitch got you guys some drinks? I'm having a mimosa. Let me know if you want one."

"This is incredible," I say. "Is anyone else coming up? This is the best spot in town."

"When the bartender shows up, if he ever shows up, Mitch'll probably come up here with a few of his friends. And a couple of my friends from school might come over a little later. We were out kinda late last night. They're probably a bit hungover. But make yourselves at home. Stake your spot now. First come, first served."

I move a chair over to the edge for Margaret, slide one over for myself, put on my sunglasses, and take a sip of my drink. Perfectly spicy, with lots of horseradish and lime juice, just the way I like it. When I look over at Margaret, her lips are curled up slightly at the corners. It's so strange to see her here, on the rooftop of a bar, drinking a Bloody Mary.

In the distance, we hear the marching band warming up to "Stars and Stripes." About a half hour later, the first few floats begin making their way down Main Street—one looks like an enormous wedding cake decorated in red, white, and blue flowers; another is a pirate ship donning a flag with a skeleton of Uncle Sam with crossbones across his face. This doesn't seem very patriotic to me, but what do I know?

A while later, Mitch and a few of his friends come up carrying a cooler of beers, and all of us sit together for hours in the sun, listening to the bugle corps and marching bands, watching the dance troupes and color guards, giving our two cents about which float should win the contest. When the parade finally ends, to the deafening roar of applause below, all of us join in on the cheering.

"So whad'ya think?" Mitch asks us as he collects empty beer cans.

"Excellent," Margaret says. "Thank you so much for letting us watch from here."

"No problem," he says.

We begin packing up our belongings when Margaret turns to me and asks if we're going back home. "I don't know. What would you like to do?"

"I want to play darts," she says.

"Darts?"

"Yes, darts. I used to be really good."

We head downstairs, treading carefully for Margaret's sake, to find that the crowd at the bar has gotten much larger and much more colorful. There are several bikers, one particularly large of frame, bald, and as red-cheeked and jolly as Santa Claus. Margaret walks right up to him and asks if the stool next to him is taken.

"It is now," he says, smiling to reveal a missing tooth. When he sees Margaret struggling a bit, he gets off his stool and offers to help her, waking me to sudden vigilance. Margaret shouldn't be sitting on a barstool. But when I try to tell her this, she tells me not to be such a stick in the mud.

"This young lady giving you a hard time?" the biker asks Margaret, winking. He is obviously going to have a little fun with me.

"No. She's just doing my worrying for me. But I don't want to think about what I can't do today."

"I don't like to think about it any day," he says. "So I usually don't. I just live my life. It's easier that way." He smiles at her conspiratorially as if I'm the prison warden about to herd all the prisoners in the yard back into their cells.

"I'm just telling you to be careful," I say.

"I've been careful for over forty years, and look where it's gotten me." The old biker tells me to stop worrying and pull up a stool, then buys us both shots. Even though this seems ill advised at twelve thirty in the afternoon, I don't even think about disobeying. Before I know it, the three of us are downing Jägermeisters with beer chasers. Salty snacks appear on the bar, and Margaret begins popping peanuts and pretzels like a college coed. "I haven't had this much fun in a long time," she says. "Hey, weren't we going to play darts?"

"There's a group of guys already playing."

"So walk up and challenge them to a game," she dares me.

"Are you kidding?"

173

"You're a beautiful woman asking a bunch of guys if you can play darts with them. Why would they say no?"

"You think I'm beautiful?" I say, entirely missing her point.

"Oh, don't go getting a big head. I'm merely flattering you so you'll go over there and claim the dartboard for us."

"Why don't you do it?" I say. "You're apparently the dart queen."

Our biker friend overhears us bickering and offers to be our intermediary.

I help Margaret off the stool, and we both follow Saint Nick across the bar through hordes of young men to the dartboard. "Excuse me," the biker says in a commanding voice, and three guys turn around. It's Mike, Trey, and Jasper.

"Noelle," Trey says. "It's you."

"Hey, welcome!" says Mike. "Happy Fourth!" It's obvious from their quite normal reactions that Jasper hasn't told them about our horrible confrontation at the Loft the other night. Jasper looks at the ground, scratches the space below his left ear.

"You know these guys?" our biker friend asks.

"My neighbors."

"Then my work is done," he says, shaking my hand and kissing Margaret on the cheek, then walking out the front door of the bar like an angel whose only purpose was to help us get a game of darts going.

"Guys, this is Margaret. Margaret, these are my neighbors, Trey and Mike. And this is . . . Jasper." There is an awkward silence as I wait to see if Margaret will visibly react to the name, then a sense of deep relief when she doesn't. I will commend her later for her excellent performance. "Margaret's been eager to play some darts," I say. "But we didn't mean to interrupt your game."

"Don't be silly," Trey says, walking to the board to retrieve the darts and handing them to Margaret. "Should we play girls against guys?"

"Girls?" Margaret says, laughing. "Yes, let's play girls against guys."

"Oh, no," I say. "I don't know how to play."

"It's easy," Mike says. "We'll start with Cricket. You need to get three points in the fifteen through twenty slices, and you can get them in any order. The fat and small pie are worth one point, the double ring worth two, the triple ring worth three." I look at him like he's speaking Swahili. "Here, we'll have a few practice rounds. Watch me, and then you can try."

Mike proceeds to demonstrate dart throwing for us, detailing his technique in exhaustive fashion. I pretend to be listening, but all I am aware of is Jasper's presence and how much I wish I could talk to him alone. When I finally sneak a glance at him, I notice he's gotten a haircut; his hair is fuzzy, like the head of a gosling. I have a tremendous urge to run my hand across it.

Mike hands Margaret the darts, and I watch as she throws them, one by one, effortlessly getting two of her darts to land in the 15 slice. "Still got it," she says.

Trey retrieves them and hands them to me. I stand in front of the dartboard, a dart in my right hand, sort of brandishing it back and forth as I've seen people do, then release it in the general direction of the board. I am so nervous that my first dart goes sailing above the board, embedding itself in the wooden paneling on the wall. The next lands in the wall below the board, probably overcompensation for my first throw. My third actually hits the board but bounces off onto the floor.

"You know, the goal is to actually hit the board," Trey says.

"Shut up," I say, angry with myself that I cannot make a stupid piece of pointed metal stick into a two-foot circle of felt.

"An auspicious beginning," Margaret says. "Did I say girls against guys? How about mixed teams?"

My mouth drops in mock indignation. "I can't believe you said that. Traitor to our sex."

"Jasper, how are you at darts?" Margaret asks.

"He's a ringer," Mike says.

"I'm not that good."

"All right," Margaret decides. "How about Jasper and Noelle versus the rest of us? He can balance out the rookie." I glare at her in disbelief. I must have her guillotined later.

And so we begin playing, Jasper hitting the double and triple rings nearly every time he throws and refusing to look at me, me seldom hitting the board at all. After a few rounds, I begin to improve. Every time I throw, I do just a little bit better, get a little bit closer to my target. But Jasper's presence right next to me is shaking my confidence. I have no idea what he's thinking, no idea whether he still hates me or not.

When Mike leaves for a bathroom break, Trey takes Margaret to the bar to get her a martini. I know I should probably have a problem with this, yet I'm suspending all my caretaking duties today and attempting to live in the moment. I go to collect the darts from the board just to have something to do, and when I turn around, Jasper is standing directly in front of me.

"God, you scared me," I say, laughing nervously and looking down.

"Sorry," he says. "I guess I have that effect on you." I laugh to diffuse the tension, but it's clear he didn't mean it as a joke. "Is that what it was? Did I scare you off? Because you warned me that you weren't ready for anything, and I came on really strong."

"No," I say, fumbling for words, "it wasn't you."

"Don't you dare say 'It wasn't you, it was me.'"

"I wasn't going to," I lie.

"Maybe it's that you're still in love with Jay?"

"No, it's not that," I say. "Look, it's complicated . . ." But before I can explain, Trey is back.

"Where's my team?" he says.

"Getting martinis."

"At two in the afternoon? What the hell?" he says. "You want one, too?" Jasper and I shake our heads vigorously, and Trey heads to the bar alone.

"So, what is it, then?" Jasper asks, so solemnly it makes my chest ache. It is really difficult to hold a conversation of this magnitude in the five-minute increments we are being allotted by our drunken teammates. I make myself look him in the eyes, then lose all resolve. With his soft, downy haircut, he looks so vulnerable, I can barely speak.

"I think I scared myself off," I finally say. "I mean, I convinced myself it wasn't going to work, you know, to try to protect myself from getting hurt."

"I can understand that. But you should have let me know what you were thinking. I could have tried to talk you out of it."

"I guess I didn't want to let myself be talked out of it," I say. "I figured you'd have so many women banging down your door by now that you'd have forgotten all about me." This attempt at levity falls completely flat.

"Do you really believe that? Jay must have really done a number on you." He begins flinging darts at the board with great force. One sails right into the wall.

"What's wrong?" I say.

He turns from the dartboard like he's going to fling one at me. "Is it so hard for you to believe that somebody might have real feelings for you? That you are worthy of someone loving you? God, you just don't get it, Noelle."

Hearing him say my name with such intensity makes my face blaze with heat. The warmth quickly spreads down to my neck. Margaret, Trey, and Mike come back with their martinis, leaving Jasper and me staring off into space to show them that we definitely weren't talking about anything serious, which of course makes it patently obvious that we were.

Jasper and I endure another awkward game together, bringing the scores of the two teams to a tie. "Let's end it here," Trey says. "Tie score."

"Are you kidding?" Margaret says. "I want to crush them."

"I do, too," Mike says, "but we're going to be late if we don't end it now. We've got people coming over for a party in about an hour. We should get going. Hey, Noelle, you're definitely stopping by when you get home, right?"

"I don't know," I say. "Margaret and I might—"

"Of course she is," Margaret says.

"But I thought you wanted to watch the fireworks," I say.

"No, I'll be too drunk by then. Hey, who drank my martini?" she asks, holding her glass upside down.

"You did," Mike says. "You should come to the party, too. You'll fit right in."

"Yeah," Trey says. "Definitely come. Noelle, please bring her. She's a party animal!"

We all say our good-byes, and Trey makes me promise I'll come tonight. Jasper barely looks at me. When they finally leave the bar, I feel so deflated I want to cry.

"I'm drunk and depressed," I say. "And I'm a lousy caretaker. Just how many drinks did you have today?"

"One," she says.

"What?"

"Only the Bloody Mary I had this morning. I faked the Jäger-meister shot, and all my martinis were virgins."

"Really?"

"Yes. And speaking of virgins, or at least virtual virgins," she says, pulling me over to an unused table, "why aren't you running after him?"

"Who?" I say.

"Who do you think? That adorable guy who just left the bar with his heart crushed."

"What are you talking about?"

"Can't you see it? The man is obviously in love, and you don't even have the decency to go after him. I felt his pain."

I let my head fall into my hands. "Oh, Margaret, I don't know. I just feel like it could never work between us."

"Why on earth not?"

"Well, he's too young, for one thing. And he's a musician. I can't compete with that. And he has this annoyingly beautiful ex-girlfriend who's always around. I think she still has a thing for him."

"Well, I didn't see her around today," Margaret says.

"I don't know. It's like, when you really like something, but other people like the same thing you like, it sort of takes something away from it, do you know what I mean?"

"No, I don't," she says, growing increasingly impatient with my whining. "The girls used to flock around Dominic all the time. You met him when he was practically an old man, but when he was young, he was quite a heartbreaker. Cheekbones to die for. And the best body. Such a slim waist and a nice muscular chest."

"Margaret . . ."

"What?"

"Get to the point."

"Look," she says, "I saw it as a challenge, being the one he loved out of all those women who adored him. It didn't take anything away from him; in fact, it only made me want him more."

"But I'm not like you. I'm not a fighter."

"Not a fighter? Like hell, you're not."

"All right, then I don't want to fight. I shouldn't have to."

"Why shouldn't you?" she says. "You think you're entitled to get what you want because you've had some misfortune in your life? That you shouldn't have to work for things anymore? Let me tell you something. I've lived on this earth twice as long as you have and I've seen far more disappointment, and I've still had to fight for everything I've wanted, every step of the way. It never gets any easier. In fact, it only gets harder. And the more you want something, the more you should fight for it. So if you see something and it's worth having, you better damn well throw your hat in the ring. Because Jasper's not going to wait around forever. And then you're going to hate yourself. More than you already do."

I press my hands into my temples, knowing she's absolutely right, but feeling powerless to do anything about it.

❧

I take Margaret back to the house, and we talk a little bit on the porch, but eventually I realize I have to go home, despite Jasper's presence at Trey and Mike's party.

Once I get back, I sneak into my house, close all the shutters and curtains, and consider hiding out all night. I turn on the television and try to distract myself with old *Frasier* episodes. But it's no use. All I can do is replay Jasper's words in my head and try to figure out where things went so very wrong. Finally, I can't take it anymore.

Quickly, I comb my hair and put on a little makeup, just enough to look presentable, and head next door to the party. The front door is open, so I step inside and scan the room for Jasper. But just my luck, who turns the corner but Jolene. I can already tell she's in supreme bitch mode, and my first instinct is to run out the door. But it's too late for that. She has already seen me and is heading my way.

"If you're looking for Jasper, he's not here," she says. "Something about being depressed after seeing you. I can see how that could happen."

"You know what, I'm really not in the mood for this. Where are Mike and Trey?"

"In the backyard. You know, I can't for the life of me figure out what Jasper sees in you. He needs some excitement in his life, not some pathetic loser who spends all her time with dogs. I mean, really, when are you going to get a life?"

"Why are you so rude?" I say. "What exactly is your problem?"

"My problem is you," she says, coming closer and towering over me like she plans to hit me.

Fortunately, Mike comes into the room and puts his arm around Jo. "Hey, what's going on in here?" he says, smiling. "Jo Jo, you drinking too much again?"

"No, your little neighbor here just can't take a hint." She shrugs Mike's arm off her shoulder and puffs her chest out at me. I can't help but laugh. "You think this is funny?" she says. "You think I'm joking?"

Other people in the room have begun to listen, and I'm beginning to feel we've become the main attraction. Carnival Girl meets the Dog Freak. Mike takes Jo aside and into the other room, giving her a brief lecture about party etiquette, while I breathe out about ten lungfuls of air.

"That was cool," I hear a voice say. "I love girl fights." It's my neighbor Dan, and he is visibly drunk—eyes glazed over with half-mast lids.

"Hi, Dan."

"You kept your cool, though. I'm impressed."

"Thanks. How are you doing?"

"Okay," he says. "You want a drink?"

"No thanks, I've already had—"

"Come on," he says, tugging on my arm.

"No, really. I had a lot to drink earlier. Where's Danielle?" I ask, hoping to distract him.

"She's at her folks'."

"On the Fourth?"

"Yeah. We kind of got into a fight."

"Oh, I'm sorry," I say. "So, how is she feeling these days? Only two more months to go."

"Well, yeah, at least she's done being sick. You'd think she'd get tired of all this after a while, you know?" He takes a long swig of his beer and looks at me.

"Tired of what?"

"Pregnancy, screaming kids running around the house. I mean, we've been married for eight years, that's how many thousand days? And I don't think I've spent one of them alone with my wife."

I laugh a little out of discomfort, as what began as an innocent question on my part seems to have opened the floodgates for a mini therapy session about Dan's marriage. I try to shift into a less dangerous gear. "How's Bebop? Is he showing less aggressive behavior?"

"Nope," he says, looking at me forlornly. "He hates me, too. Seems I'm the one always in the doghouse. I think Danielle prefers the dog over me."

"Dan," I say, desperate to stem this tide of confessional angst. "You want some coffee? A glass of water?"

"Danielle, she's just become so . . . demanding. I never thought it would be like this. Marriage, you know?"

"It's not easy," I say.

"You were married before, weren't you?"

"Yeah."

"Danielle told me. And he ended up being gay, right?"

"Well, I think he'd been gay all along." I made the mistake of telling Mike and Trey about my history with Jay at a party last year, and they promptly disseminated this information to the entire neighborhood.

"So you've been hurt. But you got over it," he says.

"Well, I wouldn't say I got over it, but I'm working on it. It does get easier." Dan reaches his hand up and grabs my arm again. "Whoa," I say. "Easy there."

"Sorry," he mutters. "You smell really great. What perfume are you wearing?"

"I'm not wearing perfume. Dan, I've got to get going. I really just came to see Jasper."

"Oh, all right. I think I'll go with you," he says. Dan follows me out of the party, and the music fades behind us.

"Well, good night," I start to say when I get near my door, but suddenly Dan is standing in front of me. He smells of beer and charcoal and maybe a little Eternity for Men. Suddenly, his lips are on mine, and for a moment my brain stalls, refusing to tell my body what to do. It reminds me of being at a college party, the smell of cologne and beer, the buzz of sexual excitement in the air.

But finally, my neurons fire and I pull away. "What the hell was that?" I say.

"You're angry."

"Not really." I am shaking my head, not angry at him but angry at myself for going to the party in the first place.

"I'm sorry," he says, quite sincerely. "I've had a bit too much to drink."

"You think?"

"I just needed someone to talk to. And you're easy to talk to."

"Well, talking usually involves your lips over there and my lips over here," I say.

"I know. I'm an idiot, what can I say? I'm really sorry."

"Don't apologize to me. Apologize to Danielle."

"Well, that's the thing," he says. "I'm thinking of leaving her."

"What?" I say.

"It's just not working between us. I don't know what else to do."

"But why?" I ask. "You guys are the perfect couple."

"No, no. She doesn't love me anymore. She doesn't need me. It's just her and the baby now."

"What are you talking about? She needs you more than ever."

"No she doesn't," he says, shaking his head drunkenly. "Her mother comes over nearly every day. She doesn't seem to even want me around anymore."

"She's probably just anxious about the new baby," I say.

"No, it's not that. She doesn't love me."

"Dan, I've seen the pictures, I've heard the stories. You guys are so in love."

"*Were* in love," he says, shaking his head. "In high school. Young love. But then she got pregnant, and everything changed. I swear, our entire marriage is based on her being pregnant. That's why we got married. That's why we stay married. But it's not enough anymore. I didn't even want to have a fourth kid. That's why I got her Bebop. I thought if she had a cute little dog to cuddle, maybe she'd finally be satisfied. But she's never going to be satisfied. We could have twelve kids, it'd be the freakin' Last Supper at our house, and she still wouldn't be satisfied." He slumps down on my front stoop and stares into his beer as if the answer might be in there. I kind of feel sorry for him.

Reluctantly, I sit down next to him. Therapist Noelle. "Listen, Dan, I can't tell you what to do. I don't know your situation, I only know that you and Danielle have three children together and you're about to have a fourth. And I really think you should be talking to Danielle about this."

"I can't talk to her," he says. "She doesn't understand. Do you know what it's like to be in a marriage where the person doesn't love you?"

"Actually, I do," I say, and he laughs bitterly.

"Right."

"But I can tell you if Jay and I had children together, I think we would have worked something out."

"What?" he says, looking up at me with pale, hazy eyes. "Are you serious?"

"If kids were involved, I think we would have found a way to make it work."

"But your husband loves men," he says. "He wouldn't have ever loved you. How could you stay in a marriage like that?"

I take a deep breath and sigh. "I don't know."

He looks at me longingly, drunkenly, then drags his fingers along my cheek. It's a testament to how lonely I've been that this physical contact actually gives me a momentary rush of feeling. "You're great, Noelle," he says.

"And you're drunk."

"I know. But Jasper's a fool if he chooses Jolene over you."

"Thanks, Dan. Go home and get some sleep. And talk to Danielle. Tomorrow."

"Maybe," he says, smiling, then staggers to his front door.

I stand outside for a few minutes longer to make sure he gets into his house before collapsing. Then I sit back down on my stoop, feeling completely spent, and think about what Dan just said to me.

Would I really have wanted Jay to stay with me in a loveless marriage so we could have children together?

But isn't this sort of what Jay is asking of me now?

The first fireworks begin to explode in the sky, and I hear Zeke barking from inside. He's going to need lots of reassurance tonight. He hates the Fourth of July.

So do I.

August

FOR SALE, Tiverton: 1880 cottage with two bedrooms, cozy living room with fireplace and floor-to-ceiling bookshelves. Rear porch overlooks small yard with herb garden. Tranquil and private. Needs TLC but priced well below market value.

Some months start out so hopeful, so full of energy and potential that for a moment, you convince yourself everything's changing for the better, that if you just let nature takes its course, the rest will fall magically into place, leaving you exactly where you were always meant to be.

The beginning of August has this wondrous aura to it. Construction crews begin clearing out the space for the addition at SASH, and blueprints circulate around the office, showing new dog residences and classrooms, skylights, outdoor dog runs. Joe tells me I am officially in charge of the new training and rehabilitation wing, and if I get the big grant I wrote, I'll be in charge of the guide dog training wing as well. I am already imagining a row of well-trained dogs in harnesses waiting to learn how to open doors, activate light switches, and pull wheelchairs. I haven't felt this excited in years. But whenever I think about how wonderful it all is, I want to share it with Jasper.

So I make a decision to do something admittedly daring and spontaneous for me. I am riding my bike to Providence to surprise him and to apologize for my foolish behavior these past few weeks. However, I am not even to Barrington when I realize I am not in nearly good enough shape for this ride. The weather has suddenly decided to go Louisiana bayou on me—hot, humid, no cloud cover anywhere. I have to stop repeatedly along the trail for water breaks, and by the time I get to Providence, I am a hot, sweaty mess. The story of my life.

I take Jasper's address out of my pocket, along with the Google map I printed out. I can do this. Follow the little blue lines and red lines and cross over the bridge and find my destination, right? I stop in a little coffee place in a trendy part of the city so I can at least wash my face off and spritz myself with the perfume I always carry with me.

When I leave the café, I follow a street diagonally from the center of town, behind the university and toward the waterfront, dominated by industrial-style buildings that have been converted into chic loft-style apartments. But as I ride farther north, the streets become more narrow and residential. When I finally find Jasper's street, tree lined with beautiful brownstones and cars parked bumper to bumper, I begin to look for the number. His is the last house on the block.

It hardly looks like the place where a bachelor would live. Container plantings out on the stoop, window boxes overflowing with flowers. Sheer curtains on the windows. I imagine the owner as some little old lady who still wears a housedress with an apron. I am embarrassed to go up to the house looking the way I do, but I've made it this far. I might as well take five more steps.

I climb the steps and buzz the second-floor button on the intercom system, wait about ten seconds, then buzz again. Maybe he's not home. I should have called. Then again, it's ten thirty on a Sunday morning. He's probably still asleep.

Finally I hear a scratchy noise from the speaker, followed by a tired voice: "Jasper, is that you?" A woman's voice. A young woman's voice.

"No," I say, panicking. "I think I have the wrong apartment." I check the intercom again, see that it's not the wrong apartment, just the wrong timing. Really wrong.

I stumble back down the stairs, feeling like I'm going to vomit. Partly from dehydration, partly from how stupid I am. What did I expect, arriving unannounced at Jasper's apartment on a Sunday morning? Did I really think a handsome guy like Jasper would be alone? Waiting for me to come to my senses? And who can blame him? After all, I did tell him I was considering adopting my ex-husband's baby *and* accuse him of lusting after his ex-girlfriend. I probably threw him right into her arms.

I grab my bike and push off, in a frenzy to ride away as quickly as possible. When I get about a block from the house, I think I see Jasper across the street, carrying a baguette in a bakery bag. I imagine he's going back to make Jolene a delicious breakfast—omelets, fresh bread with marmalade, grapefruit, maybe mimosas. Then they're going to make violent love right on his kitchen counter.

I duck down a side street and weave my way back to the center of town to the bicycle path, getting lost a few times along the way. By the time I get back to Bristol, I want to die. Just crawl into my bed with Zeke and never get out of it again. Never go to work, never eat another meal, and certainly never, ever take another bike ride again.

The next day, every one of my muscles aches, even my armpits, like I've been doing thousands and thousands of push-ups. Why didn't I just ride up to Jasper and say, *Hi, I'm here. You said stop by any time, so I did. But I gather you have company. No big deal. We'll try it again sometime.*

What if he saw me? He probably thinks I'm stalking him.

About a week after the ill-fated bike expedition to Providence, Margaret agrees to put her house on market. Apparently, Jay convinced her that it would be the best thing for everyone involved. Margaret, like someone else I know, seems unable to say no to Jay or to recognize that sometimes, he can be a bit of a selfish bastard.

So Margaret and I decide to use the weekend to look at a few assisted-living facilities. The first place we visit is awful. The minute we walk in, a woman dressed in lavender and wearing far too much eye makeup greets us at the door with a phony smile. A sickening sweet floral odor is attempting to mask the stale-sour stench of the place—scrambled eggs kept warm under heat lamps, chemical deodorizers, bed pans, soiled sheets, all tied together with a lavender fresh bow. There is no way Margaret is living here.

"I don't think this is what we're looking for," I say to the woman—Miss Julie is her name. There's something odd about a place in which you call a grown woman Miss Julie. Why not just Julie?

"Let's not rush to judgment," Margaret says, shocking me with her restraint.

"The rooms are quite lovely. Let me show you one of the private ones. You look like a private room kind of person," Miss Julie says in an attempt to curry favor with Margaret.

We follow her past the dining hall, a depressingly large room with dozens of round tables and floral chairs with plastic covers, then past the nurses' station, empty now but for one surly-looking woman, her enormous bust jutting out like a stone turret.

"Here we are," the woman says, holding her arm out, Vanna White–style. The two of us enter the room ahead of her. It's not awful—a typical hospital room with white sterile walls, a faux-wood dresser with television, a private bathroom, one window with falsely cheerful red-checkered curtains. But all the same, it is awful, in its way. There's something awful about its intentional blandness.

"Not bad," Margaret says, and I realize she's just doing this for my sake, for Jay's sake. She's trying to steel herself in case we decide this is to be her fate. I feel white-hot shame for making her do this.

"Can we have a minute alone?" I ask Miss Julie. "To discuss."

"Sure, but I still have to show you the lounge and the dining hall, and don't forget the theater. We're the only assisted-living facility that actually has a small movie theater. That's a big selling point."

"I'm sure it is," I say, "but can you excuse us anyway?"

191

"Certainly." Reluctantly she turns to leave the room, pausing at the door to give us a tight grin.

"What do you really think?" I say to Margaret.

"I don't know. It's what I expected," she says.

"Really? This is what you expected?"

"When my father's cancer got really bad, they recommended we put him into hospice care."

"Hospice care. Isn't that . . . ?"

"Yes, where people go to die. My mother and I went to check it out, and as soon as I stepped foot inside, I turned right out of there."

"But Margaret, this is supposed to be a place where people come to live. This shouldn't remind you of a place people go to die."

"No, it probably shouldn't, but it does," she says, her voice without feeling.

"Let's keep looking, then." What I want to say is *Let's stop looking*.

We go to two other places that morning, the first a modern, Swedish-looking building with lots of steel and glass, splashy paintings on the walls and unique architectural features like skylights and raised walkways that cross over the central atrium. But Margaret says it gives her the creeps; she thinks it used to be a mental institution that they gutted and renovated.

The last place is the best of the three, made to look like an enormous Victorian house surrounded by lovely paths and fountains and flower beds. But as soon as we go inside, it looks much like the first: beige, characterless, and soul killing.

We stop to get lunch at a little deli that sits over the pier in Wickford. "The last one was nice," she says, taking a bite of her salad.

"Definitely the best," I say, "but I didn't like any of them."

"Well, it's only the first day," she says. She is being far more accepting of this whole process than I am. "And that first one wasn't so bad, when you really think about it."

I think she must be joking. "Yes, and *they* have a movie theater," I say. "That's what I really look for in a quality assisted-living facility. A good movie theater."

"Noelle, stop treating this so lightly. This is where I'm going to be living. You might as well help me see the best in it."

"But I don't think that's my job at all. My job is to tell you when there's no chance in hell I'm going to let you live in one of them. The only one I'd even think about is that Victorian place."

"Luxwood Victorian Gardens."

"They make it sound so pleasant. Like you're staying in some luxurious estate, Blithewold Mansion for the physically impaired."

"Well, they have to do that to get people in the door. They can't very well call the place Let-Us-Steal-Your-Independence Gardens."

"Feed-Us-Flavorless-Food Courtyard."

"Watch-*Jeopardy*-Until-You-Die Village."

"This is a sick game we're playing," I say.

"I know." Her eyes have a hollow look that scares me.

"Margaret, are you sure you want to do this?"

"What choice do I have?" she says, pathetically. "Jay's right. You can't take care of me forever. And my condition is bound to get worse. I've come to terms with that. So I might as well look on the bright side. No more cleaning the house, no more scrubbing the toilet or dusting under the furniture. No more laundry. No more yard work."

"When was the last time you did yard work?"

"It's been a while. I actually miss being able to do it. Raking leaves. Planting bulbs. I enjoyed that."

"Yeah."

"I'll miss cooking the most. I love cooking. I used to be a good cook."

"You can come to my place and cook for me," I say.

"Can I?"

"Of course."

"Don't just say it. Because I'm going to need to get out of the place, wherever it is. You can't just put me somewhere and leave me. People do that, you know. Just leave their relatives in one of these places and never see them again."

"I would never do that, Margaret."

"Promise me?" she says.

"Margaret, I promise." Because in a strange way, I'm all Margaret's got.

❧

The next week, I am at the kitchen table, paying bills, when Zeke begins to whine. He's just finished his dinner, and he's pacing back and forth, panting and crying.

"What wrong, sweetie?" I say. "Need to go out?" I let him outside, but the minute he gets out there, he barks at the door to come back in. I pet him on the head and throat, feel his breathing. It seems rapid. "What is it?" He looks up at me, desperate, then continues to pace throughout the house.

I follow him through the rooms and finally get him to lie down on the floor. "Hold still," I say, smoothing my hand along his side, when I notice his belly looks swollen—distended and lumpy. Immediately I get up and call SASH, tell Tara I'm bringing Zeke over.

My heart is racing as I put the leash on Zeke and lead him into the car. He can barely jump up himself. I can tell he's panicking, and so am I. Along the way, I talk to him softly and soothingly, trying to reassure him that everything will be all right. At times like these, I know the proper thing to do is pay extra attention to the road, as extreme emotions are liable to get me into an accident, but what I want to do is cut in front of people and drive on the other side of the road so I can get to the clinic faster. I have a feeling he's got bloat, an excessive buildup of gas that actually twists the stomach and can kill a dog if not treated early enough.

When I arrive, Dr. Robbins, Tara, and our other vet tech, Sam, are at the front door waiting for us. Zeke doesn't want to get out of the car; in fact, when I tug at his leash, he cries out as if he's in pain. Dr. Robbins comes to the back seat and gives him a shot of a sedative just to calm his nerves.

"Anxiety can make the condition worse," she says. "Let's see if we can calm him down enough to come inside." Eventually it is clear that we're all going to have to carry him in, so the four of us crowd around him, me in the car gently pushing him out, the three of them scooping him carefully out of the car and onto a stretcher.

I follow them back into the exam room where they place Zeke on the metal table, and then Sam goes to get the X-ray machine ready. The X-rays confirm that his stomach has twisted, and if they don't perform surgery, the twist will compress the veins carrying blood to the heart, and he'll die of cardiac depression. "You know about this surgery, Noelle," Dr. Robbins tells me. "It's high risk, and it doesn't always work. The tissue damage could be so bad that he might still have cardiac problems. Sometimes even with surgery they die a few days later from complications."

"I know," I say. "What do you think I should do?"

"I'm not telling you not to do the surgery, but the survival rate isn't as high as I'd like. We could make him very comfortable, and you could be with him when he dies."

"I don't think I can do that. Not without a fight," I say. "The surgery can work, right?"

"A lot depends on the extent of the twist and the damage to the stomach tissue. You got him here right away, so there's a decent chance. It's up to you." I look at her face. She is being practical, clinical, yet I know she cares. I've been on the other side of this conversation so many times, giving a distraught owner the very same speech. People view pets in different ways—some just as pets, others as family members. I have to decide what I'm willing to put him through, what the chances of survival are, and what his quality of living will be if he does survive.

"Kate, tell me what to do. If he's in serious pain and you don't think he's going to pull through, let's put him down," I say. God, I hate that phrase. "But if you think there's a chance . . ."

"There's always a chance."

"What would you do?"

"If it were my pet?" she says.

"Yes."

"I'd probably try it. But it's expensive. That's the other thing you need to consider. Obviously we'd let you pay it off slowly . . ."

"Go ahead and prep him for surgery," I say. "I'm going to call Jay."

I dial my phone, my hands shaking uncontrollably. "Jay, it's Noelle."

"What's wrong? Is it Mom?"

"It's Zeke," I say, and tell him the situation.

"How much will it cost?" he asks. That's actually his first question.

"I don't know," I say. "It's going to be expensive, but that's really not the point."

"Well, it kind of is the point. I mean, I love Zeke. You know I'd do anything for him, but if there's a low survival rate . . ."

"If we wait too long, there's a low survival rate. But I got him here right away. Besides, I'll pay for it. I don't care how much."

"Noelle," he says, adopting the soft, soothing tone I know so well. "I know how much you love Zeke, but he's seven years old. He's had a great life. Some Great Danes only live to be seven."

"But Zeke is healthy in every other respect," I say. "I can't lose him, Jay. Not right now. I can't. He's all I have." I am almost hyperventilating.

"Noelle, calm down," he says, but I have to hang up the phone. I know it's rude, but I'm not about to engage in a financial argument while Zeke is lying there on the table waiting, his life in my hands.

I run back to the surgery room where Zeke lies, panting wildly, his big brown eyes searching mine for some explanation. I throw my arms around him, stroke his back, crying sloppy tears into the scruffy fur around his neck. He's so nervous, his hair is coming off in clumps in my hands. "Please, Zeke, pull through. You can do it. I know you're strong enough." I kiss him on the forehead about a thousand times before Dr. Robbins, wisely, makes Tara escort me back into the waiting room.

"It's going to be okay," Tara says, putting her arm around me and making me sit down.

"God, I hope so. I just love him so much."

"You know Kate. She's amazing. She's going to do the best she can."

I want to call Jasper, just like I always want to call him when I'm feeling anxious or sad. But I can't. I also know I can't go through this alone. I can't sit here waiting to hear if Zeke's going to live or die. I'll go crazy.

So I get on my phone and call the one person I know will understand what I'm feeling. I call Margaret.

September

Zeke did make it through surgery, but Kate told me I'd have to prepare myself for the possibility that it could happen again, that he might not live more than another year or so. It's hard to believe it when I see him in action. He's already back to his old ways—rolling around on the floor with his toys, begging for bites of my tuna sandwich, looking at me yearningly so I'll take him for a walk. When we get back from a walk and he's totally exhausted, he does this hilarious thing where he flops down on the floor all at once, barely bending his legs, like a horse that's just tipped over. And then he promptly falls asleep and snores.

By Labor Day weekend, it's difficult to remember he was ever sick. I think he's forgotten all about the incident, which makes me feel slightly less guilty about having to leave him with a dog-sitter this weekend.

Every Labor Day since I was about four years old, I have gone to

Old Saybrook with my family. We stay at this crazy old 1920s hotel with a giant veranda overlooking the water. My mother loves it for its Old World grandeur, not realizing how dilapidated it's become since she first came here. She's been coming here since she was a little girl and is, therefore, just a little blinded by nostalgia. Her family vacationed here in the 1950s, and their family before them vacationed here in the twenties when the hotel must have been very grand, very Gatsby. But now the wallpaper is mostly faded and torn in places, the once luxurious Oriental carpets threadbare and musty-smelling, and the expansive foyer with the carved wooden ceiling is more ominous than elegant, lending the whole place a haunted-house feel.

As kids, Nick and I used to swear we saw ghosts at night wandering around through the long dark hallways. We'd sit up in our beds telling each other scary stories, closely watching the doorknob of our door, expecting to see it turn on its own, shrieking with a pleasurable thrill when it did, only to discover it was just our father playing tricks on us.

I'm having Tara stay with Zeke at my place while I'm gone. Tara still lives with her parents, so she's more than happy to dog-sit if it means getting out of her house. Before I leave, I take her over to meet Margaret, who has agreed to let Tara give her her shots while I'm away. I will have to pay Tara most generously for this weekend.

When I arrive at the hotel, the sky is a bit overcast, with that otherworldly glow created when a little sun streaks through purple cloud cover. The geraniums on the front stairwell are glowing almost neon, and the hotel looks more like the stage set for an Agatha Christie play than a grand estate. I grab my weekend bag and head into the hotel, checking myself in at the front desk. The foyer is smaller than I remembered it but still imposing and austere, so at odds with the guests who walk here and there in flip-flops and bathing suits. I would sooner imagine flappers and bootleggers descending the stairwell carrying Gin Rickeys and long cigarettes.

When I find my family's suite, it is empty, but there's a note on the kitchen table: *At the beach. Come meet us.* I change into my bathing suit, throw on a cover-up, then head downstairs to the beach, passing through the afternoon tearoom and out past the swimming pool. From the pool patio, I can see the small, pebbly beach crowded with tourists, soaking up their last bit of sun before heading back to their apartments in the city and returning to work. I breathe in deeply, inhaling the scents of seaweed, iodine, salt air. Gulls screech overhead, soaring in loopy delirium.

I spot Dana first—the wind is tossing her red hair into a frothy tangle behind her. She is holding Miranda over her shoulder, and my brother is leaning back on his elbows next to them. My mother and father are a few feet away under a pink and green striped beach umbrella. Even though it's not a particularly sunny day, my father's fair skin would burn easily if unprotected.

When my mother sees me, I hear her squeal, "Noelle's here." This is followed by much hugging and kissing, some oohing and ahhing on my part when I see how much Miranda has grown, how she has a full head of red hair already.

It is so nice to sit down among my family, feel the sea breeze blowing my hair, the sun warming my shoulders. My mother is overly solicitous as usual—she has a cooler full of sandwiches, which she offers me every ten minutes. Nick is basking in the glow of his pretty girlfriend and lovely daughter—they actually look like a proper family now. And my dad, who has always seemed a bit out of place on the beach, looks like he may have finally begun to allow himself to relax. I can tell he's been swimming because his hair is wet, his white paunch already a bit sunburned.

"How's Zeke?" he asks.

"Much better," I say. "Thanks. The vet thinks he's going to be all right. For a while, at least."

"That's about the best any of us can say for ourselves," he says.

"How much did the surgery cost again?" Nick says.

"Don't ask."

Nick leans over and whispers to me. "I know I owe you money. I've been trying to save up to pay you back."

"Whenever you can," I whisper back. "You've got some more pressing expenses, I imagine." I glance over at Miranda. She is sleeping soundly amid a bundle of pink blankets.

"Did you ask Jay to help you out?" my mother says, listening in on our conversation. There is an awkward silence after she mentions his name, my father's face stoic and cold.

"Well, it's kind of complicated," I say.

"Complicated, my ass," says Nick. "Wasn't it his dog in the first place? He should have paid for the whole thing."

"Actually, he's saving up to adopt a baby," I say. Since telling my parents about my infertility, I've suddenly become a verbal geyser in their presence.

"What?" my mother says. "Oh, how could he? After everything he told you? Oh, Noelle, it's too much."

"He's such a dickhead," Nick says.

"Nicholas, watch your language."

"Mom, it's okay," I say.

"Really, Nick," Dana says.

"But the nerve of him," my mother goes on. "Why I'd love to go over there and—"

"Mom, really . . ."

"Hey, is anyone up for a swim?" my father says loudly. We all look over at him as if he's just suggested amateur stingray wrestling.

"Sure," I say finally. "I'll go swimming with you."

"I will, too," Dana says. "Nick, sweetie, will you watch the baby?"

Dana, my father, and I make our way down to the water's edge. Dana doesn't even test the water—just walks straight in and dives under a wave. Intrepid.

"My God," I say. "It's freezing."

"Yeah," my dad says. "But refreshing."

He follows Dana in, pushing past the breakers, ducks all the way under, then turns around to float on his back. His comb-over has flopped endearingly to the wrong side of his head. I tip my toe into the surf, fighting the urge to go lie back down on a towel, then force myself to wade in deeper. My teeth are chattering, my arms covered with goose bumps, but I am not deterred. It's actually quite therapeutic, having this vast body of water around me, letting its currents pull me in, bob me up and down, feeling the salt water work its way into my nostrils and under my skin. Finally, I take the plunge under and emerge fully drenched, but revived.

After a few minutes, the water feels like bathwater, our bodies have grown so used to it. We swim for almost a half hour, then get out to bake dry. The sun has burned off the haze and is now beating down its full strength, making the beach houses along the coast look like mirages in the desert.

"Come with your mother for a walk," my mother says. "You can help me look for beach glass."

"All right," I say.

When we get to the water's edge, I look both ways as if about to cross a street. To the east are the flat shoals and scrubby marshland of the estuary just north of here. To the west, the sun is blazing over the crescent beach, turning the stones and pebbles silver and purple. "Which way?"

"Into the sunset, of course," my mother says, smiling. We walk slowly, my mother pausing every now and then to pick up a shell or check a speck of color on the sand.

"Your hair's gotten long again," she says, reaching over to touch the wisps by my face. "It looks so pretty that way."

"Thanks."

"I know not to ask, but I hope there's some great guy who thinks so, too."

"Not at the moment," I say. "How's the salsa dancing coming along?"

"Oh, good. Your father's improved so much. I think we might stand a chance of placing. The only real competition we have is Marcia and Ted Fielding. But Ted's kind of an oaf, and Marcia . . . well, let's just say I don't picture her looking good in a slinky red dress."

I bend down to pick up a tiny piece of frosted white sea glass, cup my hand around it, and put it in the pocket of my shorts. "So Nick and Dana seem to be getting along better."

"They are. We've been helping them out a little. Just until they're on their feet."

"That's good," I say, nodding. "I'm sure they appreciate it."

"I know you've helped him yourself over the years, and that it hasn't always been easy. I just want you to know that if you ever need money, we can help you, too. You probably feel we've helped Nicky more than you over the years, but that's only because he's needed it. He's always been something of a risk taker. Like me, I guess. But I do think he's growing up. Miranda's been really good for him. He just got another temp job. Did I tell you that?"

"No, Mom. That's great."

My mom looks at me with a poker face. "But don't worry," she says. "It's not a permanent thing." And we both start laughing. I sometimes forget my mother has a sense of humor.

After we all drag ourselves off the beach and head back to the suite, my father makes us a big pitcher of gin and tonics, and we take our drinks out onto the patio. The sun is low and orange along the shoreline, the air still balmy.

"This is the life," my father says, taking a sip of his drink and leaning his head against the chair. My father's always been a bit tightly wound. Too much stress at work, too much anxiety in life. He needs a few days at the beach where he can swim in the ocean and curl his toes in the sand and drink gin and tonics from a tumbler the size of his hand.

The rest of the weekend unfolds in this leisurely way. I spend a lot of time holding and playing with the baby, and to her credit, my mother does not hover or give me looks tinged with pity, despite the fact that my infertility must be weighing on her heart like a lead apron. On mine, too.

That night, I cannot sleep. Partly the strange room, partly worrying about Zeke, partly thinking of Jasper. A knock on the door almost has me prostrate on the floor under the bed.

"Noelle, it's me," I hear Nick whisper through the giant keyhole, roughly the size of a Bartlett pear.

"God, Nick, you scared the hell out of me," I say, letting him in.

"I was hoping you'd still be awake."

"And if I wasn't I'm sure you would have taken care of it."

"I can't sleep either," he says.

"Well, come on in, and have a seat."

He comes and sits on my bed, cross-legged, then produces five dice. "Yahtzee challenge?" he says.

"You bet."

Yahtzee had always been our favorite game as kids. We made up all our own rules, bargained to get extra turns, kept the tournament going until one of us was so far ahead, the lead was insurmountable, or until we were collapsing from exhaustion.

"Are Dana and Miranda asleep?" I ask.

"Yep. I tried waking them up first."

"So I'm your second choice."

"No, I actually wanted to talk to you," he says. "I never see you anymore—you've been so busy lately, what with your thirteen jobs."

"It's not that bad," I say.

"Well, even one is better than what I've got."

"Nothing panning out?"

"I have a crappy temp position. But Dana's father wants me to come work for him. I can't believe it, but he does. I thought he'd be trying to kill me, you know? Chasing me down the street with a shotgun."

"Is her family putting pressure on you to get married?"

"Not yet. I think they want to give us a chance to get to know each other first."

"That's very thoughtful of them."

Nick rolls three sixes on his first try. "Oooh, sign of the devil," he says. "Creepy. No, her parents don't want us to rush into anything. I mean, we barely knew each other when all this happened. But now that Miranda's here . . . I don't know. I love her so much. And I think I might love Dana, too."

"Just what every girl wants to hear. I think I might love you."

"Shut up, I'm serious," he says. "And if I'm ever going to have a chance with her, I have to get a real job."

"So what does her dad do?"

"He works for a paper products company. And you'll never guess which department he has an opening in."

"What?"

"Guess."

"You said I'll never guess."

"Toilet paper."

"Toilet paper? Oh my God, Nick," I say, stifling my laughter.

"I know, right? It's in the marketing department. Did you even know they needed to market toilet paper? I mean, people are always going to need it, right?"

I am laughing so hard now I can barely answer. "I guess so. Oooh, large straight," I say, smugly writing in my forty points.

"You're kicking my ass."

"Just like old times. So, are you going to take the job?"

"I don't know. I'm having some serious . . . issues about it. I mean it's like, the least creative job I could think of."

"Oh, I could think of some less creative jobs. Besides, you've got to bite the bullet sometime."

"So everyone keeps telling me." He looks so boyish and glum that despite his years and years of avoiding responsibility and gainful employment, my heart cannot help but go out to him.

"Look, I never want to be the one to tell people to give up on their dream and just, you know, be normal, responsible citizens. You're an artist at heart, and you're very talented. But the fact of the matter is, you have a baby now. And a girlfriend who's the mother of that baby. And whether you like it or not, you're responsible for them. Some guys might use this as an excuse to hightail it out of there, but I know that's not the kind of person you are. Taking a boring nine-to-five job doesn't mean you can't still do your art. I know a guy who spends his days developing technology for the blind and his weekends writing music and playing in a band."

"Whoa, back up a minute," he says, his head low and his eyebrows raised. "You know a guy who plays in a band?"

"Yeah, so?"

"Noelle, you've always had a thing for musicians. What's the deal?" he asks, a huge, ridiculous grin on his face.

"Nothing. I was just relating a story I thought might help put things into perspective for you."

"Noelle, come on. I know you too well. Who is he?"

"Just a friend," I say, but I can feel my cheeks burning.

"Oh my God," he says. "Noelle's got a boyfriend!"

"I do not have a boyfriend," I say.

"Right. What's going on?"

"Sadly, absolutely nothing. I screwed up. Big-time."

"Dude, what happened?" he asks so earnestly I have to laugh.

"Dude, I'm an idiot. I told him I was considering adopting Jay's baby."

"Whoa, get out!"

"I know."

"What were you thinking?"

"At the time, he had this ex-girlfriend who was still hanging around, and I wasn't sure it was going to work out anyway, and I was feeling really emotional about you and Dana having a baby together, and it just . . . slipped out."

"You're not, are you?"

"Not what?"

"Adopting Jay's baby."

"I don't know, Nick. I just worry that I won't ever get another chance."

"Noelle," he says, suddenly serious, especially for Nick, the human equivalent of a Pop-Tart. "Mom and Dad told me about your . . . not being able to . . ."

"Have a baby. It's okay. I can talk about it."

"I'm so sorry. You must have felt so angry when I told you about me and Dana."

"No, Nick, I wasn't angry at all. I felt happy for you. Maybe disappointed that it could never be me, but I wasn't angry."

"Because you never know," he says. "Doctors are coming up with new methods all the time. I wouldn't give up just yet. Besides, Jay left you. Why would you adopt his baby for him unless you were getting back together? Which, I assume you're not because he's . . . well, gay."

"No," I say, laughing.

"And a dickhead."

"It's a long story," I say. "Jay has a new boyfriend. I would be more like the surrogate adoptive parent, or something."

"That just sounds effed up," he says.

"Yeah, it does actually, doesn't it? Yahtzee!" I yell. Then both of us freeze when we hear footsteps approaching from down the hall. At first, we giggle silently into our hands like guilty teenagers, worried we've woken up some poor old sod who wants us to shut up already so he can get to sleep. But then we hear a rustle, see the doorknob move almost imperceptibly.

"Holy shit," Nick whispers. "Did you see that?" I nod. "Did you lock the door after I came in?"

"No, why would I?" I say.

"Because of the Old Saybrook ghost," he says. "The woman who hanged herself when her sailor husband didn't return."

"Nick," I say, laughing at him to make myself feel better, but inside, my intestines are churning. "What good is a locked door if there's a ghost out there? They can float through walls."

"Good point," he says. Both of us sit poised, bolt upright on the bed, watching, waiting, listening. The knob begins to turn again, and the door slowly falls open, just a crack.

"Jesus Christ," Nick says, practically jumping on top of me.

The door swings wide open, and there stands the barrel-chested shape of a man, his face in shadow. We both scream out in terror, then collapse onto each other when we realize it's just Dad. "Hot damn," my father says. "I've still got it!" He grabs the doorknob, cackling to himself as he closes the door on us, and retreats back to his room down the hall. Nick and I look at each other, both of us about to keel over from relief, and then we fall to the floor laughing until tears are streaming down our faces.

⁂

When I get back home after the weekend, Zeke practically knocks me over at the door. Good old Zeke, back in action. After thanking Tara and sending her home with some cash and an art deco lamp from the hotel's gift shop, I go through that oddly comforting post-vacation routine—walking through the house to see what's been used or moved, opening the refrigerator pointlessly, checking the answering machine.

Margaret has called—nothing urgent, just wishing me a happy trip. A message from Jay, just wanting to "touch base" with me. And then, a message from Dan, saying Danielle had the baby and asking if I could let Bebop out.

I wonder to myself how long ago he left the message, how long Bebop's gone since relieving himself. Quickly I put my shoes back on, head next door, letting myself in with the key Danielle left under the mat for me.

When I walk in, Bebop practically molests my left ankle. I walk back toward the kitchen to let him out into the yard, nearly jumping three feet in the air when the refrigerator door closes to reveal Dan standing there holding a cheese sandwich.

"Oh, I'm sorry," I say, embarrassed. "I came to let Bebop out."

"Oh, yeah," he says. "I wasn't sure if you'd get the message, so I ran home to let him out myself."

"Congratulations," I say.

"Thanks."

"Girl or boy?"

"It's a beautiful girl," he says, beaming. "Annemarie. After Danielle's grandmother."

"That's pretty," I say.

"And she's the most gorgeous thing I've ever seen. It was touch and go there for a while. She was breech, so they ended up having to do a C-section. Danielle and the baby'll probably have to stay at least another night. Danielle was so exhausted. But she's such a trouper. I'm heading back over there right after I eat some lunch."

"Great," I say. He is chewing his sandwich and rifling through his mail, looking totally distracted, and totally uninterested in me. "So you're happy?"

"Thrilled. I couldn't be happier. Healthy baby, healthy wife."

"Good, because a while ago you were thinking . . ."

"What?"

"I mean, a while ago, Danielle told me you were hoping for a girl. So I'm glad it turned out to be a girl."

"You're not kidding. I don't know if we could handle another boy. The boys are at my mother-in-law's right now, thank God. Hey, did you want to come back to the hospital with me? I think Danielle would be up for—"

"No," I say, cutting him off a little too quickly. "I mean, thanks, but I'll wait until she gets home. I'm sure she'll feel more up to visitors then. But if it looks like she's going to need more time in the hospital, just give me a call. I'd be happy to watch Bebop for you."

"Yeah, about that," he says. "I think we're going to have to give him up after all."

"Oh really?" I say, looking down at Bebop, who seems to have a sixth sense about what we're talking about. He is sitting at my feet staring up at me with the most pathetic face. "That's too bad."

"He's a lot better than he was, but I just don't think we can give him the attention he needs right now, you know?"

"I'm sorry to hear that."

"We were wondering if you could . . ."

"Sure," I say. "I'll take him to the shelter. You'll have to fill out some paperwork, of course."

"Of course," he says. "But we'd appreciate it. We didn't want to have to put him down."

"No. I understand," I say, but I really don't.

"Well, I gotta get back to Danielle," he says.

"All right. You want me to take Bebop for the time being?"

"That would be great," he says. "When Danielle comes home, we won't have to worry about him causing trouble. I want to do whatever I can to make her happy."

I cannot believe this is the same guy who stumbled over all drunk and desperate sounding, telling me he wanted to leave his wife and kids. And now he's heading out the door father of the year.

Maybe it's all a matter of state of mind, of convincing yourself that some things are worth the effort. That the rewards of a certain kind of life outweigh the sacrifices and the compromises.

I'm sorry that Bebop had to be the casualty of such a compromise, but I guess some people only have so much to give. Dan and Danielle were full out. And I guess I'd rather see Bebop with someone who appreciates him for who he is.

Once he finds a home with people who make him feel wanted, I'll bet all those strange behavior problems will cease. Because I believe you can teach an old dog new tricks. It just takes patience and a whole lot of love.

I take Bebop next door with me, and Zeke goes berserk. I won't have to walk him for the next few days because he'll get so much exercise chasing Bebop around. And it'll be a losing battle, too, because Bebop is way too small and fast for Zeke.

I'm feeling sort of exhausted from the weekend and defeated from the day. So I do what I usually do when I feel edgy and overcome. I look at real estate ads online—my electronic Valium.

With all the drama and chaos of the past few weeks, I realize I haven't done this in almost a month. But today I see a listing that stops me cold: *FOR SALE, Tiverton: Elegant restored Victorian with five bedrooms, three fireplaces, formal library, enormous modern kitchen, and lovely living room with gorgeous view of the bay. Beautifully landscaped lot equipped with stables, herb garden, and cottage that could be converted into an in-law suite.*

It is Margaret's house, all itemized by selling points and noteworthy features, broken down into glorified adjectives like some mail-order bride putting out a personals ad. But this bride doesn't really want to leave her country; her family is making her go.

And suddenly I know that Margaret doesn't want to sell her house. And that she shouldn't. The idea is all wrong. We were all wrong.

That afternoon, I drive over to Tiverton to give Margaret her shot and find her sitting on her front porch, staring out at her "gorgeous view of the bay."

"What are you doing?" I say, taking a seat on the top step of the porch.

"Sitting here feeling sorry for myself," she says. "Look at these."

I glance down and see a box containing a pair of gray, thick-soled orthopedic shoes. "They came in the mail today. I had forgotten I ordered them."

"So, what's the big deal?" I say.

"They're ugly as sin."

"So? Are they comfortable? Do they help you walk?"

"Yes, yes. I don't need a lecture. It just seems like the first step in a chain. Next will be a walker, then a wheelchair, then my grave."

"Oh, stop being melodramatic," I say.

"It's ironic, isn't it?"

"What is?"

"I had so many pairs of shoes. So many. I used to adore just look-ing at them in my closet. Strappy sandals, kitten heels, pumps made of such soft leather I could fold them in half. I know it's so vain of me to mind not being able to wear nice shoes anymore, but I can't help it."

"Want to hear something funny?" I say, trying to lighten the mood. "I've never owned a pair of shoes that cost more than twenty-five dollars."

"Really," she says, as if I've just told her I've never worn under-wear.

"No, that's not entirely true. My wedding shoes—they were ex-pensive. But look where they got me." Surprisingly, Margaret laughs.

"Well, you can have all of mine," she says. "I'm an eight. What size are you?"

"I'm an eight, too. But wide. There's no way your shoes would fit." Although I'd kill to try them on anyway.

"It's just not worth it to fixate on possessions, I guess," she says. "Anything can and will be taken away from you."

"Boy, you have been having yourself a pity party," I say. "Why wasn't I invited?"

"Well, you're here now. And it's still in full swing. You know, they say that getting rid of things is the first step in getting ready to die."

"Who says that?"

"*They*," she says, holding out her palm to represent that mysterious fount of knowledge to whom we attribute all the mysteries of the universe. "And if *they* are right, I must be at death's door."

"You're nowhere near it. Besides, I think *they* are wrong. What if getting rid of things just means we've finally figured out what's important? We've shed all our irrelevant possessions so we're left with what really matters."

"And just what is that?"

"Well . . . I don't know yet. I've been thinking . . ."

"And did you enjoy it?" she says, breaking into her horsey laugh.

"I'm serious," I say. "I've been thinking a lot about your house."

"You think I'm too attached to it? An irrelevant material possession like my shoes?"

"Actually, no," I say. "I don't think a house is the same as a pair of shoes. I think a house is important. And I've been thinking it might be the one possession worth keeping."

She laughs. "It seems a little late for that, don't you think?"

"Not really."

"It's already on the market, sweetheart, and it's what Jay wants me to do."

"Well, it's not Jay's decision," I say, suddenly getting angry, more angry than the situation warrants. Because Margaret's defeat echoes all of my own defeats with Jay. "Since when does Jay get to make all the decisions in the world? Who died and left him boss?"

"My husband," she says, bleakly. "Didn't you know, Jay was the executor of his will?"

"He was?"

"It made sense, since Jay had financial expertise. I wouldn't have had any idea what to do. I think Dominic hoped Jay would take over the business. But Jay didn't want it. I couldn't really blame him. So we sold it, but got much less than it was worth."

"I thought the business had been doing well."

"Toward the end, it was getting pushed out by Internet sales and those big shoe warehouses. Dom's company had become a dinosaur."

"I had no idea."

Her eyes take on that removed quality they always get when she talks about her husband. "I remember after Dom died, Jay and I sat down to look at finances together, and he said we needed to free up some cash or we were going to be strapped. Do you remember when he sold the Land Rover?"

"Oh yeah," I say. "That was such a great car."

"I thought so, too. But Jay made me sell it, and he wanted me to sell the house, too."

"Why? Wasn't it paid off?"

"Dom had a lot of debts. He'd wanted to settle them before he died, but he never really got the chance, did he? The man liked his creature comforts—loved to eat and drink and entertain, but he didn't have much common sense. I never thought I'd be saddled with his debts, you know? I mean, I never imagined he would die.

He seemed indomitable to me. I felt totally lost. And Jay was left trying to keep things together. That's when he asked me to sell the house."

"And what did he expect you to do? Move in with us?"

"Ha! Can you imagine me living with you two back then? No, we looked at a few fifty-five-and-older communities. And do you know, I actually thought you might have been behind it."

"Me?" I say.

"You know, putting pressure on Jay so you could get your hands on some of my money and get rid of me? Put me away in some home forever. I was kind of paranoid. I guess having money has its downsides. And not having money, even more." She laughs bitterly.

"Margaret, I was never after your—"

"No, no, I know that now. Anyway, I told Jay no. Told him the house was all I had left." It's funny. Those were the exact words I said to Jay when he suggested I put Zeke to sleep. "Of course, this is precisely why I have no money now."

I shake my head in disbelief. "I always thought you were loaded. For a while there, I even thought it was you who made that anonymous donation to SASH."

"Forty thousand dollars? Ha, I wish."

"Why didn't Jay ever tell me about your . . . financial situation?"

"I told him not to. To tell you the truth, I was embarrassed."

"Why?"

"I thought it reflected poorly on me, on my standing in the community, for whatever that was worth. I'll tell you, when you suffer a tragedy like that, it really lets you know who your friends are. After Dom died, people just disappeared. Hung around for a few months to bring over casseroles and pies, then dried up when the real grieving started."

"Maybe they didn't know how much you were suffering. You can seem rather . . . impervious."

"Well, I'm not. A true friend would know the difference."

I sit there staring at her hands, so thin and delicate looking, almost vulnerable. "Well, maybe you should hang on to the house this time, too," I say.

"You know, a guy came to look at it the other day, and I swear I found myself telling him all the things that were wrong with it. Creaking floorboards, windows that stick, complicated wiring. The man looked at me like I was a nut. So did my real estate agent. And in a way, I guess I am. I love this house, even with all its flaws."

"Then why are you selling it?"

"You know why. It's the best thing for everyone."

"No, it's not. You don't really want to move into an assisted-living community."

"But what exactly am I supposed to do about my health?"

"I can still come every day. I've kind of gotten used to it. I might actually miss it if I stopped."

"No," she says. "It's too much running around. It's not fair to you."

"It's no big deal," I say.

"It'd be a whole lot easier if you lived here," she adds, chuckling to herself. I laugh, too, but then we both look at each other, and she raises her left eyebrow. "Well, why not?" she says.

"What? Me move in here with you?"

"Well, not literally here with me. But we could fix up the cottage for you. There's plenty of room down there. It's probably as big as your rental house."

"Probably bigger," I say. "Margaret, are you serious?"

She cocks her head and puts a hand to her cheek. "You know, I think I am. You're always coming here anyway, and I know how hard it is to pay rent and bills. When my parents cut me off, I had no idea if we were going to make it. I lived that part of my life terrified all the time. You don't have to live that way."

"But Margaret, you wouldn't really want me here. I've got Zeke and . . ."

"Of course, you'll bring Zeke with you. He'd have plenty of room to run around—there's an acre and a half here, and the stables."

"I know, but . . ."

"And I wouldn't have to live my life terrified either," she says, looking down at her feet. "I'd know you were right across the yard." Quietly, she adds, "You think about it, will you?"

"Okay," I say.

And I do. I really think about it.

That night, when I get home, I sit down in my backyard with the phone. Zeke and Bebop are completely worn out. Both have fallen asleep by my feet, and Zeke is whimpering in a dream like a puppy. I hope his dreams are happy, not unsettled like mine.

Since his surgery, I see him differently, like a dog back from the dead, a Lazarus dog. But I know I will not be able to hold on to him forever. I have begun to mourn his death in small increments even though he is still with me. Maybe this is what it takes to truly appreciate someone, the knowledge that he won't always be around.

I am thinking about all of this when I call Jay that night, wondering what it is that's been keeping me from giving him an answer about the adoption. We talk for almost two hours. And while I just spent a weekend holding and loving someone else's baby, longing for a child of my own, thinking how lovely it would be to nurture a life in this world, I tell Jay that I have decided I cannot adopt his baby.

I also tell him that Margaret has decided not to sell the house and that I've decided to move in with her. Jay rambles on in his rational way about how we've both lost our senses, and how did two women who used to hate each other ever come to this. He even tells me I may be making the biggest mistake of my life.

But I don't think so, I tell him. I feel really sure about this. I feel like I'm in control of my own life for maybe the first time ever.

Jay, perhaps astounded by my sudden show of strength, is speechless.

Or maybe he's just listening to me for a change.

October

FOR ADOPTION: Adorable, energetic Jack Russell free to a loving home. Previous owner could no longer meet his needs, which include lots of exercise and attention. But those willing to give him these will be rewarded with unswerving loyalty and love.

I have started a database on SASH's website of all the dogs we have for adoption, in the hopes that some wonderful family might be browsing the site and come across Bebop's photograph—see the expressive little face, the alert body poised for action, the adorable white paws that make him look like he's wearing boxing gloves—and fall in love. I love playing matchmaker for our shelter dogs, helping bring them together with people across the country looking for a companion, a beloved family pet, a best friend. So now instead of looking for homes for myself, I look for homes for them.

The first weekend of October I move into Margaret's cottage after spending the previous three weeks cleaning out the old debris and storage, scrubbing down the walls and floors, and slowly moving my things over in shifts. The cottage is built under a small grove of shade trees, making it feel like I am Thoreau come out to the woods "to live deliberately." Inside, the cottage is rustic and full of character, with interior stone walls, cedar plank beams, and cozy nooks and bookshelves built into the walls.

My first morning here, I woke up freezing; Margaret had ordered oil for the tank, but they hadn't come to fill it yet. I made a pot of coffee, then took it outside on the front stoop, my arms folded against myself, and stood braced against the wind, looking out on the bay. Yes, I actually have my own view of the water from here. On some nights, I stand outside and see the surface of the bay as still as glass, silver and dreamy; above me, hundreds of stars that I never bothered to notice before.

I'm surprised how many mornings I see Margaret, standing alone on the front porch, her narrow frame silhouetted against the crisp blue sky like a fragile summer dress hung on a line. She's lost so much weight recently. Never hungry, she says. The steroids made her starving; the new drugs make her nauseous. I begin making her a big breakfast every morning before I leave for work. It's almost like we're married now.

I miss only two things about my old house: the cardinals who used to visit my feeder and the possibility that Jasper could stop by after one of Trey and Mike's parties. As for the birds, I do not have to wait long before a practical menagerie invites itself to the new feeder I've installed behind the cottage. From the kitchen window, I watch robins, sparrows, yellow finches, and blue jays square off and take turns at the feeder; I bang the window to chase off squirrels and grackles. I stand stock still when the occasional family of deer makes its way into the yard at dusk. There are cornfields down the road at Tiverton Four Corners, and the farmers swear that the deer swim all the way from Prudence Island to the mainland to eat the corn fresh off the stalk.

Zeke loves having the run of this enormous yard, chasing birds away, no doubt pretending he's hunting big game. He's become very disobedient of late, and I've become lax as well. When I call him in from the yard, he looks up at me as if to say, *All right, woman, but only after I chase this rabbit and chew this stick and sniff this rotting fruit and roll around in these smelly weeds. Then I'll come in.* But I don't really mind. He deserves to do what he wants in his old age.

As the days grow colder, Zeke and I spend more time inside, curled up by the potbellied stove, feeling like we really are world-weary philosophers hiding away at Walden, minus the wood chopping and tax evasion. In this spirit of simplicity, I go and get myself a haircut—something really short and easy to care for. Suddenly I feel like Georgia O'Keeffe, living alone in some desert hideout. All I need are white linen pajamas, latent artistic talent, and some animal skulls lying around.

On Halloween Margaret, Zeke, and I sit together on her porch to hand out candy. It is a perfect autumn day—the sky a deep purple blush with a big, low-hanging harvest moon, the air crisp and tart and smelling of smoke and apples. Groups of children ascend the never-ending stairs with looks of excited trepidation—Margaret's house looks imposingly Gothic from the street. They are relieved but maybe a bit disappointed to find at the top of the stairs a harmless-looking older woman, a dopey dog, and me. They'd secretly hoped for a maimed psychopath, a ghostly pale ghoul, and a hound from hell. But when we drop several Kit Kats, Snickers bars, and Milky Ways into each of their bags, they run away shocked and delighted.

"So I've been thinking," Margaret says.

"Did you enjoy it?"

"Very funny. No stealing my lines."

"What have you been thinking about?"

"I've been thinking about a certain young dart player."

"Oh, right. Him." I sigh and look down at the candy bowl, pull out a Snickers bar, and unwrap it.

"Don't do that," she says.

"Do what?"

"Replacement eating. Replacing sex with chocolate."

"This is not replacement eating. It's Halloween. I'm entitled to at least one candy bar."

"Okay," she says. "Then give me one, too."

"Kit Kat?"

"Of course. Why don't you call him?"

"I don't know," I say, then think with a certain amount of shame about how I've been checking his band's website nearly every day, just to get a glimpse of him. There are a few blurry photos of him playing in some dark, hazy clubs. This is what sustains me. Pathetic. "I've been wanting to call him. Did I tell you that grant came through?"

"The one for the guide dog training?"

"Yes. I got the money."

"Congratulations! So call him and tell him, for God's sake."

"He's not home. His band is playing tonight. A Halloween concert."

"So why don't you go?" she says.

"I don't know. I think I blew it."

"You'll never know if you don't go see him," she says.

"I'm scared. I guess I'll have to tell him the truth about why I was even considering adopting with Jay. But I'm scared of what he'll think when I tell him I can't have a baby."

"He'll be thrilled!" she says. "You'll be able to have sex without a condom."

"Margaret!"

"Sorry. Bad joke. But come on. It's not the end of the world." Another cluster of children is making their way up the porch stairs. "Trick or treat," they say in unison, their eyes wide and hopeful.

One is much younger than the rest, barely three, dressed as a pirate with an oversized patch over his eye. His mother stands a few paces behind him, one hand out as if to hold him back, protect him. But she refrains from touching him, knowing he needs to feel big, just one of the kids. When he turns from us with his candy, the mother's face expands in a smile, so proud, so hopeful. I want this. I want this so much.

"All right, that's enough of this self-pity. I order you to go to that concert," Margaret says. "You need to get out of here."

"What?"

"You heard me. Get up and get dressed, get in the car, and go."

"You can't make me go, Margaret."

"Yes I can. You live in my cottage now, so you'll live on my terms. Hand me that bowl. I'm taking charge of the candy. You're going to go inside and put on some makeup and a sexy outfit. Borrow a pair of my boots, the black ones with the three-inch heels. The leather's really soft and giving, I think they might fit you."

"Margaret . . ."

"Do something spontaneous for once in your life. If you don't go, I swear you're going to wish you'd never moved in here. You think I was a bear when you first met me? You just wait till I'm through with you tonight."

"All right, all right, I get it," I say, laughing as I stand up but terrified inside. And rightfully so.

❧

The club where Jasper is playing is one of those intimidating places—swanky, sultry, a little too hip for its own good. When I get to the door, two bouncers look me up and down before collecting my ten-dollar cover charge, then deign to let me in. The bar has none of the sordid comfortableness of the Loft, nor any of its earthy, eccentric clientele. All I see are tall, lithe girls with dancers' bodies and young, startlingly handsome men with faces that look hard and arrogant.

The bar is aglow with orange and purple lights, the dance floor packed with throbbing bodies, and the music is pulsing through me, rattling my insides. As I get closer to the stage, I see fog machines rolling out billows of fake mist at the dancers' feet, giving the place the eerie feel of a graveyard. *I'm going to die here tonight,* I think.

Jasper is not onstage; another band is up there, its members thrashing their guitars and screaming incomprehensible vocals. I hate this place. I scan the room, looking for Jasper, seeing scores of faceless bodies all dressed in black, all seemingly hostile to my presence. I'd give anything to find George and Rita here.

Retreating from the noise of the stage, I claw my way back to the relative quiet of the bar, sit down, and order myself a martini. What the hell. Even though I don't really like the taste of martinis, I love the way they look in the glass, all clear and pure and ice cold. Very Hemingway. I figure there's no way I can look uncool drinking a martini. I take my first sip, relishing the feel of the vodka, like fire and ice on my tongue.

"Hello." I hear a voice behind me and swivel around to see Jasper. He is dressed in black with an eye patch over his left eye.

"Hi," I say.

"What are you doing here?" he asks. I can't tell whether the shocked tone in his voice is good or bad.

"I came to see you."

"You came to see me?" he says. "After not calling me for four months?"

"I know," I say, feeling suddenly inept at the art of conversation. "I'm sorry, it's just . . . I've been so . . ."

"Busy. Yeah, I know." He looks away from me as if my very presence disgusts him.

"No, you don't know," I say. "I mean, I *have* been busy. My brother had a baby. I moved in with Margaret. And I got that grant. You know, for the guide dog training?" He only nods. "It's really exciting. We're bringing on a trainer in January, and we're going to start recruiting dogs from the shelter. I'm finally going to get certified."

"Good for you," he says. I can't tell whether there's sarcasm in his voice.

"I've been dying to talk to you. To thank you for all your help," I say. "And thank your sister. That information she sent me was really helpful."

"You could have thanked her personally," he says. "She was up here visiting a few months ago. It's a shame we weren't speaking at the time."

"When did she visit?" I ask, my stomach clenching.

"Back in August. Why?"

"August. Oh my God."

"What?" *I am a total moron.*

"Jasper, I rode my bike up to see you in August. I even rang your bell, but some girl answered. I thought it was Jo."

"Jo? I haven't seen Jo in months. It was Cassie."

"Well, I know that now. It was stupid of me to just ride up there without calling. I just . . . wanted to surprise you. I wanted to see you. But when I thought Jo was there, I just . . ."

"Gave up?"

"No, I couldn't face you. Plus, you never called me either."

"I wanted to call you. But I didn't think you wanted anything to do with me. You made that pretty clear on the Fourth of July."

"What are you talking about?"

"The way you left Mike's party with what's his name. Your neighbor?"

"My neighbor? You mean, Dan? Who told you I left with Dan?"

"Jolene."

"And you believed her? Jasper, I did leave with Dan, but he happens to live next door to me."

"Jo told me you two looked pretty cozy."

"Dan was really drunk, and he was having problems with his wife. He was hitting on anything that moved. And given the amount of alcohol most people had consumed, I was one of the only ones left

230

moving. Why would you trust anything Jolene has to say anyway? Especially when it comes to me."

"I don't know," he says. "I guess I was angry."

"Besides, I thought you said you hadn't seen Jolene in months."

"Yes, in months. That was July, Noelle. I've waited for four months, wondering if you'd ever get your act together, and then you waltz in here unannounced and expect everything to be okay?"

"Jasper. I didn't expect anything. I just wanted to try and explain."

He is acting so cold and aloof that I really wish I could just crawl down into the floorboards. "Well, go ahead," he says. "Explain."

I stare into my martini, take a gulp to help me get through the next few minutes. I can already feel the vodka going to my head, but it isn't pleasant. "The thing is, I've been wanting to . . . I've been meaning to . . ." *God, I can't speak. At least, not sensically. Is that a word? Sensically?* "What I'm trying to say is . . . I came here tonight because I wanted to tell you . . . I'm not adopting a baby with Jay." No reaction. Jasper's face is completely hard and inscrutable. My chest feels like it's going to cave in on itself. "I don't know what I was thinking even considering that. I was just . . . scared, like you said. Worried that I'd never be with anybody. You were right, and I'm really, really sorry." I try to look into his eyes to gauge what he's thinking, but I can't read him at all because he's wearing that damn eye patch. "So . . ." I say, desperate for some opening, some sign that he might forgive me.

"So what? So I accept your apology."

My heart sinks. I was hoping for more. "Good. Because I wanted you . . . to understand. Why I acted the way I did. Why I blew my chances with you. Because I really do like you. I've liked you since

that first day I met you at that stupid New Year's party." I am babbling now because he's just standing there, stone-faced, not saying
anything.

Finally, he says, "Look, I have to go and get ready for my next
set."

"Oh, okay. But Jasper . . ."

"What?"

"Do you think there's any chance we could . . . I don't
know . . ."

"What? Be friends?"

"I don't know. Maybe . . ."

He drops his head down, stares at the floor. "Listen, Noelle. I
don't think it's going to work between us. It just seems there are too
many obstacles standing in our way."

"But there aren't anymore!"

Suddenly, he's looking at me again. "Noelle, five minutes ago
you were still giving me a hard time for talking to Jo. You just decided not to adopt a baby with your ex-husband. I think it's safe to
say you've got some issues to work out." God, that's exactly what I
accused him of almost a year ago. "I just don't think you're ready to
start a new relationship."

"But I am," I say, standing up and reaching for his arm. I feel a
bit dizzy. I probably should have eaten more than a Kit Kat for dinner. He pulls away.

"It's not that easy, Noelle," he says. "I was really hurt by you. But
I moved on. I can't get involved with someone who doesn't know
what she wants from one day to the next. It's too painful, and I can't
do it anymore." I want to object, tell him he's wrong, but I can't
speak. "I have to go. They're warming up without me. I'm sorry,

Noelle. I'm sorry it didn't work out. I really am." And he gets up and leaves to go onstage.

I slump back onto my stool, paralyzed. The bartender comes over to me and asks if I'm okay. "No. Not really," I say. "I'm not okay."

"I just meant, would you like another drink?"

And this strikes me as funny. What a jerk! Aren't bartenders supposed to listen to our problems? What kind of bartender is he, anyway? He looks at me as if I'm demented, then turns to walk away.

"Wait, I would like another," I say. He rolls his eyes and goes off to make me another drink. When my second martini comes, I suck it down like one of those 1940s dames my mother's always talking about. Cold and jaded. Tough as nails. That's who I'll be from now on. Lauren Bacall. Veronica Lake. So mysterious you've got to get past my hair if you want to talk to me.

Maybe I am demented. I keep making the same mistakes over and over again. Why did I even leave the house tonight? I'm more miserable now than I was when I left. And it's all Margaret's fault. What the hell was she doing giving me relationship advice? This woman who couldn't even be civil to me until I was saving her life.

I hear Jasper's band begin to warm up, stand up from my barstool, and reel a bit. There's no way I'm staying to hear Jasper's stupid band play stupid songs about his stupid ex-girlfriend. "Carnival Girl"? I mean, come on. What does that even mean? That she's so damned fun and exciting that dating her is like a carnival? Give me a break.

I make my way out of the club and find myself standing out in the rain. Alone. Like a Hemingway character. That's what martinis do to you. Realizing there's no way I can possibly drive myself home,

I start walking the streets of Providence, looking for a clean, well-lit place. Somewhere I can sober up.

I walk for blocks, trying to clear out the muddle in my head, letting the rain wash away all traces of the evening. Finally once I'm soaked through to the skin, I go inside a coffee shop and order a large coffee, black like my mood. People ignore me as if I'm invisible. That's the funny thing about despair: it's so hideous no one wants to acknowledge it. I wait out the rain, wondering to myself why we keep fighting, keep running after things we want, even though we know we're going to be disappointed in the end. Maybe it's better to stop trying.

Finally, after the storm subsides and the baristas are practically sweeping beneath my feet, I pick myself up and walk back outside to find my car. When I get back to Margaret's and let myself into the cottage, I flop into bed with Zeke and sleep the sleep of the dead.

❧

The next morning, my mouth feels like wet cement, quickly hardening into concrete. Slowly, the events of the previous evening come back to me in a humiliating flash, and I sit up, feel a rush of martini in my throat, and run to the bathroom to get sick.

Zeke looks worried, and to tell you the truth, so am I. I take a quick shower to wash my own stench away, then throw on my most comfortable sweatshirt and pair of pajama pants. In desperate need of counsel, I try to think of someone I can talk to.

I certainly can't call Jasper. I don't want to call Jay. And I can't face telling Margaret that her one attempt at life coaching has failed so miserably.

Much as I hate to admit it, I really want to talk to my mom. As insufferable as she can be, she's bound by parental oath to love me unconditionally, to take me in whenever I've screwed up, and to proffer sound maternal advice. So I call her and tell her I'm coming home.

When I get to my parents' house, I am comforted to see that my mom still decorates for Halloween. There are Indian corn cobs on the front door, hay bales with scarecrows, and two jack-o'-lanterns sitting on the porch stairs. Every year, my mom and dad have their own pumpkin-carving contest, in which they both carve a scary face or scene into a pumpkin, then ask the neighborhood kids to vote on the best one. My mom usually wins because she finds her designs in the *Martha Stewart* magazine, but my dad has been known to slip the kids some extra Snickers bars in return for their votes.

I have brought Zeke along with me for moral support, so when I ring the bell, Beatrix is on the other side of the door in a flash, barking manically, while Zeke strains against his leash. I can hear my mom shouting from inside, "Jim, can you get that?"

My dad finally answers the door. "Well, hi there. I didn't know you were coming."

"Hey, Dad," I say, giving him a kiss on the cheek, while Zeke and Beatrix perform their happy reunion dance.

"Come on, Trixie," my dad says. "Let Noelle and Zeke come in."

"You call her Trixie now?" I say, and my dad shrugs, embarrassed.

"So, who won?" I ask.

"The pumpkin carving? Your mother, of course. But it wasn't a fair contest."

"Why not?"

"Nick helped her."

"I didn't know that was allowed."

"Neither did I. But there's a new rule this year. We can each have one assistant."

"Very convenient."

"Exactly. Claire!" he bellows. "Noelle's here!"

My mom comes downstairs carrying a laundry basket full of socks and boxer shorts like she's in for a day of chores, but her hair looks perfectly curled and her makeup flawless. June Cleaver for the new millennium.

"Hi, sweetheart," she says, putting down the basket to give me a hug. Then she steps back and looks at me. "Oh, you got your hair cut again," she says. "Very cute. But you know I like you better with long hair." And then, for no particular reason, I start crying. "Oh, sweetheart, it's not that bad," my mother says. "You know me, it's just that long hair reminds me of when you were a little girl." And this just sets me off even more.

"God, I don't know what's wrong with me," I say, sitting down on the couch. "This is so stupid."

"Is it Zeke?" she asks.

"No," I manage to say through hiccupping sobs. My dad is visibly uncomfortable. He'd like the explanation to be something clinical. A rare disease like narcolepsy that triggers spontaneous crying instead of sleeping.

"Jim, go get Noelle a glass of water." Thankful for the chore, my father leaves the room for the kitchen.

"Did something happen with Margaret?" I shake my head. "Jay?"

"No," I snort. "Jasper."

"Jasper? Who's Jasper?"

"A guy," I say. "Didn't Nick tell you?"

"No." I sometimes forget that men don't gossip like women do. My mom sits down on the sofa next to me, and Beatrix and Zeke jump up, too, anxious to stop my crying. "Tell me what happened."

So I tell my mom all about Jasper, from the day we met last New Year's Eve to last night's Halloween fiasco. Somewhere in the middle, my dad returns with a glass of water, sets it down, then excuses himself to go watch sports or something. Outpourings of emotion just aren't his thing.

"Oh, sweetie," my mom says when I finish telling my tale. "Come into the kitchen with me. I'm going to heat you up some of my pumpkin soup. I made it last night. I got the recipe from *Martha Stewart Living*. You'll swear there's cream in it, but it's really just potatoes, pumpkin puree . . ."

"Mom," I say. "I'm sorry, but I really don't want to hear the recipe right now."

"No, you're right. Sorry."

We move into the kitchen, and my mom heats me up a bowl of soup and places it in front of me. I inhale deeply—pumpkin, chicken stock, cinnamon, nutmeg. It smells just like childhood. "Listen, your dad and I went through a lot of ups and downs before we got together for good."

"But you were high school sweethearts," I say.

"I know. But your dad got drafted, and then he was in Vietnam for a year, and I was so scared and lonely." Boy, talking to your parents really has a way of putting things in perspective. "Your father wrote to me every week, but we still went through a lot after he got home. The point is, just because things didn't go so well last night doesn't mean you and Jasper aren't going to end up together. If it's meant to be, it's meant to be."

"I don't know if I believe that anymore," I say. "I mean, look at me and Jay. I thought we'd be together forever, and that certainly didn't happen."

"But, dear, you and Jay got married for the wrong reasons. He needed some stability in his life, and you wanted to be able to give it to him."

"But that wasn't why I married him."

"No?"

"Well . . . I don't know. We were good friends, and then . . . his father got sick. And he wanted to start a family. He needed me so much." My mother manages a few seconds of silence so the truth can sink in. "Oh my God. Mom, you're right. I married him because he needed me. What the hell is wrong with me?"

"Nothing's wrong with you," my mother says. "Lots of women fall for it. We grow up feeling like our only purpose in life is to nurture others, so much so that we forget what we want, forget what makes us happy."

"But it wasn't like that for you and Dad, was it?" I say in a whisper.

"No. But it almost was for me and Ron."

"Who's Ron?" I say, and my mother puts a finger up to her lips and goes over to shut the door to the den.

"Sorry, dear," she says. "The game's too loud." Then she sits across from me and places her hands on the table. I take a sip of my soup—

it is ridiculously good. "I met Ron Samuels while I was doing my teaching internship. He was an algebra teacher. Very tall and intellectual. Truly a nice man. Of course, we had no sexual chemistry whatsoever . . ."

"Mom, please."

"Oh, that's right. You can't possibly imagine your mother being some cute young thing, walking the hallways in miniskirts and go-go boots, but I assure you, I was quite something back then."

"Okay, okay," I say. "Get on with the story."

"We used to eat lunch together, and at first, he was very shy and sweet. I used to tell him about your dad being away, about how scared I was. Ron was very reassuring. He'd tell me not to worry, and we'd talk about other things to get my mind off Jim. Eventually, he asked me to go to the opera with him. I'd never been to an opera, so of course I was excited. He promised me we'd go as friends, but when he picked me up, he was wearing a tuxedo and had a big bouquet of flowers—tacky now that I think about it. Pink carnations, of all things."

"So, he was putting the moves on you?"

"Oh, I suppose. In his own way. To be honest, he didn't even try to kiss me, which was a little annoying at the time. But he looked handsome, and I was charmed. But once we got to the opera, all I could do was think about your father over there in the jungle, sleeping in the rain, while here I was sitting on velvet seats eating chocolate-covered almonds and listening to *Tosca*."

"So, what happened?"

"You'll never believe it. At the end of the evening, that crazy man got down on one knee on my front porch and asked me to marry him."

"What?"

"I know. I was in shock. Of course, I said no. But when I got home that evening, I began to think about it. Here was this very kind and decent man—a little lonely, of course—but someone who'd provide well for me. I imagined what our life would be like. A quaint colonial on a tree-lined street, quiet nights spent at home doing the crossword together, children who would be a little homely but brilliant."

"Mom, I can't believe you even considered marrying him."

"Well, he was there, in the flesh, while your father . . . well, I didn't even know if he'd be coming back in one piece. Or if he would have fallen in love with some beautiful Asian woman. You hear of these things happening." Her voice trails off as her eyes drift into the past.

"So?"

"So what?"

"So, what happened?"

"Well, the next Monday, I gave him a lovely card thanking him for the evening, but telling him I couldn't see him anymore."

"How did he take it?"

"Oh, he was a class act. Very understanding."

"And that was that?"

"End of story."

"Does Dad know?"

"Of course. He just doesn't like to talk about it. Doesn't like to consider how close he came to getting a Dear John letter."

I sit there, staring down into my now empty bowl of soup, contemplating all she's just told me, seeing my mother in a bit of a different light. "Do you have any regrets?" I finally ask.

"God, no. Jim and I were meant to be together. Sure, we've had our problems, and we went through some tough financial patches after he got back. But I always knew I'd made the right decision."

I sigh, relieved. I was worried the story was going to end a different way, with my mother lamenting Ron Samuels as "the one who got away," wishing she had lived some other life in which Nick and I had never been born.

"Oh, speaking of your father, the dance competition is this weekend. I think we're primed to beat Marcia and Ted Fielding. You have to see how far we've come. Jim!"

My mother opens the door to the den, and my father looks up distractedly. "Where's the fire?"

"Come on, I want to show Noelle our routine."

"Now?"

"Sure," she says.

"But the game. It's the fourth quarter."

"Oh, your game's not going anywhere. Let's show Noelle the salsa."

Reluctantly, my dad gets up from the couch. Then he looks at me and says with a smirk, "Usually I need a drink to do this." I smile and follow them out to the living room, where my mother puts a record on the record player.

She walks up to my father, and he extends his hand, then they embrace in a rather stilted way, heads facing opposite directions, and wait for the music to begin.

When it does, I am flabbergasted. They're actually good! My father's leg goes forward, my mother's backward, then they change direction, back up from one another, shimmy around a bit, and come back together. It all looks a little silly because my father's wearing jeans and a flannel shirt, and my mother's in her cleaning clothes, but still, they've got the moves down, and it's more than apparent that they're having fun and that they really love each other.

When I drive home that afternoon, my faith in relationships is somewhat renewed. The soup was great, but there's nothing quite as soothing to the soul as the sight of your parents dancing together after thirty years of marriage.

November

✧

The first weekend in November, Nick and I go to the Guilford Amateur Ballroom Dancing Championships and watch my parents salsa their way to second prize. It turns out they were no match for Marcia and Ted Fielding after all.

After the awards ceremony, we all plan to meet at a local restaurant to celebrate. The restaurant is in a two-hundred-year-old building that the owners claim is haunted, adding a pleasantly creepy post-Halloween vibe to our evening.

My parents are late in arriving, no doubt congratulating their competitors, gossiping with friends, schmoozing with the judges for next year. Nick and I take a seat by the fireplace at the old stone bar and order a couple of beers.

"So, what did you think of Mom and Dad salsa dancing? Pretty weird, huh?" Nick says.

"I don't know. I thought they looked great."

"So did I, but it's still weird. They're in their sixties, you know?"

"Well, I'd rather see them salsa dancing than watching *Lawrence Welk* and playing bingo."

"Good point."

He takes a handful of the bar snacks sitting in a bowl next to him and shuffles them around in his palm before tossing them into his mouth. "Why do guys always do that?" I say.

"What?"

"That bar snack thing," I say, demonstrating for him.

"I don't know. Too much television?"

"Probably."

"This feels strange, sitting at a bar drinking beer and eating snack mix. I haven't been inside a bar in months."

"I guess Miranda's been keeping you busy?"

"Yeah, but it's great. I never thought I'd like fatherhood. But I'm loving it. I mean, don't get me wrong. I'd love to be able to get out one night a week and sling back a few beers with the guys, play some pool, but I don't really miss it that much. Dana and I are getting along really well now. The other night she said she was proud of me for stepping up my game. That's better than going out with my friends and having them tell me I'm whipped. Who cares if I am? I'm happy."

I smile at him, take a sip of my beer to hide my envy. I don't begrudge him his contentment; I just wonder what it takes to get there.

"Hey, what ever happened with that guy?" he says. I play dumb and open my eyes wide like I don't know who he's talking about. "You know, the musician? The one you thought you blew it with."

"Yeah, him," I say. "I did blow it."

"You feel like talking? I mean, I am in a successful relationship now. I could share some of the wisdom I've acquired."

"Ha-ha," I say. "I don't think even your wisdom can help me. But thanks for trying."

"Did you ever tell him you were crazy for considering adopting Jay's baby?"

"Actually, I did."

"And what happened?"

"What happened was he got really angry with me and told me I had too much baggage."

"So then what?" Nick says, motioning to the bartender to get us two more beers.

"Then nothing," I say.

"So you're just giving up because he told you you had baggage? Hell, everyone has baggage. Maybe he was just hurt. His pride needs a little soothing."

"I don't know, Nick."

"In my experience, guys are big babies. Maybe he just wants you to make the next move."

"But I did make a move. I was the one who went to see him. I tried, and it didn't work."

"Dude, try a little harder. You've been walking around for the past few months like Sulky McGrumbles, and it's really depressing."

I turn to him and burst out laughing. "Sulky McGrumbles?"

His face turns red. "That's what Dana calls me when I'm being miserable." He gives me a goofy smile. "Seriously, call the guy! Don't just accept what he told you. I'll bet you anything he wants to talk to you."

"Mom and Dad are here," I say.

"Translation: shut up?"

"Exactly."

Mom and Dad join us at the bar for a drink, then we have a lovely formal dinner in the restaurant. But I don't even taste my food because all I can think about is Jasper.

When I get home that night, I do a most cowardly thing. I e-mail him.

That's right. I e-mail Jasper to ask him if he'd be willing to meet me for coffee sometime. I realize this is just about the lamest excuse for a reconciliation gesture possible, but it's all I'm capable of at the moment. Then for four days I get no sleep and get no work done because my every waking moment is spent checking my inbox for a reply.

Finally, the following Thursday, I receive this message:

From: jfox11@comcast.net
To: nryan@yahoo.com
Subject: Meeting

Hi, Noelle,

I was surprised to get your e-mail, but I do think we should talk. I'm free Friday after work. Can you meet me at the Daily Grind around 6? Let me know.

—J

That's it? This is all the reply I am to expect? How icy. How withholding. This man is obviously not in touch with his emotions. I am almost tempted to write back and tell him to forget it, the cold bastard. Maybe he just wants another opportunity to chew me out. Or maybe he really does want us to talk.

Hoping it's the latter, I hit reply and type:

See you @ 6.

Now I'm locked in. It's a date. With destiny or disaster, I have no idea.

❧

When Friday arrives, I am a wreck. This time, I drive up to Providence rather than bike, as I'm fairly sure sweat will not help my cause. I find parking on a side street and walk three blocks to the café. It's windy and cold, and I'm feeling a major crisis of confidence. How can I face him? What will I do if he rejects me again?

When I walk into the shop, I see Jasper sitting at a table toward the back. He's staring out the window with both hands around his coffee cup, holding on for dear life, it seems. Maybe he's nervous, too.

I shake my head to banish the cobwebs from my brain, take off my gloves, and walk back toward the table. "Hi, Jasper," I say, quietly.

"Noelle." He does that endearing half stand some men still do when a woman enters the room, and I take a seat across from him.

When I look into his eyes, all the fear and resentment and anger melt away, and all I want to do is hug him.

"Do you want something?" he says. "Coffee? Tea?" I am waiting for the end of the punch line. "Me?" he might say, and we'd both start laughing, then fall into each other's arms. But instead, silence. Crickets chirping.

"I'm glad you e-mailed," he says, finally.

"You are?" I sigh. "I didn't think you ever wanted to talk to me again."

"I was just really angry the last time I saw you," he says, looking down at the table, moving a sugar packet around with his finger.

"Yes, that was obvious. I'm so sorry about everything. I really acted like an idiot."

"Agreed."

"Thanks a lot."

He smiles a little, and I begin to feel a subtle shift in the wind. A pinprick of hope. "Well, I wasn't ready to forgive you yet," he says.

"Are you now?"

"I don't know. I might be. But I'm still not sure you're ready. I'm not even sure if you're over your ex-husband yet. That's what worries me most."

I put my hands on the table, hoping he'll grab them. He doesn't. It's already grown dark outside, and for some reason, the darkness makes me bolder. I feel like I have to tell him everything and quickly, or I'll lose my nerve.

"Jasper, I assure you, I am over Jay. But there's something I didn't tell you at the bar that night. Something that I think might help explain things."

And then, he does place his hands over mine, and for the first time, I feel secure enough to tell Jasper the truth. So I do. I tell him the whole story about Jay and me, about my infertility, about thinking Jay might have been my last chance in the world to have a child.

I explain why I didn't tell him sooner. Because I was terrified he wouldn't want me anymore once he knew the truth.

When I finish speaking, Jasper looks at me with the most honest and sincere expression. "Noelle," he says, "that doesn't matter to me at all."

"It doesn't?"

"No." He puts his coffee cup down and stands up, walks over to my chair. "Come here," he says. The two best words I've heard in a long time. I stand up and lean into his chest, and his arms wrap around me and pull me closer. I put my arms around his waist and rest my head against his chest, inhaling the scent of laundry detergent in his T-shirt. When we pull away, we look at each other tentatively.

"So, what now?" he says.

"I don't know."

"Do you want to get out of here? Go for a walk or something?"

"Jasper, it's like, thirty-five degrees out."

"I know. Don't you ever do anything dangerous?"

"You know I don't," I say, smiling.

"Well, now's your big chance to live dangerously."

The two of us set outside and head down to Providence's waterfront. It is bitterly cold, but the wind has died down. The sky has a pink tinge to it, and the air has that crispness it gets right before it snows.

"It smells like snow," I say.

"Smells like snow?"

"Yeah," I say, laughing. "Don't you know what I mean?"

"No. What does snow smell like?"

"I don't know how to explain it. Kind of fresh and fizzy."

"Like champagne?"

"No, not really. Sharper than that."

"What are you, part bloodhound or something?"

I look falsely offended. "No, I am not part dog. But when you've lived in New England your whole life, you get to know when it's going to snow from the smell in the air."

"I guess I'm still a Southern boy at heart."

"Southern gentleman," I correct him.

We continue walking along the river, scanning the horizon for lights, wondering what crazy fools would be out on a boat on a night like this. Then again, we are the only two people standing out at the pier. It seems the entire world has gone inside for the night. But we stand there shivering while he catches me up on Cassie and his job, and I catch him up on Margaret and the changes at the shelter. He pauses for a moment at the railing, then turns toward me.

"What made you finally get in touch with me, even if it was by the most impersonal of methods?" he says.

I open my eyes indignantly. "At least I contacted you. But if you want to know the truth, it was my brother's idea. He told me I should stop being so stubborn and try a little harder with you."

"Well done, Nick," he says. "If he hadn't told you to, would you have ever gotten around to it?"

"I think so. It's not like you weren't on my mind all the time, I just couldn't bring myself to call you. I couldn't face the possibility that you might hate me."

"Noelle," he says, grabbing my hands in his. "Did you really think I could hate you?"

"I don't know," I say. "What I did to you wasn't fair. I'm just glad that you know the whole story now and understand why I did what I did." He looks so sweet and sexy standing above me, his hair slightly tousled from the damp breeze. Meanwhile, my nose feels red and numb, and I have no idea whether snot is dripping down my face.

"There it is again," I say, using the opportunity to grab a tissue from my coat pocket, just in case.

"What?" he says, looking out toward the water.

"The smell of snow. I'm going to teach you what snow smells like. I want you to inhale deeply." Even though I know he doesn't believe me, he's being a good sport, making a big show of inhaling the frigid air. "Tell me what you smell."

"Hmm . . ." he says, pausing for effect. "I actually do smell something. It's almost . . . electric. Like charged ions or something."

"Yes, that's what I was trying to describe. It smells like fission."

He looks at me wiping my nose with a tissue, and I want to die. If I were a supermodel, I could be out here in a bikini, and the cold wouldn't faze me. I probably wouldn't even have goose bumps.

"You're cold," he says. "Let's go back to my place."

"Your place?" Gulp. My insides flutter as if I'm thirteen again, and the cutest boy in school has just asked me to dance.

He puts an arm around me, and we walk sixteen blocks to his house, barely speaking a word. There's so much more we could say, and yet that's just it. There's too much. His arm stays wrapped around me the entire time, protecting me from the cold, but I feel anything but cold right now.

When we finally arrive at his apartment, I follow him up the stairs to the second floor, and he opens the door. I think back to my ridiculous fantasy of attacking him, Harlequin romance–style.

The boldness of it compared to my current state of paralyzing panic almost makes me laugh.

He takes off his coat and helps me with mine, then stands there holding both our coats. There is a moment of unbearable tension.

"Jasper . . ." I say. But I have no idea what I mean to tell him.

He drops his hands to my waist, squeezing almost as if to pick me up. "Noelle."

And there in that moment, hearing him say my name, I finally breathe. And listen to what my heart and body are telling me to do.

I don't exactly slam him against the door like I'd imagined, but I do take the coats from him and toss them over a chair with more force than is warranted. I move toward him and place my hand on his face.

He leans down, his hair grazing my cheek, and kisses my neck, gently at first, then more insistent. I am a puddle of sensation. When I finally regain some semblance of control, I reach up, my arms curling around his neck and shoulders, my hands in his hair, the feel of his scalp under my fingertips.

I kiss his neck, taste his skin. He grabs my face in his hands, his tongue parts my lips, and then he is kissing me with such intensity I can feel it in my toes.

His hands move down my shoulders onto my back, tugging at my shirt, clutching my waist, pulling me toward him, and all I can do is let go. Finally, let go.

Lying in his bed later, I am weightless. Buoyant. A confection. Warm and soft and light as spun sugar. The moon is shining through the window, and Jasper's face is luminescent. Right now, he is the most gorgeous human being on the face of this planet, and he's lying here with me, his lanky leg over mine, his heartbeat close enough to hear, warm and true.

When I wake the next morning, I smell coffee brewing, strong dark coffee, and hear the comforting sounds of a kitchen coming to life—a refrigerator being opened and shut, fat sizzling in a pan, a whisk against the side of a glass bowl. Jasper is making me breakfast. I am so giddy I pull the sheets up over my head and kick my legs up and down.

A few seconds later, Jasper pokes his head into the room. "Everything okay in here?"

Yup. Perfect.

I get up, brush my teeth, and throw on one of Jasper's shirts. I have always wanted to do this, but Jay never let me. He said his shirts were too nice to turn into pajamas.

With a slight pang of anxiety, I realize I have to call Margaret to ask her to let Zeke out this morning.

"Who's this?" she says.

"You know who it is."

"No, this couldn't possibly be Noelle. This person sounds way too happy."

"Margaret, can you stop gloating for two seconds so I can ask you a question?"

"Already taken care of."

"What?" I say.

"Zeke. I let him sleep with me last night," she says.

"You shameless hussy," I say.

"Look who's talking. Anyway, I had an idea Zeke might be feeling a little abandoned last night."

"How did you know?"

"Mother's intuition," she says. "Gotta run. I'll see you when I see you." Click. Never one for the mushy stuff, that Margaret.

When I walk out into Jasper's apartment, I can honestly say I didn't notice much about the decor and furnishings last night. A few of the side windows have stained-glass panels in them, so the sun streams through them, refracting the light into brightly colored mosaics on the floor. Green, leafy plants hang healthy and profuse in front of the bay window, and splashy paintings—modern but not too modern—hang from the walls. One is of a Paris café, but it's not tacky or cliché. It is quirky and vibrant and looks like it was chosen with care from a gallery a block away from the café itself. It makes me want to go there, sit in that very square, putting marmalade on a flaky croissant and sighing over the richness of coffee.

Another painting is of two Cubist lovers dancing under a bridge, the woman's head tilted back, her hair cascading in curls that echo the curves of the trees in the background. Above the small dining table is a collage of photographs: one showing a group of smiling children on a beach; one of a colorful market stall in perhaps some Indian city; one of the spire of a white temple, a miniature Taj Mahal; and the last a photograph of a perfect yellow flower.

"Good morning," Jasper says, coming out of the kitchen with two mugs of coffee, kissing me softly on the forehead.

"Morning," I say, suddenly a little shy. Everything about this day feels raw and tender—the quality of the sunlight, the sound of his voice. "Where is this?" I say, pointing to the photo of the flower.

"India. I'd love to take you there someday."

"If you can ever get me to leave Rhode Island, right?"

"I'll find a way," he says with a sexy smile, and I have a feeling he's right.

"Your apartment is beautiful," I say. "So well decorated and . . . professional."

"What were you expecting? A bachelor pad with bean-bag chairs and Star Wars posters?"

"Kind of," I say, embarrassed.

"Noelle, you make some pretty strange assumptions about people."

"I know. It's a character flaw. I'm working on it. Rent must be pretty steep for such a nice place, though."

"Not for me," he says, going back into the kitchen to check on our food. I follow him in.

"What do you mean, not for you?"

"I own the place."

"What do you mean?"

"Own, as in pay a monthly mortgage? Rent out the other units?"

"You own this place?"

"Yeah, I thought you knew that," he says, pouring us both a cup of coffee.

"No. I definitely did not know that."

"I bought it a few years ago when the market was good. I'd been saving up for a while. And it wasn't this nice when I bought it. I've done a lot of renovations."

"But still, how did you afford it? This place is enormous."

He sets out two plates and begins serving the eggs. "Noelle, I own my own company," he says, matter-of-factly.

"OpticGate? OpticGate's yours?"

"Yeah. Where have you been?" he says.

"Jasper, I swear you never told me that."

255

"Hmm . . . must have slipped my mind," he says. "When I got the patent on the voice-recognition software, I made a lot of money."

"Oh," I say. It's all I can say.

"You seem sort of freaked out by this."

"No, no. It's just unexpected, is all." I laugh. "See, I had this idea about you."

"You thought I was a bum, like your brother. Because I played in a band."

"Well, yeah. At first. But then later I just thought you were kind of . . . a wanderer, you know? Like Indiana Jones or something. I thought you might not be the safest bet for a stable relationship."

"Is that what you thought? That I was going to run off on you?"

"I don't know," I say, embarrassed. "Jay did. You did from your family. You're in a band called the Nomads. I had reasons for thinking you might."

"Noelle. I love to travel. And yes, it took me a while to settle down and figure out what I wanted. But I don't care where I am as long as I'm happy. And right now, I'm really, really happy."

And, I realize, so am I.

Even when I leave his apartment later that day and find a parking ticket on my windshield, I am still smiling. It's the best forty dollars I ever spent.

When I pull open the shades of the cottage on Thanksgiving morning, the day looks sunny, clear, and cold. The floor feels like an ice-skating rink under the soles of my feet. I take a longer shower than usual, lingering under the spray of hot water and steam, then quickly get dressed in my favorite faded jeans, a cozy sweater, and brown leather boots lined with fleece—perfect attire for cooking, eating, watching football.

I call home, wondering if my mother's finally ready to speak to me again after what will hereafter be referred to as the "Thanksgiving Betrayal." My father answers the phone.

"Is she still angry?" I ask him.

"Let me see. Claire, are you still angry at Noelle?" he shouts.

"Is that Noelle? Let me talk to her," I hear my mother say in the background, and a second later, she is on the phone, my father a distant memory. I don't think my father and I have ever had a phone conversation that's lasted over three sentences.

"Mom, I didn't even get to wish Dad a happy Thanksgiving."

"Oh, you actually care about your parents now?" she says dramatically.

"Mom, I've explained it to you a hundred times."

"You could have come here for dinner."

"I know," I say, "but Margaret really wanted to have Thanksgiving here at her house while she's still able to cook. She doesn't know what her condition's going to be like next year."

"Well, why couldn't she make dinner for her own son? Why my daughter?"

"Mom, Jay's spending Thanksgiving with Taj's family in Atlanta."

"He always has some excuse, doesn't he?"

"What do you mean?"

"It just seems like Jay never comes home anymore, and you end up being Margaret's surrogate child. Don't get me wrong, I think it's very charitable of you, but it'd be nice if you were as thoughtful about your own mother."

"Mom, you're being ridiculous," I say, trying very hard to maintain my cool in the face of her histrionics. "You know I love you and Dad and Nick. But I'm living here now, and I promised Margaret I'd spend Thanksgiving with her."

"Well, you'd better come here for Christmas," she says.

"You know I will. And if all goes well, I might be bringing someone with me."

"Who?" she says. "Not another dog."

"No," I say.

"Noelle, honey, what are you talking about?"

"Never mind, Mom," I say. I don't want to jinx it. "I've got to go. I'm making some side dishes."

"Oh, sweetheart, are you making stuffing?" she says. "Don't forget to use more butter than you think, okay?"

"Okay, Mom."

"Sage and celery are most important."

"Okay, Mom."

"And I hope you're not using cranberry from a can."

"I like cranberry from the can," I say. "That's what we always had as kids."

"Well, that's when I didn't know any better. Martha Stewart has this wonderful recipe for cranberry and orange compote . . ."

"Mom, I gotta go. I love you."

"I love you, too, sweetheart," she says, and I think she's crying a little. I hang up reluctantly, staring at the phone.

Jasper's sister, Cassie, is visiting, and Margaret has invited us all to dinner. In fact, they are both staying here for the night so no one has to drive home after an afternoon of eating and drinking to excess. I'm excited to meet Cassie but a bit nervous, too. We're having this iconic holiday meal with a makeshift family, and I'm not sure how everyone is going to get along.

I pack up some shopping bags with all my ingredients, and then Zeke and I head up to the house. Margaret is already in the kitchen hovering over the bird, tenting the tinfoil around it. Zeke sidles up next to her, knowing an easy mark when he sees one, and I have to warn her not to feed him anything strange today. I have become a bit overly cautious about his diet since his surgery.

"Margaret, it smells wonderful."

"It does, doesn't it?" she says. She's not wearing her orthopedic shoes but is in her stocking feet. She has tied a pale yellow apron over her plum-colored silk pantsuit, and her hair is elegantly pinned up like a ballerina's. Without thinking, I give her a kiss on the cheek. She smiles, embarrassed, then changes the subject. "When are they getting here?" she asks.

"Soon," I say. "Apparently, Cassie's a big football fan."

"Really? Even though she can't see the game?"

"Jasper says she likes listening to the commentators argue and yell. So, what can I do?" I ask.

"Why don't you set the table? The good china's in the sideboard, and the crystal's in the cabinet." I go out to the dining room and am almost finished setting the table when the doorbell rings.

"I'll get it," I shout, but Margaret comes out of the kitchen, still the perfect host. Like Katharine Hepburn in *Guess Who's Coming to Dinner*. She uses a cane now, but it doesn't seem to bother her. She opens the front door, and there is a cacophony of noise in the foyer—the dog barking, boots squeaking, luggage being thrown into corners, people talking over one another, making introductions. I like Cassie immediately. She is wearing large Audrey Hepburn sunglasses that suit her pixie face. The minute her hands find Zeke's head, she leans her cane against the wall and bends down to give him a hearty scratch behind the ears.

"Hello, there. Who are you?" she says.

"This is Zeke."

"He's so big."

"But gentle," Jasper says. "A real sweetheart."

"I hear you like football," Margaret says.

"I love it."

"Jasper, if you'd be so kind, maybe you could move the television into the kitchen? That way we can listen to the game while we cook."

"Sounds great," Cassie says. Jasper follows Margaret into the living room, and I take Cassie's arm and lead her into the kitchen to get her a drink.

"What are you serving?" she says, taking a stool by the island.

"Margaret's got a pretty well-stocked bar. I imagine you could have whatever you want," I say. "Now whether or not I know how to make it is another story."

"Oh, that's okay. I'm an excellent bartender," she says.

"Really?"

"Oh yeah. I actually tended bar for a few years after college."

"If you don't mind me asking, how did you know what was what?"

"The owners and I had a system. Always kept things in the same spot, and Jasper made me a Braille label maker."

Jasper comes into the kitchen, wheeling the television in on a cart, and smiles at me. Margaret resumes her place at the oven and begins making conversation. I envy her generation's ability to multitask, to stick a hand in a turkey's insides while asking how someone's flight was.

"So, what do you do?" she asks Cassie.

"I'm an air traffic controller," Cassie says.

Margaret looks at me quizzically, and Jasper laughs. "Cassie, they don't know your sense of humor yet."

"Sorry," she says. "I'm back in school to get certified to teach science. I want to teach at the institute where I went to school. But I want to let the kids do real science labs with chemicals and do dissections and go on field trips to museums and nature centers. Being blind has changed quite a bit since the days of Helen Keller."

"Thanks to people like your brother," Margaret says. "Jasper, Noelle tells me you work for a company that makes products for the blind."

"Actually," I say, "he owns the company."

"Ohhh," Margaret says, looking straight at me, her eyebrows about a mile above her eyes.

"I was inspired by Cassie," Jasper says.

"Don't be so modest," Cassie says. "Before OpticGate, I wouldn't have been able to take a lot of the classes I've taken. Most regular universities still don't have accommodations for the blind. I remember having to rely on my roommate to read me these long lab reports before they were available in Braille. And doing assignments on the Internet before they had voice translation and Braille keyboards was a nightmare."

While Cassie is telling us this story, she is mixing us a pitcher of Manhattans. I am impressed, and I think Margaret is, too. I bring over some glasses and set them down in front of her.

"I'm still not the greatest at pouring," she says, laughing.

"No problem," I say, pouring the drinks for all of us, dropping a cherry in each glass.

"To your health," Cassie says, raising her glass, and I glance over at Margaret. She winks at me, and suddenly I know the weekend is going to be just fine.

As the turkey is cooking, Margaret asks Jasper if he'd like to see the library, but I think she really just wants a chance to have him all to herself, the shameless flirt. Cassie and I stay in the kitchen to begin prepping vegetables, thickening gravies, all those things I watched my mother do a hundred times but that now seem quite daunting. While I'm chopping celery, Cassie turns to me and asks, point-blank: "So, tell me. What are your intentions with my brother?" I freeze for a moment, my knife poised in the air. But then Cassie laughs, a charmingly uninhibited laugh. "Of course, I'm joking," she says. "But he is my big brother, and I do have quite a soft spot for him. And I can tell he's smitten."

"Really?"

"Really?" She imitates my inflection. "Come on, Noelle. I'm the blind one here."

"How do you know?" I say.

"I'm his sister. And Jasper's not an overly effusive guy. So when he gushes on and on about you for half an hour on the phone, I know something's up."

"I really like him, too."

"I'm glad he's not in the room right now. He might puke."

"Why?" I say, laughing.

"You *like* him? The boy's head over heels about you, and you say you *like* him?"

"Listen," I say, heading to the refrigerator to find something to do. Even though her eyes are covered, I feel like this girl can see right through me. "I don't know if he told you the whole story about me, but I've had a difficult year. When I met Jasper, I was just getting over a divorce."

"Yes, he told me. A divorce from a gay guy. No offense, but I don't see the reason for the three-year mourning period."

"Oh my God," I say.

"You're blushing, aren't you?"

"No," I lie. "It's just that you know everything."

"Not everything," she says. "But enough to know he loves you."

"He does not. I mean, I know he likes me a lot. He's been so good to me. Did he tell you about the fund-raiser for my dog shelter?"

"Ad nauseam."

"Who else would offer to help a virtual stranger like that?"

"I don't think he thought of you as a virtual stranger. He was already torturing me with e-mails about you, way back then."

"He was? I just thought he liked dogs."

"Noelle, he does like dogs, but even he doesn't like dogs enough to make a forty-thousand-dollar donation to a charity he just heard about."

"What?" I say, spinning around with the potato masher in my hands.

"The donation. To the shelter. Surely you knew that was Jasper."

"No, I didn't," I say.

"Jasper told me you were smart. Noelle, his company is making so much money these days that he gives a lot to charity. This year, he chose your charity. Not the March of Dimes, not the humanitarian crisis in Darfur. Your dog shelter."

"Oh my God," I say.

"Yes, oh my freakin' God."

Jasper and Margaret come back into the kitchen laughing, and Cassie puts a finger up to her lips. I look at Jasper, smiling so warmly at Margaret, completely unaware of how wonderful he is.

During dinner, I tell everyone about the tradition we have in my family of going around the table and saying what we're thankful for. It's kind of corny, but even with all the overbearing nonsense my family can dish out, I sort of miss them right now. This is my way of paying tribute to them.

"I'll start," I say. "I'm thankful to both Jasper and Cassie for helping me find the courage to start a guide dog training program at SASH. I don't think I would have been able to continue working there without a new project to look forward to. And I'm thankful to Margaret for inviting me into her home and into her life."

Margaret looks uncharacteristically emotional, almost like she's shaking tears away. "Jasper, you're next," she says.

"Me?" Jasper says. "Okay, well, I'm thankful that Margaret has been so kind as to invite us to her house for an amazing dinner, and I'm thankful that Cassie and I get to spend our holiday with two people who feel more like family than our own family ever did."

Cassie nods her head at me, then raises her drink. "And I am thankful that I will no longer have to listen to my brother complaining about this girl named Noelle who refuses to call him back. And I'm thankful to have my brother in my life, the only man in my life right now regrettably. But if you're only going to have one, let it be him."

"Hear, hear," says Margaret, smiling at me.

"Margaret, you're last but not least," Cassie says.

Margaret grabs her drink and sighs. "It's so strange. I've spent most of this year hating my life. And I can't say I've thanked many people these past few months. But I really should have. I need to thank Noelle for coming into my home and taking care of me, even when she knew how awful I could be. And I want to thank you all for being here right now, despite being young and having lives of your own. Thank you so much for sharing this day with me. It means a lot." She stops talking as if she can't go on, but it seems there's a lot more she wishes she could say. Then she adds, almost as an afterthought, "Amen."

And for some reason, this seems wonderfully funny and appropriate, and we all begin laughing, released by this final affirmation of life. Amen. Amen. Amen.

After dinner, Margaret and I clean up the dishes while Jasper goes upstairs to help Cassie get situated in the guest room. "Noelle, honey," she says to me, "he is so adorable."

"I know."

"I didn't get to know him on the Fourth of July. He was . . . not really himself."

"I know."

"But he's so nice."

"I know."

"And helpful in the kitchen."

"I know."

"And did I mention how cute he is?"

"Margaret, what are you trying to do, give me a heart attack right here? I know. He's perfect."

"No, I'm sure he's not perfect. But you have as long as you want to find out all his flaws. I have a feeling this one's going to stick around."

When Jasper comes back downstairs, he actually kisses Margaret good night on the cheek. Later we walk down from the house to the cottage, stumbling in the dark over divots and shrubbery, Zeke racing ahead of us in the night. The sky is lit with stars, the moon nowhere to be found. We stand outside in the cold night air, shivering, not wanting to go inside just yet.

"Cassie's great," I say.

"She is. So is Margaret. I wish I had a mother like that."

"She's pretty amazing. She was a bit mushy tonight. For Margaret, anyway."

"Well, she realizes she's got a good thing in you."

"I don't know if that's it."

Jasper turns to me and pulls me into his arms. His clothes smell warm and spicy, like baked apples and pumpkin pie. "Come on, you do so much for her. That's one of the things I love about you. Your selflessness. You give so much."

"No more than usual," I say.

"Noelle," he says, "believe me. A lot more than usual. Margaret's really lucky her son married you."

"Yeah, well, aren't we all so fortunate that I came into Jay's life?" I say, not even attempting to conceal my sarcasm.

"Yes, actually," he says. "Even me. Just think if you'd married the perfect man—good-looking, successful, *and* heterosexual. I'd be out of luck."

I laugh. "So you're saying it's a good thing I married Jay?"

"Well, good for me, and for Margaret, and for Jay. You've gone way beyond what any ex-wife would do for her mother-in-law."

"Well, that's because Jay and I are still friends. We take care of each other."

"I don't want to argue with you tonight, Noelle," he says, stroking my cheek and moving a stray wisp of hair out of my face. "It's been too perfect a day. I just feel . . . frustrated. I think the situation ends up benefiting him more than you."

"I'm fine," I say. "Look, I've got this great little cottage, I've got my job, I've got you . . ."

"Yes, you've got me," he says, hugging me tightly. "And a job that leaves you so little time to see me. Plus the responsibilities of taking care of Margaret all on your own."

"I don't mind," I say, reverting into my Saint Noelle mode. "She's helped me a lot, too."

"I know. It just bothers me that Jay's off cavorting around with his boyfriend, living his life clear and free and easy."

"He lives in Atlanta. I don't expect him to come all the way up here every week," I say, for some reason still feeling a need to defend Jay.

"No, not every week," he says, "but every month maybe? He chose to move to Atlanta and to stay down there even after his mother got sick. And you, someone who doesn't owe Jay anything . . . I'm sorry. It's not my place to say."

"I don't want you to feel that way," I say. "It is your place to say. We're involved now, and I care what you think. I want your opinion."

He pulls away and looks at me. "I just feel he abandoned you."

"He had reason."

"No," he says. "He had reason not to marry you in the first place, but he did for his own selfish motives. And I think that's why you were so scared to get involved with me. Why you always thought I was going to run off on you. Jay never should have married you in the first place. He knew he couldn't ever love you. But I can. And I do. I love you, Noelle. And I want you to be happy."

My breath has just stopped, but my heart is still clanging away like one of those mechanical cymbal-clapping monkeys.

He loves me. He wants me to be happy. But let's go back to that first one. He loves me.

I feel as if I have to say something, but I don't just want to repeat the words back to him. I don't want it to seem like an automatic response. So instead of saying anything, I look up and kiss him softly, tenderly this time.

Moments later, we stumble into the cottage, flooded with emotion and relief, and fall asleep in each other's arms with Zeke lying comfortably at the foot of the bed. Snoring loudly.

The next day after we have a big meal of leftovers and make our good-byes, Cassie and Jasper leave and I retreat to my little cottage in the woods. I notice that Jasper refilled my bird feeder while he was packing his things—there are six birds all perched along its ledges sharing a meal together.

Last night there would have been six of us at the dinner table, if only Jay and Taj had been able to make it home. Margaret didn't complain about anything, but I know it bothered her far more than she let on. While my mother drives me crazy, she's always been able to talk to me, to let me know when something's bothering her. Margaret isn't able to do that with Jay. I'm not sure why.

So I decide to do it for her.

I call Jay. And I tell him everything I've been thinking about since last night.

When I ask him whether he's coming home to spend Christmas with Margaret, things start to get ugly. "I have to go to my parents' for Christmas or they'll kill me," I tell him. "I've already lost about three thousand good-daughter points for spending Thanksgiving with your mom."

"I don't know if we'll be able to make it up, sweetheart," Jay says, as if I'm asking him to trek to Antarctica. He sounds very far away. "We've been looking into adopting here in the States since it looks like India's not going to happen. Taj and I have a ton of paperwork to fill out if we're going to move forward with our life together."

"Paperwork? Paperwork, Jay? Look," I tell him, "Margaret loves you, and she's not ever going to say anything to you, but I feel I have to say something for her. I want you and Taj to be happy, I really do. I want you to be able to adopt and move on with your life together, but I have a life, too. And the fact is, I need a little help here. I've been taking care of your mother for the past twelve months, and I don't mind doing it. But Margaret loves you. And aside from me, you're all she has left. So you better be here for Christmas."

"Jesus, what's gotten into you, Noelle? Have you been taking my mother's meds?"

"Don't get glib," I say. "I'm serious. This isn't fair to your mom."

"My mother's independent and tough. You said it yourself."

"She's not as tough as you think," I say. "But while we're on the subject, it's not fair to me either. I have a life, too, and I'd like to be able to live it."

There is a brief silence over the line as Jay weighs his next words, trying to decide between being snide or sincere. "Oh, all of a sudden, you have a life," he says. "What, is it that new man of yours?"

His condescending tone just about sets me over the edge. "Yes, as a matter of fact it is. We've been dating for a few months now."

"Really? Why didn't you tell me? You used to tell me everything."

"Well, you've been so busy lately," I say sarcastically. "It's hard to pin you down for even two seconds."

"Well, which one is he?" Jay asks, a teasing quality in his voice.

"There's only ever been one. Jasper. He's the musician I told you about."

"Like, a year ago?" he says, his voice a disbelieving guffaw.

"It took me a while to figure out what I wanted."

"Really?" Jay says, a hint of disappointment in his voice. "Noelle, this sounds serious. I can hear it in your voice. Something's changed."

You bet it has, I think to myself.

December

This morning Margaret wants to go to the beach. Yes, it's December and bitterly cold, but she says she doesn't care whether her legs won't cooperate or whether a blizzard is forecast to descend on our town—she wants to see the ocean.

So I help her bundle up, we get her cane and shoes, and we drive my hatchback to the point. Margaret is trying her hardest to be strong, to remain independent, but it's getting harder and harder for her to maintain this illusion.

After I help her out of the car, we trek out onto the deserted beach, and Margaret shrugs off my assisting arm, insisting on making her own way down the narrow beach to the shoreline with her cane. Actually, she looks quite beautiful, her white hair tossing back in the breeze, her elegant profile silhouetted against the wintry blue skyline. The water is the blue-green color of jewels, even under the low, slanting sun. I allow Margaret a few moments alone by the water's edge before joining her down there, staring at the ragged hem of the ocean. "You know," she says, turning toward me, pulling her hair into a knot at the back of her head. "Things are probably going to get a lot worse. I'll understand if you're not up for it."

"What are you talking about?" I say.

"The doctors say it may get ugly."

"Look, the doctors say you're going to have good months and bad months, that's the nature of the disease. But I'm going to be here to help you get through both. And so is Jasper. It's okay."

"But what if I end up in a wheelchair?"

"Then you end up in a wheelchair, and I come wheel you out onto the beach. You can pop wheelies in the sand." This gets a slight laugh out of her.

"But I'll understand if you can't do it anymore. You deserve a life of your own."

"Margaret, we've had this conversation before. My life is here, at the shelter, with Jasper, and with you."

"But maybe I should have gone into one of those . . . homes, those assisted-living places. Maybe I shouldn't have been so stubborn about keeping the house."

"If you'll remember, I was the one being stubborn. I practically ran you out of those places. That's not what you need. You need people. You need me. And I didn't want to tell you this, but since you're feeling so sorry for yourself, Jasper and I were talking, and we want to get you a dog. An assistance dog."

"What?" she says, looking at me as if I've grown an extra limb.

"I start my training in January, and I've talked to the guy who runs the East Coast facility. He says he has a dog he thinks would be perfect as my first trainee. He's a German shepherd, abused as a puppy, but apparently the sweetest, smartest dog. You'd actually be doing me a favor by letting me train him to be your guide dog," I say, trying to soften the blow to her pride. But she still looks uncertain. "These dogs can do everything. Open doors, turn on lights. Screw in lightbulbs for you, change the bed linens, make veal saltimbocca." I am trying to make her laugh again but failing miserably. "Jasper and I want to do this for you, sort of as a Christmas present. But only if you're comfortable with it." And then, to my surprise, Margaret begins to cry. "What?" I say. "What is it?"

"I don't know," she says, wiping her eyes self-consciously. "It's just that ever since I got this disease, I've felt like I've lost so many things I used to think were important. But now . . ."

"What?"

"You, and Jasper. You've been so good to me. I feel like I've been given a gift I don't deserve. I haven't been a very good person in my life. I was so selfish for so long. I never thought I'd be saying this, but I don't deserve you."

"That's ridiculous. And it's a terrible way to think," I say. "But one I happen to be in touch with."

"Yes, I know," she says, laughing through her tears. "Since when did we both become such self-hating, guilt-ridden martyrs?"

"I don't know," I say, laughing.

"God, I'm so emotional lately. I never cry. I guess I can blame it on the meds. I suppose I should just be grateful and say thank you."

"Or tell me to screw off," I say. "That's what the old Margaret would have probably said."

"True," she says, wiping her face with a sleeve. "But don't worry.

She's still around here somewhere. Waiting to strike when you least expect it."

"Good," I say. "I was beginning to worry." And I offer her my arm, which she does not reject, and the two of us walk down the beach together, two former enemies, who despite their best efforts, have ended up as friends.

Two weekends before Christmas I take Margaret shopping, and the next week she takes Jasper and me to see the Boston Pops as an early birthday present. On our way home, we stop at a tree farm to buy one of those Christmas trees that still has the root ball intact. That way we can plant it after the holiday is over. No more throwing trees to the curb after New Year's.

When we get back to the house, Jasper and I trim the tree under Margaret's supervision and listen to Christmas carols on her record player. Jasper even sings an incredibly corny version of "The First Noel," complete with his own lyrics about me.

By Christmas Eve Margaret is feeling overwhelmed from all the holiday hustle and bustle. Even though I really wanted her to meet my parents, she says she's not feeling up to coming to their place for Christmas. I feel guilty leaving her alone, especially since Jay and Taj said they won't be able to make it home until New Year's Eve.

But on Christmas morning, Jasper and I bring a few presents up to the house, make Margaret one of my famous omelets, then change back into our pajamas and head out to my parents' house for the annual holiday extravaganza. Before we are even fully through the doorway, my mother becomes a one-woman firing squad, asking Jasper at least five questions a minute, barely giving him time to formulate answers—I knew I must have gotten this trait from somewhere. My father is in a particularly convivial mood, shaking Jasper's hand with the force of a locomotive engine and pumping him for information.

I can tell what's going on here: my parents are seeing if he's husband material. This is obvious and humiliating, but Jasper doesn't seem to mind. Soon everyone begins to talk over one other, Nick asking Jasper about his band, running to get his guitar from his old room, Dana trying to calm an overly stimulated Miranda, my mother fawning all over Jasper like a 1960s stewardess.

We open presents right away, sort of as an icebreaker. Beatrix is in her glory, running around panting and wagging joyfully, trying to squirrel away a few balls of wrapping paper to play with later. Jasper loves the way she appears to be winking at everyone, like she's in on the cosmic joke of human existence.

After we open presents, we head into the dining room for brunch. As we're trying to choose seats, my father shoves me lightly in the shoulder. "Did you see your mother's theme this year?" he says.

I glance around the room searching for clues, finding things that at first seem anomalous to Christmas: Santa in stirrups and cowboy boots, cacti strung with colored lights, and most hilarious of all, a Christmas tree with the star of Texas at the top. This seems somewhat sacrilegious for my mother, but I let it slide.

"Get it?" my father says. "The lone star of Bethlehem?"

"It's a Texas Christmas," my mother shouts, coming in with a platter heaping with fried food. "I'm even serving steak and eggs with onion rings in honor of Jasper."

"Wow, thanks," Jasper says, looking flattered by this absurd display.

"Mom, Jasper may be from Texas, but he's not a cowboy, for God's sake."

"Noelle, do you think it might be possible for you to refrain from using the Lord's name in vain, especially considering what day it is?"

"Sorry," I mumble, relegated to preteen status in my home once again. Jasper looks at me and smiles, grabs my hand and squeezes. He likes my family, God bless him.

Brunch is a hilarious overture of compliments about my mother's cooking, embarrassing childhood stories meant to humiliate me, frequent rolled eyes between me and Nick, and lots of good-natured chatting between my father and Jasper.

After we finish eating, Nick leaves the room and comes back in holding a bottle of champagne. Dana pulls some plastic champagne flutes from her diaper bag and passes them around the table. Before I can even make sense of what's happening, Nick is filling our glasses.

"Mom, Dad, Noelle, Jasper. Dana and I have an announcement to make," he says. My mother looks like she's about to keel over in her chair. "We've decided to get married."

"Oh my goodness, Nicky!" my mother screeches, standing up and throwing her arms up in ecstasy. Everything Nick does tends to give her this reaction.

My father smiles softly and gives Nick one of his hand-crushing handshakes, then leans over to Dana, giving her a quick shoulder squeeze, his version of a hug. I stand up and hug them both. "Oh, sweetheart," my mother gushes, "this is the best Christmas gift ever. We're so thrilled!"

"I can't believe you said yes," my father says.

"Jim," scolds my mother. "I can't believe you just said that."

"I finally said yes because he finally got a job," Dana says, smiling. "Well, that and because I love him."

She gives my brother a look that's so private, so entirely their own, I can feel the lump rising in my throat, feel the constriction in the bridge of my nose. "Congratulations," I manage to say, squelching my tears.

"Nick, what's the job?" my father asks, cutting past the nonsense to get to the heart of the matter.

"It's with Dana's father's company. They're actually going to let me work on their website," he says. He runs into the other room and grabs his laptop, setting it up right on the dining room table between our dirty dishes. "Here, look," he says once the website loads up. "Let me show you the demo."

We all gather round the monitor, watching as white, vertical perforated stripes appear on the page and begin spinning in a blur, finally stopping to reveal a toilet paper roll with six squares hanging down. Each square contains a link to a page on the website. Jasper and I begin cracking up.

"That's hilarious," Jasper says. "Really creative."

"Well, I figured if someone has to browse the toilet paper website, they might as well have fun while they're trying to decide between single or double ply or between a plumpness factor of two or five."

"Is there really such a thing as plumpness factor?" I ask, bursting into laughter again.

"Oh, you don't know the half of it," he says. "There's a whole unknown world of toilet paper just waiting to be discovered. And

I'm the webmaster waiting to take you on that journey." Dana rolls her eyes at me, then shakes her head into Nick's shoulder with stifled laughter.

I'm glad Nick has found the humor in working a boring nine-to-five job, and more than that, I'm glad he has finally decided to grow up, even if it means the next few years of our lives will be inundated with toilet-related humor.

After champagne we settle into the living room and sit around the tree singing Christmas carols to Jasper's guitar. Even Dana, whom I had always perceived as being incredibly shy, joins in on the singing, and I find myself feeling full of holiday spirit and love for my nutty, exasperating family. I am reminded of how I felt this same time last year—alone, depressed, hopeless. What a difference a year makes if only you're willing to take some chances.

Later that afternoon, Jasper and Nick play video games in the den like eight-year-old boys while my father frolics with Miranda on the floor and Dana helps my mother and me clean up the kitchen, one of the liberated Ryan women already. When the baby starts to cry, Dana leaves us to feed her, and I am left alone with my mother, even more of an emotional basket case at Christmastime than usual.

"Can't you and Jasper stay overnight?" she asks me for the third time.

"No, Mom. I think we'll be more comfortable at home. Besides, I don't want Margaret to be alone. What with Jay being too busy to come and see his dear old mother on Christmas Day." I turn to my mother to see if I've managed to crack a smile out of her, but instead, she looks like she's about to cry. "What on earth is wrong?" I say.

"You called it home," she says, openly sobbing now.

"What are you talking about?"

"Margaret's house," she says. "You called it home."

"Well, it is where I live now," I say.

"I know, but I wanted you kids to always consider this your home," she sputters, in between sobs. "To know you could always come back here."

"We do know that, Mom."

She dries her hands on the dishrag and turns to face me, her face red and splotchy with tears. "I just love it when everyone's here, safe under one roof. I enjoy cooking for everyone and turning down your beds and even cleaning up after you. I've never minded any of it."

"I know, Mom," I say. "You were a great mom."

And this just sets her off again. "Were?" she says. "*Were?*"

"*Are* a great mom," I correct myself, laughing a little. I can't help it. "Mom, you're being ridiculous. You're still a great mom, and grand-mom."

"But I don't have a big fancy house like Margaret. I'm not rich and beautiful and tortured like she is. You're always trying to please her. But what about me? Doesn't anyone care about pleasing me?"

"Of course, Mom," I say. "But what exactly would please you?"

"I don't know," she says. "It's just so nice having you all home again, feeling needed. You never stop wanting your kids to need you."

And that's the moment when I realize where it came from. My love of hearth and home, my fixation with houses, my irrational fear of people abandoning me, as if love were encased in mortar and stone instead of hearts and minds.

"Mom, I will always need you," I tell her, hugging her tightly. "I may leave home and go out into the world, just like Nick's going to do, and eventually even Miranda. But we'll always need you. And we'll be here for you when you decide you need us, too."

This seems to make her happy because she is able to stop herself from crying for a minute and face me head on. I put my arm around her and lead her out of the kitchen into the living room. My father looks at us as we enter, shakes his head at his emotional car wreck of a wife, then throws his arm over the sofa as an invitation for my mother to sit down next to him. I sit down next to Dana, and she hands the baby to me. I smile down at her, this tiny miracle that entered my family just when we needed her most, and she suddenly grabs my index finger and squeezes, an unspoken promise of things to come—of what, I have no idea.

After Jasper and I finally extricate ourselves from my family's Irish good-byes, we drive back to Margaret's. As we walk up to the front porch we hear voices inside. When we open the door, I am startled to see Jay on the floor playing with Zeke, Margaret laughing, throwing her head back like a much younger woman, and a man I can only presume is Taj standing in the archway smiling at us. He is tall and handsome, with beautiful almond-shaped eyes and a sweet, gentle face.

"What are you doing here?" I say to Jay. "I thought you said you couldn't make it."

"They wanted to surprise me," Margaret says, totally oblivious to all the conversations I've had with Jay over the past few months about coming home for Christmas. Introductions are made all around, accompanied by the constant thwacking of Zeke's tail against the walls.

Jasper looks like the little boy who's just found out the bicycle with the big red bow sitting under the tree is for somebody else. I squeeze his hand to assure him this will all be fine. But I'm not so sure myself.

Jasper decides to give himself an occupation, asking for drink orders all around. "Oh, aren't you sweet, Jasper? Actually there's a bottle of champagne in the fridge. I think this moment calls for a little bubbly, don't you?"

I follow Jasper and help him grab the champagne flutes. "Are you all right?" I ask him tentatively. We had both been looking forward to a quiet night with Margaret, and this was definitely not going to be that.

"Sure, why wouldn't I be okay?" he says.

"I don't know. It's just sort of unexpected. I'd understand if you felt uncomfortable."

"No, I'm actually relieved. He's not nearly as good-looking as me," he says, turning to flash me a cocky grin.

"No, he absolutely isn't."

We pour the champagne, go back out and make some Christmas toasts, and settle down in the living room to get to know each other better. Taj is very serious and earnest. I can tell he lets Jay be the funny one. Just like I used to do. Margaret is in her glory, telling stories about Jay to Taj, making us all laugh. Any minute, I swear she's going to get the photo albums out.

"Noelle, tell Taj about Jay's abnormal aversion to mayonnaise," she says.

"It's almost pathological," I say, sneaking a glance at Jasper, whose jaw is clenching. How awful for him to have to sit and listen to me and Margaret reminisce about Jay's endearing foibles. If Jasper were sitting here talking about Jolene's fondness for wasabi, I'd have to slap him.

"Well, listen to you two ganging up on poor me," Jay says. "You of all people. The dueling duo. I told Taj I thought we might come back to find you'd scratched each other's eyes out."

Taj laughs. "Yes, Jay told me that setting you two together was like putting two cats with arched backs in the same room together." He and Jay begin laughing conspiratorially, but I can tell everyone else in the room is experiencing an emotion other than mirth.

Margaret forces a false smile. "You know, it turned out to be a happy ending," she says, "but you were kind of a shit for doing that to us."

Jay looks over at his mother, his smile frozen in place. Flummoxed, I think. I don't recall that Margaret has ever criticized her son for anything in his life. "Mom, you know it was all for the best. I knew Noelle would take good care of you."

"Yes, I know, dear, but . . ." she says, biting her tongue.

"I think what Margaret is trying to say is we're happy you threw us together, but we'd rather you not refer to us as a couple of enraged felines from now on."

Jay's head keeps swiveling from his mom to me, as if he's hoping we'll both start laughing any minute and let him off the hook. In a moment of poor judgment, his eyes settle on Jasper. "Don't look at me," Jasper says.

Taj looks nervous and uncomfortable; he is, no doubt, used to Jay's way of saying something slick to get out of any awkward situation. It turns out Jay still has the touch.

"Well, since I've got your attention now, I have a little announcement to make," he says. I look over at Jasper, who grimaces and shrugs his shoulders. "Taj and I have been talking a lot about the future. After the adoption didn't work out, we decided that maybe we'd been jumping the gun in trying to adopt a child before we were even married. So we thought, first steps first. We decided to get married."

"What?" Margaret says, all her hardness disappearing in a fog of motherly love.

"But that's not all. We thought to ourselves, where can two gay men get married in this crazy country? And we realized it was right across the border from you, Mom, in Massachusetts. So we're coming back here to live." Margaret is speechless. I am speechless. "We've already started looking at houses right over the state line. We're hoping to live less than thirty minutes away from you, Mom."

"Oh, Jay," Margaret finally says.

"We're going to be here for you from now on."

"This makes me so happy," she says, standing up to hug her son and soon-to-be son-in-law.

For some reason, even though I'm happy for Margaret and a bit relieved, I feel somewhat disappointed, a little possessive of Margaret. I don't know if I want someone else to take care of her. Now Jay gets to sweep back into her life and be the hero?

Jasper stands up, which makes me realize I should stand as well. He goes over to shake Jay's hand and offer them both congratulations. For some reason, I cannot speak, so I let Jasper take care of the polite formalities I am incapable of at the moment. Sensing my discomfort, Jasper offers to check on the hors d'oeuvres and takes me with him back to the kitchen.

"You all right?" he says.

"Wow, didn't I ask you that just an hour ago?"

"Yeah, but you seem a little . . . weird. Are you upset Jay's getting remarried?"

"Oh, no. Not at all. It's just . . . unexpected."

I meet Jasper's eyes and see true anxiety there. "Are you sure? You seem really freaked out by this."

I grab his hand, turn it over, and kiss his knuckles. "I am a little freaked out, but it has nothing to do with Jay. It has to do with Margaret. I don't want her to get hurt. I mean, I hope to God he means it. I really hope Jay and Taj can pull through for her."

He puts his arms around me and pulls me close. "Have a little faith in people," he says.

During dinner, I find myself realizing that all of us have a future that involves Margaret, and she deserves to have Jay in her life as much as possible. As the wine bottles empty and Zeke prowls the room for handouts, we begin to relax and enjoy each other's company, figuring out how we will all fit ourselves into this new, unexpected equation. Even Taj begins to assert himself, complimenting Margaret on her fine taste, teasing Jay about his fussy eating style, asking Jasper questions about his travels in India, and giving me the sweetest, most formal smiling nods. There is genuine trust and respect in his eyes, and I feel he is the kind of man who will make Jay live up to his promises.

Later after the meal is over, Jasper offers to clean up so we can all talk, but Jay insists on helping him in the kitchen. I am astounded. Taj helps me carry the desserts into the living room, where we settle down to watch *White Christmas*. But we're doing a lot more talking than watching, mostly discussing what kind of house Jay and Taj are looking for.

"You ought to hire Noelle as your real estate agent," Margaret says. "She always picks the best house on the market."

"Is this true? You know the housing market?" Taj asks, looking at me eagerly. While I am trying my hardest to stay engaged in this conversation, all I can imagine is the conversation going on in the kitchen. I assure Taj that my interest in the housing market is purely recreational, that I am actually a poor judge of a house's true value, having become too frequently enamored with arbitrary features like granite countertops, luxurious master suites, and Jacuzzi tubs.

"Will you excuse me for a second?" I say, unable to contain my curiosity for another minute. I grab some empty plates as an excuse to go into the kitchen and eavesdrop.

Quietly I open the swinging kitchen door and see Jasper and Jay over at the sink by the window, washing the stemware and silver.

"I've wanted to punch you so many times over the past months," Jasper says, and my hand reflexively goes up to cover my mouth as if I'm the one who just said it. But Jay is laughing.

"I know. I've been a jerk," he says. "It wasn't fair to do to Noelle, or to Mom. I'm sorry you had to deal with that."

"It's okay," Jasper says. "I got the best part of the bargain. It's not a burden to take care of Noelle. Or your mom."

"If it makes you feel any better, I still really care about Noelle. In fact, I was a bit worried when she first told me about you. I thought you might turn out to be a psycho."

"Why did you think that?" Jasper says.

"Just overprotective."

"Are you feeling better about me now?"

"A little," Jay says. "But I was kind of hoping you'd be some scrawny, pasty scientist, not a sexy guitar player with muscles." Jasper is laughing now, too, and I am in disbelief that this conversation is taking place.

Two men, squaring off and trading barbs over a dishful of suds.

With a certain amount of perverse pleasure, I imagine them both as puppies, crouching down in play pose, but baring their teeth now and again just to make sure the other knows he's no slouch. Finally I decide to make my presence known, practically clanging two dessert plates together like cymbals to let them know I'm coming in.

"Hey," Jasper says.

"Hey yourself. What's going on in here?"

"Just doing the dishes," he says.

"I'm shocked," I say, raising an eyebrow at Jay.

"Well, I'm letting Jay dry," Jasper says. "He's already informed me that he'd hate to ruin his beautiful hands with dish detergent."

"Oh, of course," I say. "How thoughtful of you." We all smile to diffuse the tension, and then Jay puts down his rag.

"Noelle," Jay says. "Can I talk to you for a minute?"

Jasper shakes his hands off and grabs a clean towel. "Noelle, why don't you take over from here?" he says. "Just the silverware left."

"Okay, sure," I say, and he kisses me on my temple, then joins the others in the living room.

"Noelle," Jay says after an awkward silence, "it's good to see you so happy."

"You, too," I say, keeping my head focused on the bubbles in the sink. The water is scalding hot, but it feels good.

"I hope we didn't throw too much on you all at once," he says. "It's just that once Taj and I decided to get married, we couldn't wait to get up here and tell everyone."

"No, I think it's great," I say. "I'm really happy for you."

"Are you?" he says, cocking his head like Zeke.

"I really am this time," I say, laughing. "It's taken me a while, but I've finally gotten over you, Jay Salazar."

He frowns for a quick second, then smiles. "Well, I guess that's good, isn't it? But I can't say I'm not a little jealous."

"Jealous?"

"Yeah," he says. "You were my first love. And now you're over me."

"Jay," I say. "You're the one getting married."

"I know, I know. But there was a part of me that wanted you to love me forever. I know that sounds awful, but I can't help it."

"I know what you mean," I say. "I was jealous of Taj for a long time. But he's wonderful, and you guys seem perfect together."

"We are," he says. "And Jasper seems great."

"He really is."

"And what a body," he adds, giving me a mischievous smile.

"Don't even start with me," I say, and he laughs and grabs me by both shoulders, pulling me into one of his irresistible hugs. And I wait for that usual breathless response I have whenever I am physically close to Jay. There he stands in front of me, tall and golden and gorgeous and smelling of cool, expensive things. But I feel nothing.

"All right, all right," he says, pulling away from me. "You're getting dish water on my suit."

"I guess some things never change."

"What are you talking about?" he says, falsely offended. "I've changed a lot. Taj has been good for me. No more Mr. Selfish. I'm Mr. Loving and Giving now."

"Really?" I say, skeptically. "Well, Mr. Loving and Giving, do you think you might want to adopt a dog once you're living up here?"

"Why, do you want to give us Zeke?" he says, his eyes lighting up.

"No way! Are you kidding? I mean another dog we have at the

shelter. He's the cutest little Jack Russell, looks just like Eddie from *Frasier*."

"What's wrong with him?" Jay asks.

"Nothing. The owners had a new baby, and they didn't have time for him anymore. He's a little high strung, just like you."

"Thanks a lot. I'll have to talk to Taj, but it might be a good test before we adopt a baby, you know?"

"Good," I say, "because he needs a happy ending, too." We finish putting the last of the silver in the dish drainer, then sit down at the stools around the island.

"Oh, that reminds me," Jay says, grabbing two clean glasses and pouring us the dregs of the bottle of champagne. "I know it's a little belated, but happy birthday, Noelle."

"You remembered?" I say, smiling like a little girl.

"Of course," he says, clinking my glass and giving me a kiss on the cheek.

It may not be earth-shattering, but it's something. And I think to myself, if dogs can be rehabilitated, can learn to love and trust again, maybe we can, too.

A New Year

After Christmas, Jay and Taj return to Atlanta to begin closing up their affairs down there. Jasper closes his office for the week between Christmas and New Year's, so he practically moves in with me in the cottage, and I can't say I mind.

By New Year's Day, Margaret, Jasper, Zeke, and I have established a strange sort of life together. I know it's impermanent, but it works. This afternoon, we are putting the Christmas decorations away while listening to my favorite Nat King Cole Christmas album, especially bittersweet when you hear it on January first, and know it will be another eleven months before you get to hear that honeyed voice again.

Margaret watches us from the couch, her eyes kind of dreamy and faraway. But she looks happy. Jasper hands us two cups containing the last of the eggnog, heavily spiked with rum à la Nick Ryan's recipe. Margaret takes a sip, her eyes pop wide open, and she smiles and winks at Jasper.

"When Jay comes back, you two aren't going to desert me, are you?" she says.

"Of course not. You're not getting rid of us that easily. You're going to be seeing a lot of me this year with the guide dog training," I say. "In fact, you're probably going to be sick to death of me. When I show up here at six o'clock on a Saturday morning with a leash and two cups of Dunkin' Donuts coffee ready to start work, you're going to want to slam the door in my face."

"No, I won't," she says. "I'm looking forward to training. What do you think I should name my dog?"

"Well, I've always thought Jasper was a good name for a dog," Jasper says. "Especially if it's a beagle."

"Shut up," I say, tossing a stuffed reindeer at him.

"Jasper, promise me one thing," Margaret says.

"What's that?"

"Once Jay and Taj are up here, take this woman on a vacation, would you? She works harder than anyone I know. For a very long time, I've felt she was in desperate need of a good . . ."

"Yes, Margaret," I say. "I'm quite aware of what you think I need."

Her mouth is open in mock horror. "I was going to say holiday."

"I have to agree," Jasper says, pulling me into a bear hug. "But I'm way ahead of you, Margaret. I've already booked us two round-trip tickets to India."

"India? Isn't that where the *Kama Sutra* was written?"

"Margaret, please. Spare us," I say.

"Well, good for you, Jasper. Noelle needs to get out of this . . . puritanical New England environment. When are you going?"

"Easter week," Jasper says.

"Easter week? The season of miracles." She gives me what's meant to be a private look, but Jasper knows exactly what we're both thinking. "Maybe you can get Noelle to relax for a few days. That'll be a miracle."

"Oh, once she sees this beach, she'll relax."

"I can't wait," I say.

"So long as you don't plan to stay there forever," Margaret says. "I'm still going to need you both. I mean, I don't expect you to live here for the rest of your lives. Eventually, I hope you two get married and get a place of your own and adopt lots of dogs and babies. But not just yet."

I laugh, embarrassed she's said something I've been thinking, almost like she can read my mind. But Jasper doesn't laugh—he just smiles at me, the last strand of the Christmas lights twinkling in his eyes.

Margaret stretches her arms in the air and leans down into the sofa, pulling an afghan around her. "What a pleasant afternoon," she says. "Do you two want help with the decorations?"

"No, just rest. We'll take care of everything," I say. And we quietly pack the remaining ornaments away, letting Margaret drift slowly to sleep.

After we finish dismantling the tree, we decide to take it outside and plant it in the yard. Zeke follows behind, then tears off across the lawn beyond us. It's just begun to flurry, and Zeke puts his nose into the air and breathes in, like he's really savoring the moment— the crisp winter air, the smell of snow in the sky, the chance to romp and frolic once again. His second chance at life.

Together, we carry the tree out to the hole Jasper dug out last week, now filled with compost and leaves. We hoist the tree up and gingerly place it inside its new home. I hold the tree upright as Jasper fetches a shovel and a wheelbarrow full of soil. He gently shovels the fresh soil around the roots, while I hold the tree.

As we work, I watch Jasper, who's wearing this funny little hat scrunched over his ears. He has the look of a kid on the first snow day, and I realize then that I am totally in love with him. I want to tell him this, but his hat's down over his ears and the wind's blowing and he's too absorbed in his task to hear me. I'll have plenty of time to tell him later.

When we're all finished, he grabs my waist from behind and pulls me into his arms. We stand there in the slowly falling snow, looking at our new tree, vibrant and green and still cherished, even after the lights and tinsel have fallen.

And here in this swirl of flurries, standing on a bluff above the bay with the smell of snow in the air, I watch a tree take root in the ground. And I realize this may be as close as I ever get to giving new life to the planet. This tree, on this field, on this first day of the new year.

But I think it might be enough.

READERS GUIDE
FOR

Free to a
Good Home

Discussion Questions

1. Dogs play a large role in the novel, particularly shelter dogs. What rewards can be gained by adopting an animal that has gone through difficult circumstances?

2. Why do you think humans traditionally have had such close ties to their dogs and pets? What is it that pets provide us that sometimes our human counterparts do not?

3. Many of the characters in the novel are searching for a sense of belonging or stability. What does the notion of *home* mean to each of them? What does it mean to you?

4. Noelle has two very different maternal relationships, one with Margaret and one with her own mother. How do our relationships with our mothers both ground us and exasperate us? Why do you think the mother-child relationship is so complicated?

5. Initially Jay does not want to consider placing his mother in a nursing home, asking Noelle to care for her instead. Would you agree to care for a former family member? What are some of the complexities of leaving a family member in someone else's care?

6. In the novel, Noelle comes to terms with her infertility. How does not having children, whether by choice or circumstance, affect one's sense of self?

7. Noelle makes assumptions about Jasper and almost lets her own insecurities sabotage their relationship. How much do our past relationships affect our ability to enter into new ones? What does the loss of a marriage do to a person's faith in relationships?

8. Jay and Noelle get married for perhaps the wrong reasons. Does it ever make sense to stay in a marriage just for companionship?

9. Ultimately, Jay and his boyfriend move back to Massachusetts so they can get married and, eventually, adopt a child. How do you feel about gay couples marrying? How about adopting children?

10. Debilitating diseases such as MS or ALS can take away an individual's independence and sense of worth. What determines how people react to such losses? What do you see as the most important factors in responding to a disease with strength and grace?

Visit the author's website at evemariemont.com.